THE TALES OF CHEKHOV
VOLUME 4

THE PARTY
AND OTHER STORIES

D1565154

THE TALES OF CHEKHOV

THE PARTY

AND OTHER STORIES

By
ANTON CHEKHOV

Translated By
CONSTANCE GARNETT

The Ecco Press
New York

Library of Congress Cataloging in Publication Data
Chekhov, Anton Pavlovich, 1860–1904.
The party and other stories.
(The Tales of Chekhov; vol. 4)
Reprint. Originally published: New York: Macmillan, 1917.
Contents: The party–Terror–A woman's kingdom–[etc.]
I. Title. II. Series: Chekhov, Anton Pavlovich, 1860–1904.
Short stories. English; vol. 4
PG3456.A15G3   1984   vol. 4   891.73'3s [891.73'3]   84-6122
ISBN   0-88001-051-7   (pbk.)

CONTENTS

THE TALES OF CHEKHOV
VOLUME 4

THE PARTY
AND OTHER STORIES

THE PARTY
AND OTHER STORIES

THE PARTY

I

AFTER the festive dinner with its eight courses and its endless conversation, Olga Mihalovna, whose husband's name-day was being celebrated, went out into the garden. The duty of smiling and talking incessantly, the clatter of the crockery, the stupidity of the servants, the long intervals between the courses, and the stays she had put on to conceal her condition from the visitors, wearied her to exhaustion. She longed to get away from the house, to sit in the shade and rest her heart with thoughts of the baby which was to be born to her in another two months. She was used to these thoughts coming to her as she turned to the left out of the big avenue into the narrow path. Here in the thick shade of the plums and cherry-trees the dry branches used to scratch her neck and shoulders; a spider's web would settle on her face, and there would rise up in

3

her mind the image of a little creature of undetermined sex and undefined features, and it began to seem as though it were not the spider's web that tickled her face and neck caressingly, but that little creature. When, at the end of the path, a thin wicker hurdle came into sight, and behind it podgy beehives with tiled roofs; when in the motionless, stagnant air there came a smell of hay and honey, and a soft buzzing of bees was audible, then the little creature would take complete possession of Olga Mihalovna.   She used to sit down on a bench near the shanty woven of branches, and fall to thinking.

This time, too, she went on as far as the seat, sat down, and began thinking; but instead of the little creature there rose up in her imagination the figures of the grown-up people whom she had just left. She felt dreadfully uneasy that she, the hostess, had deserted her guests, and she remembered how her husband, Pyotr Dmitritch, and her uncle, Nikolay Nikolaitch, had argued at dinner about trial by jury, about the press, and about the higher education of women.   Her husband, as usual, argued in order to show off his Conservative ideas before his visitors — and still more in order to disagree with her uncle, whom he disliked.   Her uncle contradicted him and wrangled over every word he uttered, so as to show the company that he, Uncle Nikolay Nikolaitch, still retained his youthful freshness of spirit and free-thinking in spite of his fifty-nine years. And towards the end of dinner even Olga Mihalovna herself could not resist taking part and unskilfully attempting to defend university education for women — not that that education stood in need of her defence, but simply because she wanted to annoy her husband, who to her mind was unfair. The guests were wearied by this discussion, but they all thought it necessary to take part in it, and talked a great deal, although none of them took any interest in trial by jury or the higher education of women. . . .

Olga Mihalovna was sitting on the nearest side of the hurdle near the shanty. The sun was hidden behind the clouds. The trees and the air were overcast as before rain, but in spite of that it was hot and stifling. The hay cut under the trees on the previous day was lying ungathered, looking melancholy, with here and there a patch of colour from the faded flowers, and from it came a heavy, sickly scent. It was still. The other side of the hurdle there was a monotonous hum of bees. . . .

Suddenly she heard footsteps and voices; some one was coming along the path towards the bee-house.

"How stifling it is!" said a feminine voice. "What do you think — is it going to rain, or not?"

"It is going to rain, my charmer, but not before

night," a very familiar male voice answered languidly. " There will be a good rain."

Olga Mihalovna calculated that if she made haste to hide in the shanty they would pass by without seeing her, and she would not have to talk and to force herself to smile. She picked up her skirts, bent down and crept into the shanty. At once she felt upon her face, her neck, her arms, the hot air as heavy as steam. If it had not been for the stuffiness and the close smell of rye bread, fennel, and brush-wood, which prevented her from breathing freely, it would have been delightful to hide from her visitors here under the thatched roof in the dusk, and to think about the little creature. It was cosy and quiet.

" What a pretty spot! " said a feminine voice. " Let us sit here, Pyotr Dmitritch."

Olga Mihalovna began peeping through a crack between two branches. She saw her husband, Pyotr Dmitritch, and Lubotchka Sheller, a girl of seven-teen who had not long left boarding-school. Pyotr Dmitritch, with his hat on the back of his head, languid and indolent from having drunk so much at dinner, slouched by the hurdle and raked the hay into a heap with his foot; Lubotchka, pink with the heat and pretty as ever, stood with her hands behind her, watching the lazy movements of his big handsome person.

Olga Mihalovna knew that her husband was attractive to women, and did not like to see him with them. There was nothing out of the way in Pyotr Dmitritch's lazily raking together the hay in order to sit down on it with Lubotchka and chatter to her of trivialities; there was nothing out of the way, either, in pretty Lubotchka's looking at him with her soft eyes; but yet Olga Mihalovna felt vexed with her husband and frightened and pleased that she could listen to them.

"Sit down, enchantress," said Pyotr Dmitritch, sinking down on the hay and stretching. "That's right. Come, tell me something."

"What next! If I begin telling you anything you will go to sleep."

"Me go to sleep? Allah forbid! Can I go to sleep while eyes like yours are watching me?"

In her husband's words, and in the fact that he was lolling with his hat on the back of his head in the presence of a lady, there was nothing out of the way either. He was spoilt by women, knew that they found him attractive, and had adopted with them a special tone which every one said suited him. With Lubotchka he behaved as with all women. But, all the same, Olga Mihalovna was jealous.

"Tell me, please," said Lubotchka, after a brief silence —"is it true that you are to be tried for something?"

"I? Yes, I am . . . numbered among the transgressors, my charmer."

" But what for? "

" For nothing, but just . . . it's chiefly a question of politics," yawned Pyotr Dmitritch —" the antagonisms of Left and Right. I, an obscurantist and reactionary, ventured in an official paper to make use of an expression offensive in the eyes of such immaculate Gladstones as Vladimir Pavlovitch Vladimirov and our local justice of the peace — Kuzma Grigoritch Vostryakov."

Pytor Dmitritch yawned again and went on:

" And it is the way with us that you may express disapproval of the sun or the moon, or anything you like, but God preserve you from touching the Liberals! Heaven forbid! A Liberal is like the poisonous dry fungus which covers you with a cloud of dust if you accidentally touch it with your finger."

" What happened to you? "

" Nothing particular. The whole flare-up started from the merest trifle. A teacher, a detestable person of clerical associations, hands to Vostryakov a petition against a tavern-keeper, charging him with insulting language and behaviour in a public place. Everything showed that both the teacher and the tavern-keeper were drunk as cobblers, and that they behaved equally badly. If there had been insulting behaviour, the insult had anyway been mutual.

Vostryakov ought to have fined them both for a
breach of the peace and have turned them out of the
court — that is all. But that's not our way of doing
things. With us what stands first is not the person
— not the fact itself, but the trade-mark and label.
However great a rascal a teacher may be, he is
always in the right because he is a teacher; a tavern-
keeper is always in the wrong because he is a tavern-
keeper and a money-grubber. Vostryakov placed
the tavern-keeper under arrest. The man appealed
to the Circuit Court; the Circuit Court triumphantly
upheld Vostryakov's decision. Well, I stuck to my
own opinion. . . . Got a little hot. . . . That was
all."

Pyotr Dmitritch spoke calmly with careless irony.
In reality the trial that was hanging over him worried him extremely. Olga Mihalovna remembered
how on his return from the unfortunate session he
had tried to conceal from his household how troubled
he was, and how dissatisfied with himself. As an
intelligent man he could not help feeling that he had
gone too far in expressing his disagreement; and how
much lying had been needful to conceal that feeling
from himself and from others! How many unnecessary conversations there had been! How
much grumbling and insincere laughter at what was
not laughable! When he learned that he was to be
brought up before the Court, he seemed at once

harassed and depressed; he began to sleep badly, stood oftener than ever at the windows, drumming on the panes with his fingers.   And he was ashamed to let his wife see that he was worried, and it vexed her.

"They say you have been in the province of Poltava?" Lubotchka questioned him.

"Yes," answered Pyotr Dmitritch.   "I came back the day before yesterday."

"I expect it is very nice there."

"Yes, it is very nice, very nice indeed; in fact, I arrived just in time for the haymaking, I must tell you, and in the Ukraine the haymaking is the most poetical moment of the year.   Here we have a big house, a big garden, a lot of servants, and a lot going on, so that you don't see the haymaking; here it all passes unnoticed.   There, at the farm, I have a meadow of forty-five acres as flat as my hand. You can see the men mowing from any window you stand at.   They are mowing in the meadow, they are mowing in the garden.   There are no visitors, no fuss nor hurry either, so that you can't help seeing, feeling, hearing nothing but the haymaking.   There is a smell of hay indoors and outdoors.   There's the sound of the scythes from sunrise to sunset.   Altogether Little Russia is a charming country.   Would you believe it, when I was drinking water from the rustic wells and filthy vodka in some Jew's tavern, when on quiet evenings the strains of the Little Russian fiddle and the tambourines reached me, I was tempted by a fascinating idea — to settle down on my place and live there as long as I chose, far away from Circuit Courts, intellectual conversations, philosophizing women, long dinners. . . ."

Pyotr Dmitritch was not lying. He was unhappy and really longed to rest. And he had visited his Poltava property simply to avoid seeing his study, his servants, his acquaintances, and everything that could remind him of his wounded vanity and his mistakes.

Lubotchka suddenly jumped up and waved her hands about in horror.

"Oh! A bee, a bee!" she shrieked. "It will sting!"

"Nonsense; it won't sting," said Pyotr Dmitritch. "What a coward you are!"

"No, no, no," cried Lubotchka; and looking round at the bees, she walked rapidly back.

Pyotr Dmitritch walked away after her, looking at her with a softened and melancholy face. He was probably thinking, as he looked at her, of his farm, of solitude, and — who knows? — perhaps he was even thinking how snug and cosy life would be at the farm if his wife had been this girl — young, pure, fresh, not corrupted by higher education, not with child. . . .

When the sound of their footsteps had died away, Olga Mihalovna came out of the shanty and turned towards the house. She wanted to cry. She was by now acutely jealous. She could understand that her husband was worried, dissatisfied with himself and ashamed, and when people are ashamed they hold aloof, above all from those nearest to them, and are unreserved wtih strangers; she could understand, also, that she had nothing to fear from Lubotchka or from those women who were now drinking coffee indoors. But everything in general was terrible, incomprehensible, and it already seemed to Olga Mihalovna that Pyotr Dmitritch only half belonged to her. . . .

"He has no right to do it!" she muttered, trying to formulate her jealousy and her vexation with her husband. "He has no right at all. I will tell him so plainly!"

She made up her mind to find her husband at once and tell him all about it: it was disgusting, absolutely disgusting, that he was attractive to other women and sought their admiration as though it were some heavenly manna; it was unjust and dishonourable that he should give to others what belonged by right to his wife, that he should hide his soul and his conscience from his wife to reveal them to the first pretty face he came across. What harm had his wife done him? How was she to blame? Long ago she had been sickened by his lying: he was for ever posing, flirting, saying what he did not think, and trying to seem different from what he was and what he ought to be. Why this falsity? Was it seemly in a decent man? If he lied he was demeaning himself and those to whom he lied, and slighting what he lied about. Could he not understand that if he swaggered and posed at the judicial table, or held forth at dinner on the prerogatives of Government, that he, simply to provoke her uncle, was showing thereby that he had not a ha'p'orth of respect for the Court, or himself, or any of the people who were listening and looking at him?

Coming out into the big avenue, Olga Mihalovna assumed an expression of face as though she had just gone away to look after some domestic matter. In the verandah the gentlemen were drinking liqueur and eating strawberries: one of them, the Examining Magistrate — a stout elderly man, *blagueur* and wit — must have been telling some rather free anecdote, for, seeing their hostess, he suddenly clapped his hands over his fat lips, rolled his eyes, and sat down. Olga Mihalovna did not like the local officials. She did not care for their clumsy, ceremonious wives, their scandal-mongering, their frequent visits, their flattery of her husband, whom they all hated. Now, when they were drinking, were replete with food and showed no signs of going away, she felt their pres-

ence an agonizing weariness; but not to appear im-
polite, she smiled cordially to the Magistrate, and
shook her finger at him.   She walked across the
dining-room and drawing-room smiling, and looking
as though she had gone to give some order and make
some arrangement.   " God grant no one stops me,"
she thought, but she forced herself to stop in the
drawing-room to listen from politeness to a young
man who was sitting at the piano playing: after
standing for a minute, she cried, " Bravo, bravo, M.
Georges ! " and clapping her hands twice, she went
on.

She found her husband in his study.   He was
sitting at the table, thinking of something.   His face
looked stern, thoughtful, and guilty.   This was not
the same Pyotr Dmitritch who had been arguing at
dinner and whom his guests knew, but a different
man — wearied, feeling guilty and dissatisfied with
himself, whom nobody knew but his wife.   He must
have come to the study to get cigarettes.   Before
him lay an open cigarette-case full of cigarettes, and
one of his hands was in the table drawer; he had
paused and sunk into thought as he was taking the
cigarettes.

Olga Mihalovna felt sorry for him.   It was as
clear as day that this man was harassed, could find
no rest, and was perhaps struggling with himself.
Olga Mihalovna went up to the table in silence:

wanting to show that she had forgotten the argument at dinner and was not cross, she shut the cigarette-case and put it in her husband's coat pocket.

"What should I say to him?" she wondered; "I shall say that lying is like a forest — the further one goes into it the more difficult it is to get out of it. I will say to him, 'You have been carried away by the false part you are playing; you have insulted people who were attached to you and have done you no harm. Go and apologize to them, laugh at yourself, and you will feel better. And if you want peace and solitude, let us go away together.' "

Meeting his wife's gaze, Pyotr Dmitritch's face immediately assumed the expression it had worn at dinner and in the garden — indifferent and slightly ironical. He yawned and got up.

"It's past five," he said, looking at his watch. "If our visitors are merciful and leave us at eleven, even then we have another six hours of it. It's a cheerful prospect, there's no denying!"

And whistling something, he walked slowly out of the study with his usual dignified gait. She could hear him with dignified firmness cross the dining-room, then the drawing-room, laugh with dignified assurance, and say to the young man who was playing, "Bravo! bravo!" Soon his footsteps died away: he must have gone out into the garden. And now not jealousy, not vexation, but real hatred of his footsteps, his insincere laugh and voice, took possession of Olga Mihalovna. She went to the window and looked out into the garden. Pyotr Dmitritch was already walking along the avenue. Putting one hand in his pocket and snapping the fingers of the other, he walked with confident swinging steps, throwing his head back a little, and looking as though he were very well satisfied with himself, with his dinner, with his digestion, and with nature. . . .

Two little schoolboys, the children of Madame Tchizhevsky, who had only just arrived, made their appearance in the avenue, accompanied by their tutor, a student wearing a white tunic and very narrow trousers. When they reached Pyotr Dmitritch, the boys and the student stopped, and probably congratulated him on his name-day. With a graceful swing of his shoulders, he patted the children on their cheeks, and carelessly offered the student his hand without looking at him. The student must have praised the weather and compared it with the climate of Petersburg, for Pyotr Dmitritch said in a loud voice, in a tone as though he were not speaking to a guest, but to an usher of the court or a witness:

"What! It's cold in Petersburg? And here, my good sir, we have a salubrious atmosphere and the fruits of the earth in abundance. Eh? What?"

And thrusting one hand in his pocket and snapping the fingers of the other, he walked on. Till he had disappeared behind the nut bushes, Olga Mihalovna watched the back of his head in perplexity. How had this man of thirty-four come by the dignified deportment of a general? How had he come by that impressive, elegant manner? Where had he got that vibration of authority in his voice? Where had he got these " what's," " to be sure's," and " my good sir's "?

Olga Mihalovna remembered how in the first months of her marriage she had felt dreary at home alone and had driven into the town to the Circuit Court, at which Pyotr Dmitritch had sometimes presided in place of her godfather, Count Alexey Petrovitch. In the presidential chair, wearing his uniform and a chain on his breast, he was completely changed. Stately gestures, a voice of thunder, " what," " to be sure," careless tones. . . . Everything, all that was ordinary and human, all that was individual and personal to himself that Olga Mihalovna was accustomed to seeing in him at home, vanished in grandeur, and in the presidential chair there sat not Pyotr Dmitritch, but another man whom every one called Mr. President. This consciousness of power prevented him from sitting still in his place, and he seized every opportunity to ring his bell, to glance sternly at the public, to shout. . . . Where had he got his short-sight and his deafness when he suddenly began to see and hear with difficulty, and, frowning majestically, insisted on people speaking louder and coming closer to the table? From the height of his grandeur he could hardly distinguish faces or sounds, so that it seemed that if Olga Mihalovna herself had gone up to him he would have shouted even to her, " Your name? " Peasant witnesses he addressed familiarly, he shouted at the public so that his voice could be heard even in the street, and behaved incredibly with the lawyers. If a lawyer had to speak to him, Pyotr Dmitritch, turning a little away from him, looked with half-closed eyes at the ceiling, meaning to signify thereby that the lawyer was utterly superfluous and that he was neither recognizing him nor listening to him; if a badly-dressed lawyer spoke, Pyotr Dmitritch pricked up his ears and looked the man up and down with a sarcastic, annihilating stare as though to say: " Queer sort of lawyers nowadays! "

" What do you mean by that? " he would interrupt.

If a would-be eloquent lawyer mispronounced a foreign word, saying, for instance, " factitious " instead of " fictitious," Pyotr Dmitritch brightened up at once and asked, " What? How? Factitious? What does that mean? " and then observed impressively: " Don't make use of words you do not understand." And the lawyer, finishing his speech, would walk away from the table, red and perspiring, while Pyotr Dmitritch; with a self-satisfied smile, would lean back in his chair triumphant. In his manner with the lawyers he imitated Count Alexey Petrovitch a little, but when the latter said, for instance, " Counsel for the defence, you keep quiet for a little! " it sounded paternally good-natured and natural, while the same words in Pyotr Dmitritch's mouth were rude and artificial.

II

There were sounds of applause. The young man had finished playing. Olga Mihalovna remembered her guests and hurried into the drawing-room.

" I have so enjoyed your playing," she said, going up to the piano. " I have so enjoyed it. You have a wonderful talent! But don't you think our piano's out of tune? "

At that moment the two schoolboys walked into the room, accompanied by the student.

" My goodness! Mitya and Kolya," Olga Mihalovna drawled joyfully, going to meet them: " How big they have grown! One would not know you! But where is your mamma? "

" I congratulate you on the name-day," the student began in a free-and-easy tone, " and I wish you all happiness.   Ekaterina Andreyevna sends her congratulations and begs you to excuse her.   She is not very well."

" How unkind of her !   I have been expecting her all day.   Is it long since you left Petersburg ? " Olga Mihalovna asked the student.   " What kind of weather have you there now ? "   And without waiting for an answer, she looked cordially at the schoolboys and repeated :

" How tall they have grown !   It is not long since they used to come with their nurse, and they are at school already !   The old grow older while the young grow up. . . . Have you had dinner ? "

" Oh, please don't trouble ! " said the student.

" Why, you have not had dinner ? "

" For goodness' sake, don't trouble ! "

" But I suppose you are hungry ? " Olga Mihalovna said it in a harsh, rude voice, with impatience and vexation — it escaped her unawares, but at once she coughed, smiled, and flushed crimson.   " How tall they have grown ! " she said softly.

" Please don't trouble ! " the student said once more.

The student begged her not to trouble; the boys said nothing; obviously all three of them were hungry.   Olga Mihalovna took them into the dining-room and told Vassily to lay the table.

" How unkind of your mamma! " she said as she made them sit down. " She has quite forgotten me. Unkind, unkind, unkind . . . you must tell her so. What are you studying?" she asked the student.

" Medicine."

" Well, I have a weakness for doctors, only fancy. I am very sorry my husband is not a doctor. What courage any one must have to perform an operation or dissect a corpse, for instance! Horrible! Aren't you frightened? I believe I should die of terror! Of course, you drink vodka?"

" Please don't trouble."

" After your journey you must have something to drink. Though I am a woman, even I drink sometimes. And Mitya and Kolya will drink Malaga. It's not a strong wine; you need not be afraid of it. What fine fellows they are, really! They'll be thinking of getting married next."

Olga Mihalovna talked without ceasing; she knew by experience that when she had guests to entertain it was far easier and more comfortable to talk than to listen. When you talk there is no need to strain your attention to think of answers to questions, and to change your expression of face. But unawares she asked the student a serious question; the student began a lengthy speech and she was forced to listen. The student knew that she had once been at the University, and so tried to seem a serious person as he talked to her.

" What subject are you studying? " she asked, forgetting that she had already put that question to him.

" Medicine."

Olga Mihalovna now remembered that she had been away from the ladies for a long while.

" Yes? Then I suppose you are going to be a doctor? " she said, getting up. " That's splendid. I am sorry I did not go in for medicine myself. So you will finish your dinner here, gentlemen, and then come into the garden. I will introduce you to the young ladies."

She went out and glanced at her watch: it was five minutes to six. And she wondered that the time had gone so slowly, and thought with horror that there were six more hours before midnight, when the party would break up. How could she get through those six hours? What phrases could she utter? How should she behave to her husband?

There was not a soul in the drawing-room or on the verandah. All the guests were sauntering about the garden.

" I shall have to suggest a walk in the birch-wood before tea, or else a row in the boats," thought Olga Mihalovna, hurrying to the croquet ground, from which came the sounds of voices and laughter.

" And sit the old people down to *vint.* . . ."
She met Grigory the footman coming from the
croquet ground with empty bottles.

"Where are the ladies?" she asked.

" Among the raspberry-bushes. The master's
there, too."

" Oh, good heavens!" some one on the croquet
lawn shouted with exasperation. " I have told you
a thousand times over! To know the Bulgarians
you must see them! You can't judge from the
papers!"

Either because of the outburst or for some other
reason, Olga Mihalovna was suddenly aware of a
terrible weakness all over, especially in her legs and
in her shoulders. She felt she could not bear to
speak, to listen, or to move.

" Grigory," she said faintly and with an effort,
" when you have to serve tea or anything, please
don't appeal to me, don't ask me anything, don't
speak of anything. . . . Do it all yourself, and . . .
and don't make a noise with your feet, I entreat
you. . . . I can't, because . . ."

Without finishing, she walked on towards the
croquet lawn, but on the way she thought of the
ladies, and turned towards the raspberry-bushes.
The sky, the air, and the trees looked gloomy again
and threatened rain; it was hot and stifling. An immense flock of crows, foreseeing a storm, flew caw-

ing over the garden.   The paths were more over-
grown, darker, and narrower as they got nearer the
kitchen garden.   In one of them, buried in a thick
tangle of wild pear, crab-apple, sorrel, young oaks,
and hopbine, clouds of tiny black flies swarmed round
Olga Mihalovna.   She covered her face with her
hands and began forcing herself to think of the little
creature. . . . There floated through her imagination the figures of Grigory, Mitya, Kolya, the faces
of the peasants who had come in the morning to
present their congratulations. . . .

She heard footsteps, and she opened her eyes.
Uncle Nikolay Nikolaitch was coming rapidly
towards her.

" It's you, dear?   I am very glad . . ." he began, breathless.   " A couple of words. . . ."   He
mopped with his handkerchief his red shaven chin,
then suddenly stepped back a pace, flung up his
hands and opened his eyes wide.   " My dear girl,
how long is this going on? " he said rapidly, splut-
tering.   " I ask you: is there no limit to it?   I say
nothing of the demoralizing effect of his martinet
views on all around him, of the way he insults all that
is sacred and best in me and in every honest thinking man — I will say nothing about that, but he
might at least behave decently!   Why, he shouts, he
bellows, gives himself airs, poses as a sort of Bona-
parte, does not let one say a word. . . . I don't

know what the devil's the matter with him! These lordly gestures, this condescending tone; and laughing like a general! Who is he, allow me to ask you? I ask you, who is he? The husband of his wife, with a few paltry acres and the rank of a titular who has had the luck to marry an heiress! An upstart and a *junker,* like so many others! A type out of Shtchedrin! Upon my word, it's either that he's suffering from megalomania, or that old rat in his dotage, Count Alexey Petrovitch, is right when he says that children and young people are a long time growing up nowadays, and go on playing they are cabmen and generals till they are forty!"

"That's true, that's true," Olga Mihalovna assented. "Let me pass."

"Now just consider: what is it leading to?" her uncle went on, barring her way. "How will this playing at being a general and a Conservative end? Already he has got into trouble! Yes, to stand his trial! I am very glad of it! That's what his noise and shouting has brought him to — to stand in the prisoner's dock. And it's not as though it were the Circuit Court or something: it's the Central Court! Nothing worse could be imagined, I think! And then he has quarrelled with every one! He is celebrating his name-day, and look, Vostryakov's not here, nor Yahontov, nor Vladimirov, nor Shevud, nor the Count. . . . There is no one, I imagine,

more Conservative than Count Alexey Petrovitch,
yet even he has not come.   And he never will come
again.   He won't come, you will see ! "

" My God ! but what has it to do with me ? " asked
Olga Mihalovna.

" What has it to do with you?   Why, you are
his wife !   You are clever, you have had a university education, and it was in your power to make him
an honest worker ! "

" At the lectures I went to they did not teach us
how to influence tiresome people.   It seems as
though I should have to apologize to all of you for
having been at the University," said Olga Mihalovna
sharply.   " Listen, uncle.   If people played the
same scales over and over again the whole day long
in your hearing, you wouldn't be able to sit still and
listen, but would run away.   I hear the same thing
over again for days together all the year round.
You must have pity on me at last."

Her uncle pulled a very long face, then looked at
her searchingly and twisted his lips into a mocking
smile.

" So that's how it is," he piped in a voice like an
old woman's.   " I beg your pardon ! " he said, and
made a ceremonious bow.   " If you have fallen
under his influence yourself, and have abandoned
your convictions, you should have said so before.   I
beg your pardon ! "

"Yes, I have abandoned my convictions," she cried. "There; make the most of it!"

"I beg your pardon!"

Her uncle for the last time made her a ceremonious bow, a little on one side, and, shrinking into himself, made a scrape with his foot and walked back.

"Idiot!" thought Olga Mihalovna. "I hope he will go home."

She found the ladies and the young people among the raspberries in the kitchen garden. Some were eating raspberries; others, tired of eating raspberries, were strolling about the strawberry beds or foraging among the sugar-peas. A little on one side of the raspberry bed, near a branching apple-tree propped up by posts which had been pulled out of an old fence, Pyotr Dmitritch was mowing the grass. His hair was falling over his forehead, his cravat was untied. His watch-chain was hanging loose. Every step and every swing of the scythe showed skill and the possession of immense physical strength. Near him were standing Lubotchka and the daughters of a neighbour, Colonel Bukryeev — two anaemic and unhealthily stout fair girls, Natalya and Valentina, or, as they were always called, Nata and Vata, both wearing white frocks and strikingly like each other. Pyotr Dmitritch was teaching them to mow.

" It's very simple," he said.   " You have only to
know how to hold the scythe and not to get too hot
over it — that is, not to use more force than is necessary!   Like this. . . . Wouldn't you like to try? "
he   said,   offering   the   scythe   to   Lubotchka.
" Come! "

Lubotchka took the scythe clumsily, blushed crimson, and laughed.

" Don't be afraid, Lubov Alexandrovna! " cried
Olga Mihalovna, loud enough for all the ladies to
hear that she was with them.   " Don't be afraid!
You must learn!   If you marry a Tolstoyan he will
make you mow."

Lubotchka raised the scythe, but began laughing
again, and, helpless with laughter, let go of it at
once.   She was ashamed and pleased at being talked
to as though grown up.   Nata, with a cold, serious
face, with no trace of smiling or shyness, took the
scythe, swung it and caught it in the grass; Vata,
also without a smile, as cold and serious as her sister,
took the scythe, and silently thrust it into the earth.
Having done this, the two sisters linked arms and
walked in silence to the raspberries.

Pyotr Dmitritch laughed and played about like a
boy, and this childish, frolicsome mood in which he
became exceedingly good-natured suited him far better than any other.   Olga Mihalovna loved him
when he was like that.   But his boyishness did not

usually last long. It did not this time; after playing
with the scythe, he for some reason thought it necessary to take a serious tone about it.

"When I am mowing, I feel, do you know,
healthier and more normal," he said. "If I were
forced to confine myself to an intellectual life I believe I should go out of my mind. I feel that I was
not born to be a man of culture! I ought to mow,
plough, sow, drive out the horses."

And Pyotr Dmitritch began a conversation with
the ladies about the advantages of physical labour,
about culture, and then about the pernicious effects
of money, of property. Listening to her husband,
Olga Mihalovna, for some reason, thought of her
dowry.

"And the time will come, I suppose," she thought,
"when he will not forgive me for being richer than
he. He is proud and vain. Maybe he will hate
me because he owes so much to me."

She stopped near Colonel Bukryeev, who was
eating raspberries and also taking part in the conversation.

"Come," he said, making room for Olga Mihalovna and Pyotr Dmitritch. "The ripest are
here. . . . And so, according to Proudhon," he
went on, raising his voice, "property is robbery.
But I must confess I don't believe in Proudhon, and
don't consider him a philosopher. The French are

not authorities, to my thinking — God bless them! "

" Well, as for Proudhons and Buckles and the rest of them, I am weak in that department," said Pyotr Dmitritch. " For philosophy you must apply to my wife. She has been at University lectures and knows all your Schopenhauers and Proudhons by heart. . . ."

Olga Mihalovna felt bored again. She walked again along a little path by apple and pear trees, and looked again as though she was on some very important errand. She reached the gardener's cottage. In the doorway the gardener's wife, Varvara, was sitting together with her four little children with big shaven heads. Varvara, too, was with child and expecting to be confined on Elijah's Day. After greeting her, Olga Mihalovna looked at her and the children in silence and asked:

" Well, how do you feel? "

" Oh, all right. . . ."

A silence followed. The two women seemed to understand each other without words.

" It's dreadful having one's first baby," said Olga Mihalovna after a moment's thought. " I keep feeling as though I shall not get through it, as though I shall die."

" I fancied that, too, but here I am alive. . . . One has all sorts of fancies."

Varvara, who was just going to have her fifth,

looked down a little on her mistress from the height
of her experience and spoke in a rather didactic tone,
and Olga Mihalovna could not help feeling her authority; she would have liked to have talked of her
fears, of the child, of her sensations, but she was
afraid it might strike Varvara as naïve and trivial.
And she waited in silence for Varvara to say something herself.

"Olya, we are going indoors," Pyotr Dmitritch
called from the raspberries.

Olga Mihalovna liked being silent, waiting and
watching Varvara. She would have been ready to
stay like that till night without speaking or having
any duty to perform. But she had to go. She had
hardly left the cottage when Lubotchka, Nata, and
Vata came running to meet her. The sisters
stopped short abruptly a couple of yards away;
Lubotchka ran right up to her and flung herself on
her neck.

"You dear, darling, precious," she said, kissing
her face and her neck. "Let us go and have tea
on the island!"

"On the island, on the island!" said the precisely
similar Nata and Vata, both at once, without a smile.

"But it's going to rain, my dears."

"It's not, it's not," cried Lubotchka with a woe-
begone face. "They've all agreed to go. Dear!
darling!"

" They are all getting ready to have tea on the island," said Pyotr Dmitritch, coming up.   " See to arranging things. . . . We will all go in the boats, and the samovars and all the rest of it must be sent in the carriage with the servants."

He walked beside his wife and gave her his arm. Olga Mihalovna had a desire to say something disagreeable to her husband, something biting, even about her dowry perhaps — the crueller the better, she felt.   She thought a little, and said:

" Why is it Count Alexey Petrovitch hasn't come? What a pity! "

" I am very glad he hasn't come," said Pyotr Dmitritch, lying.   " I'm sick to death of that old lunatic."

" But yet before dinner you were expecting him so eagerly! "

III

Half an hour later all the guests were crowding on the bank near the pile to which the boats were fastened.   They were all talking and laughing, and were in such excitement and commotion that they could hardly get into the boats.   Three boats were crammed with passengers, while two stood empty. The keys for unfastening these two boats had been somehow mislaid, and messengers were continually running from the river to the house to look for them. Some said Grigory had the keys, others that the bailiff had them, while others suggested sending for a blacksmith and breaking the padlocks. And all talked at once, interrupting and shouting one another down. Pyotr Dmitritch paced impatiently to and fro on the bank, shouting:

"What the devil's the meaning of it! The keys ought always to be lying in the hall window! Who has dared to take them away? The bailiff can get a boat of his own if he wants one!"

At last the keys were found. Then it appeared that two oars were missing. Again there was a great hullabaloo. Pyotr Dmitritch, who was weary of pacing about the bank, jumped into a long, narrow boat hollowed out of the trunk of a poplar, and, lurching from side to side and almost falling into the water, pushed off from the bank. The other boats followed him one after another, amid loud laughter and the shrieks of the young ladies.

The white cloudy sky, the trees on the riverside, the boats with the people in them, and the oars, were reflected in the water as in a mirror; under the boats, far away below in the bottomless depths, was a second sky with the birds flying across it. The bank on which the house and gardens stood was high, steep, and covered with trees; on the other, which was sloping, stretched broad green water-

meadows with sheets of water glistening in them.
The boats had floated a hundred yards when, behind
the mournfully drooping willows on the sloping
banks, huts and a herd of cows came into sight; they
began to hear songs, drunken shouts, and the strains
of a concertina.

Here and there on the river fishing-boats were
scattered about, setting their nets for the night.   In
one of these boats was the festive party, playing on
home-made violins and violoncellos.

Olga Mihalovna was sitting at the rudder; she
was smiling affably and talking a great deal to entertain her visitors, while she glanced stealthily at her
husband.   He was ahead of them all, standing up
punting with one oar.   The light sharp-nosed canoe,
which all the guests called the " death-trap "— while
Pyotr Dmitritch, for some reason, called it *Penderaklia* — flew along quickly; it had a brisk, crafty
expression, as though it hated its heavy occupant and
was looking out for a favourable moment to glide
away from under his feet.   Olga Mihalovna kept
looking at her husband, and she loathed his good
looks which attracted every one, the back of his
head, his attitude, his familiar manner with women;
she hated all the women sitting in the boat with her,
was jealous, and at the same time was trembling
every minute in terror that the frail craft would upset and cause an accident.

"Take care, Pyotr!" she cried, while her heart fluttered with terror. "Sit down! We believe in your courage without all that!"

She was worried, too, by the people who were in the boat with her. They were all ordinary good sort of people like thousands of others, but now each one of them struck her as exceptional and evil. In each one of them she saw nothing but falsity. "That young man," she thought, "rowing, in gold-rimmed spectacles, with chestnut hair and a nice-looking beard: he is a mamma's darling, rich, and well-fed, and always fortunate, and every one considers him an honourable, free-thinking, advanced man. It's not a year since he left the University and came to live in the district, but he already talks of himself as 'we active members of the Zemstvo.' But in another year he will be bored like so many others and go off to Petersburg, and to justify running away, will tell every one that the Zemstvos are good-for-nothing, and that he has been deceived in them. While from the other boat his young wife keeps her eyes fixed on him, and believes that he is 'an active member of the Zemstvo,' just as in a year she will believe that the Zemstvo is good-for-nothing. And that stout, carefully shaven gentleman in the straw hat with the broad ribbon, with an expensive cigar in his mouth: he is fond of saying, 'It is time to put away dreams and set to work!'"

He has Yorkshire pigs, Butler's hives, rape-seed, pine-apples, a dairy, a cheese factory, Italian book-keeping by double entry; but every summer he sells his timber and mortgages part of his land to spend the autumn with his mistress in the Crimea. And there's Uncle Nikolay Nikolaitch, who has quarrelled with Pyotr Dmitritch, and yet for some reason does not go home."

Olga Mihalovna looked at the other boats, and there, too, she saw only uninteresting, queer creatures, affected or stupid people. She thought of all the people she knew in the district, and could not remember one person of whom one could say or think anything good. They all seemed to her mediocre, insipid, unintelligent, narrow, false, heartless; they all said what they did not think, and did what they did not want to. Dreariness and despair were stifling her; she longed to leave off smiling, to leap up and cry out, " I am sick of you," and then jump out and swim to the bank.

" I say, let's take Pyotr Dmitritch in tow! " some one shouted.

" In tow, in tow! " the others chimed in. " Olga Mihalovna, take your husband in tow."

To take him in tow, Olga Mihalovna, who was steering, had to seize the right moment and to catch hold of his boat by the chain at the beak. When she bent over to the chain Pyotr Dmitritch frowned and looked at her in alarm.

" I hope you won't catch cold," he said.

" If you are uneasy about me and the child, why do you torment me? " thought Olga Mihalovna.

Pyotr Dmitritch acknowledged himself vanquished, and, not caring to be towed, jumped from the *Penderaklia* into the boat which was overful already, and jumped so carelessly that the boat lurched violently, and every one cried out in terror.

" He did that to please the ladies," thought Olga Mihalovna; " he knows it's charming." Her hands and feet began trembling, as she supposed, from boredom, vexation from the strain of smiling and the discomfort she felt all over her body. And to conceal this trembling from her guests, she tried to talk more loudly, to laugh, to move.

" If I suddenly begin to cry," she thought, " I shall say I have toothache. . . ."

But at last the boats reached the " Island of Good Hope," as they called the peninsula formed by a bend in the river at an acute angle, covered with a copse of old birch-trees, oaks, willows, and poplars. The tables were already laid under the trees; the samovars were smoking, and Vassily and Grigory, in their swallow-tails and white knitted gloves, were already busy with the tea-things. On the other bank, opposite the " Island of Good Hope," there stood the carriages which had come with the provisions. The baskets and parcels of provisions were carried across to the island in a little boat like the *Penderaklia*. The footmen, the coachmen, and even the peasant who was sitting in the boat, had the solemn expression befitting a name-day such as one only sees in children and servants.

While Olga Mihalovna was making the tea and pouring out the first glasses, the visitors were busy with the liqueurs and sweet things. Then there was the general commotion usual at picnics over drinking tea, very wearisome and exhausting for the hostess. Grigory and Vassily had hardly had time to take the glasses round before hands were being stretched out to Olga Mihalovna with empty glasses. One asked for no sugar, another wanted it stronger, another weak, a fourth declined another glass. And all this Olga Mihalovna had to remember, and then to call, " Ivan Petrovitch, is it without sugar for you ? " or, " Gentlemen, which of you wanted it weak ? " But the guest who had asked for weak tea, or no sugar, had by now forgotten it, and, absorbed in agreeable conversation, took the first glass that came. Depressed-looking figures wandered like shadows at a little distance from the table, pretending to look for mushrooms in the grass, or reading the labels on the boxes — these were those for whom there were not glasses enough. "Have you had tea?" Olga Mihalovna kept asking, and the guest so addressed begged her not to trouble, and said, "I will wait," though it would have suited her better for the visitors not to wait but to make haste.

Some, absorbed in conversation, drank their tea slowly, keeping their glasses for half an hour; others, especially some who had drunk a good deal at dinner, would not leave the table, and kept on drinking glass after glass, so that Olga Mihalovna scarcely had time to fill them. One jocular young man sipped his tea through a lump of sugar, and kept saying, "Sinful man that I am, I love to indulge myself with the Chinese herb." He kept asking with a heavy sigh: "Another tiny dish of tea more, if you please." He drank a great deal, nibbled his sugar, and thought it all very amusing and original, and imagined that he was doing a clever imitation of a Russian merchant. None of them understood that these trifles were agonizing to their hostess, and, indeed, it was hard to understand it, as Olga Mihalovna went on all the time smiling affably and talking nonsense.

But she felt ill. . . . She was irritated by the crowd of people, the laughter, the questions, the jocular young man, the footmen harassed and run off their legs, the children who hung round the table; she was irritated at Vata's being like Nata, at Kolya's being like Mitya, so that one could not tell which of them had had tea and which of them had not. She felt that her smile of forced affability was passing into an expression of anger, and she felt every minute as though she would burst into tears.

" Rain, my friends," cried some one.

Every one looked at the sky.

"Yes, it really is rain . . ." Pyotr Dmitritch assented, and wiped his cheek.

Only a few drops were falling from the sky — the real rain had not begun yet; but the company abandoned their tea and made haste to get off. At first they all wanted to drive home in the carriages, but changed their minds and made for the boats. On the pretext that she had to hasten home to give directions about the supper, Olga Mihalovna asked to be excused for leaving the others, and went home in the carriage.

When she got into the carriage, she first of all let her face rest from smiling. With an angry face she drove through the village, and with an angry face acknowledged the bows of the peasants she met. When she got home, she went to the bedroom by the back way and lay down on her husband's bed.

" Merciful God! " she whispered. " What is all

this hard labour for? Why do all these people hustle each other here and pretend that they are enjoying themselves? Why do I smile and lie? I don't understand it."

She heard steps and voices. The visitors had come back.

"Let them come," thought Olga Mihalovna; "I shall lie a little longer."

But a maid-servant came and said:

"Marya Grigoryevna is going, madam."

Olga Mihalovna jumped up, tidied her hair and hurried out of the room.

"Marya Grigoryevna, what is the meaning of this?" she began in an injured voice, going to meet Marya Grigoryevna. "Why are you in such a hurry?"

"I can't help it, darling! I've stayed too long as it is; my children are expecting me home."

"It's too bad of you! Why didn't you bring your children with you?"

"If you will let me, dear, I will bring them on some ordinary day, but to-day . . ."

"Oh, please do," Olga Mihalovna interrupted; "I shall be delighted! Your children are so sweet! Kiss them all for me. . . . But, really, I am offended with you! I don't understand why you are in such a hurry!"

"I really must, I really must. . . . Good-bye,

dear.   Take care of yourself.   In your condition, you know . . ."

And the ladies kissed each other.   After seeing the departing guest to her carriage, Olga Mihalovna went in to the ladies in the drawing-room.   There the lamps were already lighted and the gentlemen were sitting down to cards.

IV

The party broke up after supper about a quarter past twelve.   Seeing her visitors off, Olga Mihalovna stood at the door and said:

" You really ought to take a shawl!   It's turning a little chilly.   Please God, you don't catch cold!"

" Don't trouble, Olga Mihalovna," the ladies answered as they got into the carriage.   " Well, good-bye.   Mind now, we are expecting you; don't play us false!"

" Wo-o-o!" the coachman checked the horses.

" Ready, Denis!   Good-bye, Olga Mihalovna!"

" Kiss the children for me!"

The carriage started and immediately disappeared into the darkness.   In the red circle of light cast by the lamp in the road, a fresh pair or trio of impatient horses, and the silhouette of a coachman with his hands held out stiffly before him, would

come into view. Again there began kisses, re-
proaches, and entreaties to come again or to take
a shawl. Pyotr Dmitritch kept running out and
helping the ladies into their carriages.

"You go now by Efremovshtchina," he directed
the coachman; "it's nearer through Mankino, but
the road is worse that way. You might have an
upset. . . . Good-bye, my charmer. *Mille compli-
ments* to your artist!"

"Good-bye, Olga Mihalovna, darling! Go indoors, or you will catch cold! It's damp!"

"Wo-o-o! you rascal!"

"What horses have you got here?" Pyotr Dmitritch asked.

"They were bought from Haidorov, in Lent," answered the coachman.

"Capital horses. . . ."

And Pyotr Dmitritch patted the trace horse on
the haunch.

"Well, you can start! God give you good
luck!"

The last visitor was gone at last; the red circle on
the road quivered, moved aside, contracted and
went out, as Vassily carried away the lamp from
the entrance. On previous occasions when they had
seen off their visitors, Pyotr Dmitritch and Olga
Mihalovna had begun dancing about the drawing-
room, facing each other, clapping their hands and

singing: "They've gone! They've gone!" But now Olga Mihalovna was not equal to that. She went to her bedroom, undressed, and got into bed.

She fancied she would fall asleep at once and sleep soundly. Her legs and her shoulders ached painfully, her head was heavy from the strain of talking, and she was conscious, as before, of discomfort all over her body. Covering her head over, she lay still for three or four minutes, then peeped out from under the bed-clothes at the lamp before the ikon, listened to the silence, and smiled.

"It's nice, it's nice," she whispered, curling up her legs, which felt as if they had grown longer from so much walking. "Sleep, sleep. . . ."

Her legs would not get into a comfortable position; she felt uneasy all over, and she turned on the other side. A big fly blew buzzing about the bedroom and thumped against the ceiling. She could hear, too, Grigory and Vassily stepping cautiously about the drawing-room, putting the chairs back in their places; it seemed to Olga Mihalovna that she could not go to sleep, nor be comfortable till those sounds were hushed. And again she turned over on the other side impatiently.

She heard her husband's voice in the drawing-room. Some one must be staying the night, as Pyotr Dmitritch was addressing some one and speaking loudly:

" I don't say that Count Alexey Petrovitch is an impostor. But he can't help seeming to be one, because all of you gentlemen attempt to see in him something different from what he really is. His craziness is looked upon as originality, his familiar manners as good-nature, and his complete absence of opinions as Conservatism. Even granted that he is a Conservative of the stamp of '84, what after all is Conservatism? "

Pyotr Dmitritch, angry with Count Alexey Petrovitch, his visitors, and himself, was relieving his heart. He abused both the Count and his visitors, and in his vexation with himself was ready to speak out and to hold forth upon anything. After seeing his guest to his room, he walked up and down the drawing-room, walked through the dining-room, down the corridor, then into his study, then again went into the drawing-room, and came into the bed-room. Olga Mihalovna was lying on her back, with the bed-clothes only to her waist (by now she felt hot), and with an angry face, watched the fly that was thumping against the ceiling.

" Is some one staying the night? " she asked.

" Yegorov."

Pyotr Dmitritch undressed and got into his bed. Without speaking, he lighted a cigarette, and he, too, fell to watching the fly. There was an uneasy and forbidding look in his eyes. Olga Mihalovna looked at his handsome profile for five minutes in silence. It seemed to her for some reason that if her husband were suddenly to turn facing her, and to say, " Olga, I am unhappy," she would cry or laugh, and she would be at ease. She fancied that her legs were aching and her body was uncomfortable all over because of the strain on her feelings.

" Pyotr, what are you thinking of ? " she said.

" Oh, nothing . . ." her husband answered.

" You have taken to having secrets from me of late : that's not right."

" Why is it not right ? " answered Pyotr Dmitritch drily and not at once. " We all have our personal life, every one of us, and we are bound to have our secrets."

" Personal life, our secrets . . . that's all words ! Understand you are wounding me ! " said Olga Mihalovna, sitting up in bed. " If you have a load on your heart, why do you hide it from me ? And why do you find it more suitable to open your heart to women who are nothing to you, instead of to your wife ? I overheard your outpourings to Lubotchka by the bee-house to-day."

" Well, I congratulate you. I am glad you did overhear it."

This meant " Leave me alone and let me think." Olga Mihalovna was indignant. Vexation, hatred, and wrath, which had been accumulating within her during the whole day, suddenly boiled over; she wanted at once to speak out, to hurt her husband without putting it off till to-morrow, to wound him, to punish him. . . . Making an effort to control herself and not to scream, she said:

"Let me tell you, then, that it's all loathsome, loathsome, loathsome! I've been hating you all day; you see what you've done."

Pyotr Dmitritch, too, got up and sat on the bed.

"It's loathsome, loathsome, loathsome," Olga Mihalovna went on, beginning to tremble all over. "There's no need to congratulate me; you had better congratulate yourself! It's a shame, a disgrace. You have wrapped yourself in lies till you are ashamed to be alone in the room with your wife! You are a deceitful man! I see through you and understand every step you take!"

"Olya, I wish you would please warn me when you are out of humour. Then I will sleep in the study."

Saying this, Pyotr Dmitritch picked up his pillow and walked out of the bedroom. Olga Mihalovna had not foreseen this. For some minutes she remained silent with her mouth open, trembling all over and looking at the door by which her husband had gone out, and trying to understand what it meant. Was this one of the devices to which deceitful people have recourse when they are in the wrong, or was it a deliberate insult aimed at her pride? How was she to take it? Olga Mihalovna remembered her cousin, a lively young officer, who often used to tell her, laughing, that when " his spouse nagged at him " at night, he usually picked up his pillow and went whistling to spend the night in his study, leaving his wife in a foolish and ridiculous position. This officer was married to a rich, capricious, and foolish woman whom he did not respect but simply put up with.

Olga Mihalovna jumped out of bed. To her mind there was only one thing left for her to do now; to dress with all possible haste and to leave the house forever. The house was her own, but so much the worse for Pyotr Dmitritch. Without pausing to consider whether this was necessary or not, she went quickly to the study to inform her husband of her intention (" Feminine logic! " flashed through her mind), and to say something wounding and sarcastic at parting. . . .

Pyotr Dmitritch was lying on the sofa and pretending to read a newspaper. There was a candle burning on a chair near him. His face could not be seen behind the newspaper.

" Be so kind as to tell me what this means? I am asking you."

" Be so kind . . ." Pyotr Dmitritch mimicked her, not showing his face. " It's sickening, Olga!

Upon my honour, I am exhausted and not up to
it. . . . Let us do our quarrelling to-morrow."

" No, I understand you perfectly!" Olga Mihalovna went on. " You hate me! Yes, yes! You
hate me because I am richer than you! You will
never forgive me for that, and will always be lying
to me!" (" Feminine logic!" flashed through her
mind again.) " You are laughing at me now. . . .
I am convinced, in fact, that you only married me
in order to have property qualifications and those
wretched horses. . . . Oh, I am miserable!"

Pyotr Dmitritch dropped the newspaper and got
up. The unexpected insult overwhelmed him.
With a childishly helpless smile he looked desperately at his wife, and holding out his hands to her
as though to ward off blows, he said imploringly:

" Olya!"

And expecting her to say something else awful,
he leaned back in his chair, and his huge figure
seemed as helplessly childish as his smile.

" Olya, how could you say it?" he whispered.

Olga Mihalovna came to herself. She was suddenly aware of her passionate love for this man,
remembered that he was her husband, Pyotr Dmitritch, without whom she could not live for a day,
and who loved her passionately, too. She burst
into loud sobs that sounded strange and unlike her,
and ran back to her bedroom.

She fell on the bed, and short hysterical sobs, choking her and making her arms and legs twitch, filled the bedroom.   Remembering there was a visitor sleeping three or four rooms away, she buried her head under the pillow to stifle her sobs, but the pillow rolled on to the floor, and she almost fell on the floor herself when she stooped to pick it up. She pulled the quilt up to her face, but her hands would not obey her, but tore convulsively at everything she clutched.

She thought that everything was lost, that the falsehood she had told to wound her husband had shattered her life into fragments.   Her husband would not forgive her.   The insult she had hurled at him was not one that could be effaced by any caresses, by any vows. . . . How could she convince her husband that she did not believe what she had said?

"It's all over, it's all over!" she cried, not noticing that the pillow had slipped on to the floor again.   "For God's sake, for God's sake!"

Probably roused by her cries, the guest and the servants were now awake; next day all the neighbourhood would know that she had been in hysterics and would blame Pyotr Dmitritch.   She made an effort to restrain herself, but her sobs grew louder and louder every minute.

"For God's sake," she cried in a voice not like

her own, and not knowing why she cried it. "For God's sake!"

She felt as though the bed were heaving under her and her feet were entangled in the bed-clothes. Pyotr Dmitritch, in his dressing-gown, with a candle in his hand, came into the bedroom.

"Olya, hush!" he said.

She raised herself, and kneeling up in bed, screwing up her eyes at the light, articulated through her sobs:

"Understand . . . understand! . . ."

She wanted to tell him that she was tired to death by the party, by his falsity, by her own falsity, that it had all worked together, but she could only articulate:

"Understand . . . understand!"

"Come, drink!" he said, handing her some water.

She took the glass obediently and began drinking, but the water splashed over and was spilt on her arms, her throat and knees.

"I must look horribly unseemly," she thought.

Pyotr Dmitritch put her back in bed without a word, and covered her with the quilt, then he took the candle and went out.

"For God's sake!" Olga Mihalovna cried again. "Pyotr, understand, understand!"

Suddenly something gripped her in the lower

part of her body and back with such violence that her wailing was cut short, and she bit the pillow from the pain.   But the pain let her go again at once, and she began sobbing again.

The maid came in, and arranging the quilt over her, asked in alarm:

" Mistress, darling, what is the matter? "

" Go out of the room," said Pyotr Dmitritch sternly, going up to the bed.

"Understand . . . understand! . . ." Olga Mihalovna began.

" Olya, I entreat you, calm yourself," he said. " I did not mean to hurt you.   I would not have gone out of the room if I had known it would have hurt you so much; I simply felt depressed.   I tell you, on my honour . . ."

" Understand! . . . You were lying, I was lying. . . ."

" I understand. . . . Come, come, that's enough! I understand," said Pyotr Dmitritch tenderly, sitting down on her bed.   " You said that in anger; I quite understand.   I swear to God I love you beyond anything on earth, and when I married you I never once thought of your being rich.   I loved you immensely, and that's all . . . I assure you.   I have never been in want of money or felt the value of it, and so I cannot feel the difference between your fortune and mine. It always seemed to me we were equally well off. And that I have been deceitful in little things, that . . . of course, is true. My life has hitherto been arranged in such a frivolous way that it has somehow been impossible to get on without paltry lying. It weighs on me, too, now. . . . Let us leave off talking about it, for goodness' sake!"

Olga Mihalovna again felt in acute pain, and clutched her husband by the sleeve.

"I am in pain, in pain, in pain . . ." she said rapidly. "Oh, what pain!"

"Damnation take those visitors!" muttered Pyotr Dmitritch, getting up. "You ought not to have gone to the island to-day!" he cried. "What an idiot I was not to prevent you! Oh, my God!"

He scratched his head in vexation, and, with a wave of his hand, walked out of the room.

Then he came into the room several times, sat down on the bed beside her, and talked a great deal, sometimes tenderly, sometimes angrily, but she hardly heard him. Her sobs were continually interrupted by fearful attacks of pain, and each time the pain was more acute and prolonged. At first she held her breath and bit the pillow during the pain, but then she began screaming on an unseemly piercing note. Once seeing her husband near her, she remembered that she had insulted him, and without pausing to think whether it were really Pyotr Dmitritch or whether she were in delirium, clutched his hand in both hers and began kissing it.

"You were lying, I was lying . . ." she began justifying herself. "Understand, understand. . . . They have exhausted me, driven me out of all patience."

"Olya, we are not alone," said Pyotr Dmitritch.

Olga Mihalovna raised her head and saw Varvara, who was kneeling by the chest of drawers and pulling out the bottom drawer. The top drawers were already open. Then Varvara got up, red from the strained position, and with a cold, solemn face began trying to unlock a box.

"Marya, I can't unlock it!" she said in a whisper. "You unlock it, won't you?"

Marya, the maid, was digging a candle end out of the candlestick with a pair of scissors, so as to put in a new candle; she went up to Varvara and helped her to unlock the box.

"There should be nothing locked . . ." whispered Varvara. "Unlock this basket, too, my good girl. Master," she said, "you should send to Father Mihail to unlock the holy gates! You must!"

"Do what you like," said Pyotr Dmitritch, breathing hard, "only, for God's sake, make haste and fetch the doctor or the midwife! Has Vassily gone? Send some one else. Send your husband!"

" It's the birth," Olga Mihalovna thought. " Varvara," she moaned, " but he won't be born alive ! "

" It's all right, it's all right, mistress," whispered Varvara. " Please God, he will be alive ! he will be alive ! "

When Olga Mihalovna came to herself again after a pain she was no longer sobbing nor tossing from side to side, but moaning. She could not refrain from moaning even in the intervals between the pains. The candles were still burning, but the morning light was coming through the blinds. It was probably about five o'clock in the morning. At the round table there was sitting some unknown woman with a very discreet air, wearing a white apron. From her whole appearance it was evident she had been sitting there a long time. Olga Mihalovna guessed that she was the midwife.

" Will it soon be over ? " she asked, and in her voice she heard a peculiar and unfamiliar note which had never been there before. " I must be dying in childbirth," she thought.

Pyotr Dmitritch came cautiously into the bedroom, dressed for the day, and stood at the window with his back to his wife. He lifted the blind and looked out of window.

" What rain ! " he said.

" What time is it ? " asked Olga Mihalovna, in

order to hear the unfamiliar note in her voice again.

" A quarter to six," answered the midwife.

" And what if I really am dying? " thought Olga Mihalovna, looking at her husband's head and the window-panes on which the rain was beating. " How will he live without me?   With whom will he have tea and dinner, talk in the evenings, sleep? "

And he seemed to her like a forlorn child; she felt sorry for him and wanted to say something nice, caressing and consolatory. She remembered how in the spring he had meant to buy himself some harriers, and she, thinking it a cruel and dangerous sport, had prevented him from doing it.

" Pyotr, buy yourself harriers," she moaned.

He dropped the blind and went up to the bed, and would have said something; but at that moment the pain came back, and Olga Mihalovna uttered an unseemly, piercing scream.

The pain and the constant screaming and moaning stupefied her. She heard, saw, and sometimes spoke, but hardly understood anything, and was only conscious that she was in pain or was just going to be in pain. It seemed to her that the nameday party had been long, long ago — not yesterday, but a year ago perhaps; and that her new life of agony had lasted longer than her childhood, her school-days, her time at the University, and her marriage, and would go on for a long, long time, endlessly. She saw them bring tea to the midwife, and summon her at midday to lunch and afterwards to dinner; she saw Pyotr Dmitritch grow used to coming in, standing for long intervals by the window, and going out again; saw strange men, the maid, Varvara, come in as though they were at home. . . . Varvara said nothing but, " He will, he will," and was angry when any one closed the drawers and the chest. Olga Mihalovna saw the light change in the room and in the windows: at one time it was twilight, then thick like fog, then bright daylight as it had been at dinner-time the day before, then again twilight . . . and each of these changes lasted as long as her childhood, her school-days, her life at the University. . . .

In the evening two doctors — one bony, bald, with a big red beard; the other with a swarthy Jewish face and cheap spectacles — performed some sort of operation on Olga Mihalovna. To these unknown men touching her body she felt utterly indifferent. By now she had no feeling of shame, no will, and any one might do what he would with her. If any one had rushed at her with a knife, or had insulted Pyotr Dmitritch, or had robbed her of her right to the little creature, she would not have said a word.

They gave her chloroform during the operation. When she came to again, the pain was still there

and insufferable. It was night. And Olga Mihalovna remembered that there had been just such a
night with the stillness, the lamp, with the midwife
sitting motionless by the bed, with the drawers of
the chest pulled out, with Pyotr Dmitritch standing
by the window, but some time very, very long
ago. . . .

V

" I am not dead . . ." thought Olga Mihalovna
when she began to understand her surroundings
again, and when the pain was over.

A bright summer day looked in at the widely
open windows; in the garden below the windows,
the sparrows and the magpies never ceased chat-
tering for one instant.

The drawers were shut now, her husband's bed
had been made. There was no sign of the midwife or of the maid, or of Varvara in the room,
only Pyotr Dmitritch was standing, as before, motionless by the window looking into the garden.
There was no sound of a child's crying, no one was
congratulating her or rejoicing, it was evident that
the little creature had not been born alive.

" Pyotr! "

Olga Mihalovna called to her husband.

Pyotr Dmitritch looked round. It seemed as

though a long time must have passed since the last guest had departed and Olga Mihalovna had insulted her husband, for Pyotr Dmitritch was perceptibly thinner and hollow-eyed.

"What is it?" he asked, coming up to the bed.

He looked away, moved his lips and smiled with childlike helplessness.

"Is it all over?" asked Olga Mihalovna.

Pyotr Dmitritch tried to make some answer, but his lips quivered and his mouth worked like a toothless old man's, like Uncle Nikolay Nikolaitch's.

"Olya," he said, wringing his hands; big tears suddenly dropping from his eyes. "Olya, I don't care about your property qualification, nor the Circuit Courts . . ." (he gave a sob) "nor particular views, nor those visitors, nor your fortune. . . . I don't care about anything! Why didn't we take care of our child? Oh, it's no good talking!"

With a despairing gesture he went out of the bedroom.

But nothing mattered to Olga Mihalovna now, there was a mistiness in her brain from the chloroform, an emptiness in her soul. . . . The dull indifference to life which had overcome her when the two doctors were performing the operation still had possession of her.

1888

TERROR

TERROR

MY FRIEND'S STORY

DMITRI PETROVITCH SILIN had taken his degree and entered the government service in Petersburg, but at thirty he gave up his post and went in for agriculture. His farming was fairly successful, and yet it always seemed to me that he was not in his proper place, and that he would do well to go back to Petersburg. When sunburnt, grey with dust, exhausted with toil, he met me near the gates or at the entrance, and then at supper struggled with sleepiness and his wife took him off to bed as though he were a baby; or when, overcoming his sleepiness, he began in his soft, cordial, almost imploring voice, to talk about his really excellent ideas, I saw him not as a farmer nor an agriculturist, but only as a worried and exhausted man, and it was clear to me that he did not really care for farming, but that all he wanted was for the day to be over and " Thank God for it."

I liked to be with him, and I used to stay on his farm for two or three days at a time. I liked his house, and his park, and his big fruit garden, and the river — and his philosophy, which was clear, though rather spiritless and rhetorical. I suppose I was fond of him on his own account, though I can't say that for certain, as I have not up to now succeeded in analysing my feelings at that time. He was an intelligent, kind-hearted, genuine man, and not a bore, but I remember that when he confided to me his most treasured secrets and spoke of our relation to each other as friendship, it disturbed me unpleasantly, and I was conscious of awkwardness. In his affection for me there was something inappropriate, tiresome, and I should have greatly preferred commonplace friendly relations.

The fact is that I was extremely attracted by his wife, Marya Sergeyevna. I was not in love with her, but I was attracted by her face, her eyes, her voice, her walk. I missed her when I did not see her for a long time, and my imagination pictured no one at that time so eagerly as that young, beautiful, elegant woman. I had no definite designs in regard to her, and did not dream of anything of the sort, yet for some reason, whenever we were left alone, I remembered that her husband looked upon me as his friend, and I felt awkward. When she played my favourite pieces on the piano or told me something interesting, I listened with pleasure, and yet at the same time for some reason the reflection that she loved her husband, that he was my friend, and that she herself looked upon me as his friend, obtruded themselves upon me, my spirits flagged, and I became listless, awkward, and dull. She noticed this change and would usually say:

"You are dull without your friend. We must send out to the fields for him."

And when Dmitri Petrovitch came in, she would say:

"Well, here is your friend now. Rejoice."

So passed a year and a half.

It somehow happened one July Sunday that Dmitri Petrovitch and I, having nothing to do, drove to the big village of Klushino to buy things for supper. While we were going from one shop to another the sun set and the evening came on — the evening which I shall probably never forget in my life. After buying cheese that smelt like soap, and petrified sausages that smelt of tar, we went to the tavern to ask whether they had any beer. Our coachman went off to the blacksmith to get our horses shod, and we told him we would wait for him near the church. We walked, talked, laughed over our purchases, while a man who was known in the district by a very strange nickname, "Forty Martyrs," followed us all the while in silence with a mysterious air like a detective. This Forty Martyrs was no other than Gavril Syeverov, or more simply Gavryushka, who had been for a short time in my service as a footman and had been dismissed by me for drunkenness. He had been in Dmitri Petrovitch's service, too, and by him had been dismissed for the same vice. He was an inveterate drunkard, and indeed his whole life was as drunk and disorderly as himself. His father had been a priest and his mother of noble rank, so by birth he belonged to the privileged class; but however carefully I scrutinized his exhausted, respectful, and always perspiring face, his red beard now turning grey, his pitifully torn reefer jacket and his red shirt, I could not discover in him the faintest trace of anything we associate with privilege. He spoke of himself as a man of education, and used to say that he had been in a clerical school, but had not finished his studies there, as he had been expelled for smoking; then he had sung in the bishop's choir and lived for two years in a monastery, from which he was also expelled, but this time not for smoking but for " his weakness." He had walked all over two provinces, had presented petitions to the Consistory, and to various government offices, and had been four times on his trial. At last, being stranded in our district, he had served as a footman, as a forester, as a kennelman, as a sexton, had married a cook who was a widow and rather a loose character, and had so hopelessly sunk into a menial position, and had grown so used to filth and dirt, that he even spoke of his privileged origin with a certain scepticism, as of some myth. At the time I am describing, he was hanging about without a job, calling himself a carrier and a huntsman, and his wife had disappeared and made no sign.

From the tavern we went to the church and sat in the porch, waiting for the coachman. Forty Martyrs stood a little way off and put his hand before his mouth in order to cough in it respectfully if need be. By now it was dark; there was a strong smell of evening dampness, and the moon was on the point of rising. There were only two clouds in the clear starry sky exactly over our heads: one big one and one smaller; alone in the sky they were racing after one another like mother and child, in the direction where the sunset was glowing.

"What a glorious day!" said Dmitri Petrovitch.

"In the extreme . . ." Forty Martyrs assented, and he coughed respectfully into his hand. "How was it, Dmitri Petrovitch, you thought to visit these parts?" he asked in an ingratiating voice, evidently anxious to get up a conversation.

Dmitri Petrovitch made no answer. Forty Martyrs heaved a deep sigh and said softly, not looking at us:

"I suffer solely through a cause to which I must answer to Almighty God. No doubt about it, I am a hopeless and incompetent man; but believe me, on my conscience, I am without a crust of bread and worse off than a dog. . . . Forgive me, Dmitri Petrovitch."

Silin was not listening, but sat musing with his head propped on his fists. The church stood at the end of the street on the high river-bank, and through the trellis gate of the enclosure we could see the river, the water-meadows on the near side of it, and the crimson glare of a camp fire about which black figures of men and horses were moving. And beyond the fire, further away, there were other lights, where there was a little village. They were singing there. On the river, and here and there on the meadows, a mist was rising. High narrow coils of mist, thick and white as milk, were trailing over the river, hiding the reflection of the stars and hovering over the willows. Every minute they changed their form, and it seemed as though some were embracing, others were bowing, others lifting up their arms to heaven with wide sleeves like priests, as though they were praying. . . . Probably they reminded Dmitri Petrovitch of ghosts and of the dead, for he turned facing me and asked with a mournful smile:

" Tell me, my dear fellow, why is it that when we want to tell some terrible, mysterious, and fantastic story, we draw our material, not from life, but in-

variably from the world of ghosts and of the shadows beyond the grave."

" We are frightened of what we don't understand."

" And do you understand life? Tell me: do you
understand life better than the world beyond the
grave ? "

Dmitri Petrovitch was sitting quite close to me,
so that I felt his breath upon my cheek. In the
evening twilight his pale, lean face seemed paler
than ever and his lark beard was black as soot.
His eyes were sad, truthful, and a little frightened,
as though he were about to tell me something horrible. He looked into my eyes and went on in his
habitual imploring voice:

" Our life and the life beyond the grave are
equally incomprehensible and horrible. If any one
is afraid of ghosts he ought to be afraid, too, of
me, and of those lights and of the sky, seeing that,
if you come to reflect, all that is no less fantastic
and beyond our grasp than apparitions from the
other world. Prince Hamlet did not kill himself
because he was afraid of the visions that might
haunt his dreams after death. I like that famous
soliloquy of his, but, to be candid, it never touched
my soul. I will confess to you as a friend that in
moments of depression I have sometimes pictured

to myself the hour of my death.   My fancy invented thousands of the gloomiest visions, and I have succeeded in working myself up to an agonizing exaltation, to a state of nightmare, and I assure you that that did not seem to me more terrible than reality. What I mean is, apparitions are terrible, but life is terrible, too.   I don't understand life and I am afraid of it, my dear boy; I don't know.   Perhaps I am a morbid person, unhinged.   It seems to a sound, healthy man that he understands everything he sees and hears, but that 'seeming' is lost to me, and from day to day I am poisoning myself with terror.   There is a disease, the fear of open spaces, but my disease is the fear of life.   When I lie on the grass and watch a little beetle which was born yesterday and understands nothing, it seems to me that its life consists of nothing else but fear, and in it I see myself."

"What is it exactly you are frightened of?" I asked.

"I am afraid of everything.   I am not by nature a profound thinker, and I take little interest in such questions as the life beyond the grave, the destiny of humanity, and, in fact, I am rarely carried away to the heights.   What chiefly frightens me is the common routine of life from which none of us can escape.   I am incapable of distinguishing what is true and what is false in my actions, and they worry me. I recognize that education and the conditions of life have imprisoned me in a narrow circle of falsity, that my whole life is nothing else than a daily effort to deceive myself and other people, and to avoid noticing it; and I am frightened at the thought that to the day of my death I shall not escape from this falsity. To-day I do something and to-morrow I do not understand why I did it. I entered the service in Petersburg and took fright; I came here to work on the land, and here, too, I am frightened. . . . I see that we know very little and so make mistakes every day. We are unjust, we slander one another and spoil each other's lives, we waste all our powers on trash which we do not need and which hinders us from living; and that frightens me, because I don't understand why and for whom it is necessary. I don't understand men, my dear fellow, and I am afraid of them. It frightens me to look at the peasants, and I don't know for what higher objects they are suffering and what they are living for. If life is an enjoyment, then they are unnecessary, superfluous people; if the object and meaning of life is to be found in poverty and unending, hopeless ignorance, I can't understand for whom and what this torture is necessary. I undestand no one and nothing. Kindly try to understand this specimen, for instance," said Dmitri Petrovitch, pointing to Forty Martyrs. "Think of him!"

Noticing that we were looking at him, Forty Martyrs coughed deferentially into his fist and said:

" I was always a faithful servant with good masters, but the great trouble has been spirituous liquor. If a poor fellow like me were shown consideration and given a place, I would kiss the ikon. My word's my bond."

The sexton walked by, looked at us in amazement, and began pulling the rope. The bell, abruptly breaking upon the stillness of the evening, struck ten with a slow and prolonged note.

"It's ten o'clock, though," said Dmitri Petrovitch. "It's time we were going. Yes, my dear fellow," he sighed, "if only you knew how afraid I am of my ordinary everyday thoughts, in which one would have thought there should be nothing dreadful. To prevent myself thinking I distract my mind with work and try to tire myself out that I may sleep sound at night. Children, a wife — all that seems ordinary with other people; but how that weighs upon me, my dear fellow!"

He rubbed his face with his hands, cleared his throat, and laughed.

" If I could only tell you how I have played the fool in my life!" he said. "They all tell me that I

have a sweet wife, charming children, and that I am
a good husband and father. They think I am very
happy and envy me. But since it has come to that,
I will tell you in secret: my happy family life is only
a grievous misunderstanding, and I am afraid of it."

His pale face was distorted by a wry smile. He
put his arm round my waist and went on in an under-
tone:

"You are my true friend; I believe in you and
have a deep respect for you. Heaven gave us
friendship that we may open our hearts and escape
from the secrets that weigh upon us. Let me take
advantage of your friendly feeling for me and tell
you the whole truth. My home life, which seems to
you so enchanting, is my chief misery and my chief
terror. I got married in a strange and stupid way.
I must tell you that I was madly in love with Masha
before I married her, and was courting her for two
years. I asked her to marry me five times, and she
refused me because she did not care for me in the
least. The sixth, when burning with passion I
crawled on my knees before her and implored her to
take a beggar and marry me, she consented. . . .
What she said to me was: 'I don't love you, but I
will be true to you. . . .' I accepted that condition
with rapture. At the time I understood what that
meant, but I swear to God I don't understand it now.
'I don't love you, but I will be true to you.' What

does that mean?   It's a fog, a darkness.   I love her
now as intensely as I did the day we were married,
while she, I believe, is as indifferent as ever, and I
believe she is glad when I go away from home.   I
don't know for certain whether she cares for me or
not — I don't know, I don't know; but, as you see,
we live under the same roof, call each other ' thou,'
sleep together, have children, our property is in common. . . . What does it mean, what does it mean?
What is the object of it?   And do you understand it
at all, my dear fellow?   It's cruel torture!   Because
I don't understand our relations, I hate, sometimes
her, sometimes myself, sometimes both at once.
Everything is in a tangle in my brain; I torment myself and grow stupid.   And as though to spite me,
she grows more beautiful every day, she is getting
more wonderful. . . . I fancy her hair is marvellous, and her smile is like no other woman's.   I
love her, and I know that my love is hopeless.
Hopeless love for a woman by whom one has two
children!   Is that intelligible?   And isn't it terrible?   Isn't it more terrible than ghosts? "

He was in the mood to have talked on a good deal
longer, but luckily we heard the coachman's voice.
Our horses had arrived.   We got into the carriage,
and Forty Martyrs, taking off his cap, helped us
both into the carriage with an expression that suggested that he had long been waiting for an oppor-

tunity to come in contact with our precious persons.

"Dmitri Petrovitch, let me come to you," he said, blinking furiously and tilting his head on one side. "Show divine mercy! I am dying of hunger!"

"Very well," said Silin. "Come, you shall stay three days, and then we shall see."

"Certainly, sir," said Forty Martyrs, overjoyed. "I'll come today, sir."

It was a five miles' drive home. Dmitri Petrovitch, glad that he had at last opened his heart to his friend, kept his arm round my waist all the way; and speaking now, not with bitterness and not with apprehension, but quite cheerfully, told me that if everything had been satisfactory in his home life, he should have returned to Petersburg and taken up scientific work there. The movement which had driven so many gifted young men into the country was, he said, a deplorable movement. We had plenty of rye and wheat in Russia, but absolutely no cultured people. The strong and gifted among the young ought to take up science, art, and politics; to act otherwise meant being wasteful. He generalized with pleasure and expressed regret that he would be parting from me early next morning, as he had to go to a sale of timber.

And I felt awkward and depressed, and it seemed to me that I was deceiving the man. And at the same time it was pleasant to me. I gazed at the immense crimson moon which was rising, and pictured the tall, graceful, fair woman, with her pale face, always well-dressed and fragrant with some special scent, rather like musk, and for some reason it pleased me to think she did not love her husband.

On reaching home, we sat down to supper. Marya Sergeyevna, laughing, regaled us with our purchases, and I thought that she certainly had wonderful hair and that her smile was unlike any other woman's.   I watched her, and I wanted to detect in every look and movement that she did not love her husband, and I fancied that I did see it.

Dmitri Petrovitch was soon struggling with sleep. After supper he sat with us for ten minutes and said:

" Do as you please, my friends, but I have to be up at three o'clock tomorrow morning.   Excuse my leaving you."

He kissed his wife tenderly, pressed my hand with warmth and gratitude, and made me promise that I would certainly come the following week. That he might not oversleep next morning, he went to spend the night in the lodge.

Marya Sergeyevna always sat up late, in the Petersburg fashion, and for some reason on this occasion I was glad of it.

" And now," I began when we were left alone, " and now you'll be kind and play me something."

I felt no desire for music, but I did not know how

to begin the conversation. She sat down to the piano and played, I don't remember what. I sat down beside her and looked at her plump white hands and tried to read something on her cold, indifferent face. Then she smiled at something and looked at me.

" You are dull without your friend," she said.

I laughed.

" It would be enough for friendship to be here once a month, but I turn up oftener than once a week."

Saying this, I got up and walked from one end of the room to the other. She too got up and walked away to the fireplace.

" What do you mean to say by that? " she said, raising her large, clear eyes and looking at me.

I made no answer.

" What you say is not true," she went on, after a moment's thought. " You only come here on account of Dmitri Petrovitch. Well, I am very glad. One does not often see such friendships nowadays."

" Aha ! " I thought, and, not knowing what to say, I asked: " Would you care for a turn in the garden? "

" No."

I went out upon the verandah. Nervous shudders were running over my head and I felt chilly

with excitement.   I was convinced now that our conversation would be utterly trivial, and that there was
nothing particular we should be able to say to one
another, but that, that night, what I did not dare to
dream of was bound to happen — that it was bound
to be that night or never.

"What lovely weather!" I said aloud.

"It makes absolutely no difference to me," she
answered.

I went into the drawing-room.   Marya Sergeyevna was standing, as before, near the fireplace,
with her hands behind her back, looking away and
thinking of something.

"Why does it make no difference to you?" I
asked.

"Because I am bored.   You are only bored without your friend, but I am always bored.   However
. . . that is of no interest to you."

I sat down to the piano and struck a few chords,
waiting to hear what she would say.

"Please don't stand on ceremony," she said, looking angrily at me, and she seemed as though on the
point of crying with vexation.   "If you are sleepy,
go to bed.   Because you are Dmitri Petrovitch's
friend, you are not in duty bound to be bored with
his wife's company.   I don't want a sacrifice.
Please go."

I did not, of course, go to bed.   She went out on

the verandah while I remained in the drawing-room
and spent five minutes turning over the music.
Then I went out, too. We stood close together in
the shadow of the curtains, and below us were the
steps bathed in moonlight. The black shadows of
the trees stretched across the flower beds and the
yellow sand of the paths.

" I shall have to go away tomorrow, too," I said.

" Of course, if my husband's not at home you can't
stay here," she said sarcastically. " I can imagine
how miserable you would be if you were in love with
me! Wait a bit: one day I shall throw myself on
your neck. . . . I shall see with what horror you
will run away from me. That would be interesting."

Her words and her pale face were angry, but her
eyes were full of tender passionate love. I already
looked upon this lovely creature as my property, and
then for the first time I noticed that she had golden
eyebrows, exquisite eyebrows. I had never seen such
eyebrows before. The thought that I might at once
press her to my heart, caress her, touch her wonderful hair, seemed to me such a miracle that I laughed
and shut my eyes.

" It's bed-time now. . . . A peaceful night," she
said.

" I don't want a peaceful night," I said, laughing,
following her into the drawing-room. " I shall
curse this night if it is a peaceful one."

Pressing her hand, and escorting her to the door, I saw by her face that she understood me, and was glad that I understood her, too.

I went to my room.   Near the books on the table lay Dmitri Petrovitch's cap, and that reminded me of his affection for me.   I took my stick and went out into the garden.   The mist had risen here, too, and the same tall, narrow, ghostly shapes which I had seen earlier on the river were trailing round the trees and bushes and wrapping about them.   What a pity I could not talk to them!

In the extraordinarily transparent air, each leaf, each drop of dew stood out distinctly; it was all smiling at me in the stillness half asleep, and as I passed the green seats I recalled the words in some play of Shakespeare's: "How sweetly falls the moonlight on yon seat!"

There was a mound in the garden; I went up it and sat down.   I was tormented by a delicious feeling. I knew for certain that in a moment I should hold in my arms, should press to my heart her magnificent body, should kiss her golden eyebrows; and I wanted to disbelieve it, to tantalize myself, and was sorry that she had cost me so little trouble and had yielded so soon.

But suddenly I heard heavy footsteps.   A man of medium height appeared in the avenue, and I recognized him at once as Forty Martyrs.   He sat down on the bench and heaved a deep sigh, then crossed himself three times and lay down. A minute later he got up and lay on the other side. The gnats and the dampness of the night prevented his sleeping.

" Oh, life! " he said. " Wretched, bitter life! "

Looking at his bent, wasted body and hearing his heavy, noisy sighs, I thought of an unhappy, bitter life of which the confession had been made to me that day, and I felt uneasy and frightened at my blissful mood. I came down the knoll and went to the house.

" Life, as he thinks, is terrible," I thought, " so don't stand on ceremony with it, bend it to your will, and until it crushes you, snatch all you can wring from it."

Marya Sergeyevna was standing on the verandah. I put my arms round her without a word, and began greedily kissing her eyebrows, her temples, her neck. . . .

In my room she told me she had loved me for a long time, more than a year. She vowed eternal love, cried and begged me to take her away with me. I repeatedly took her to the window to look at her face in the moonlight, and she seemed to me a lovely dream, and I made haste to hold her tight to convince myself of the truth of it. It was long since I had known such raptures. . . . Yet somewhere far away at the bottom of my heart I felt an awkwardness, and I was ill at ease.   In her love for me there was something incongruous and burdensome, just as in Dmitri Petrovitch's friendship.   It was a great, serious passion with tears and vows, and I wanted nothing serious in it — no tears, no vows, no talk of the future.   Let that moonlight night flash through our lives like a meteor and — *basta!*

At three o'clock she went out of my room, and, while I was standing in the doorway, looking after her, at the end of the corridor Dmitri Petrovitch suddenly made his appearance; she started and stood aside to let him pass, and her whole figure was expressive of repulsion.   He gave a strange smile, coughed, and came into my room.

" I forgot my cap here yesterday," he said without looking at me.

He found it and, holding it in both hands, put it on his head; then he looked at my confused face, at my slippers, and said in a strange, husky voice unlike his own:

" I suppose it must be my fate that I should understand nothing. . . . If you understand anything, I congratulate you.   It's all darkness before my eyes."

And he went out, clearing his throat.   Afterwards from the window I saw him by the stable, harnessing the horses with his own hands.   His hands were trembling, he was in nervous haste and kept looking round at the house; probably he was feeling terror. Then he got into the gig, and, with a strange expression as though afraid of being pursued, lashed the horses.

Shortly afterwards I set off, too. The sun was already rising, and the mist of the previous day clung timidly to the bushes and the hillocks. On the box of the carriage was sitting Forty Martyrs; he had already succeeded in getting drunk and was muttering tipsy nonsense.

"I am a free man," he shouted to the horses. "Ah, my honeys, I am a nobleman in my own right, if you care to know!"

The terror of Dmitri Petrovitch, the thought of whom I could not get out of my head, infected me. I thought of what had happened and could make nothing of it. I looked at the rooks, and it seemed so strange and terrible that they were flying.

"Why have I done this?" I kept asking myself in bewilderment and despair. "Why has it turned out like this and not differently? To whom and for what was it necessary that she should love me in earnest, and that he should come into my room to fetch his cap? What had a cap to do with it?"

I set off for Petersburg that day, and I have not seen Dmitri Petrovitch nor his wife since. I am told that they are still living together.

1892

A WOMAN'S KINGDOM

A WOMAN'S KINGDOM

I

CHRISTMAS EVE

HERE was a thick roll of notes. It came from the bailiff at the forest villa; he wrote that he was sending fifteen hundred roubles, which he had been awarded as damages, having won an appeal. Anna Akimovna disliked and feared such words as " awarded damages " and " won the suit." She knew that it was impossible to do without the law, but for some reason, whenever Nazaritch, the manager of the factory, or the bailiff of her villa in the country, both of whom frequently went to law, used to win lawsuits of some sort for her benefit, she always felt uneasy and, as it were, ashamed. On this occasion, too, she felt uneasy and awkward, and wanted to put that fifteen hundred roubles further away that it might be out of her sight.

She thought with vexation that other girls of her age — she was in her twenty-sixth year — were now busy looking after their households, were weary and would sleep sound, and would wake up tomorrow morning in holiday mood; many of them had long been married and had children.   Only she, for some reason, was compelled to sit like an old woman over these letters, to make notes upon them, to write answers, then to do nothing the whole evening till midnight, but wait till she was sleepy; and tomorrow they would all day long be coming with Christmas greetings and asking for favours; and the day after tomorrow there would certainly be some scandal at the factory — some one would be beaten or would die of drinking too much vodka, and she would be fretted by pangs of conscience; and after the holidays Nazaritch would turn off some twenty of the work-people for absence from work, and all of the twenty would hang about at the front door, without their caps on, and she would be ashamed to go out to them, and they would be driven away like dogs. And all her acquaintances would say behind her back, and write to her in anonymous letters, that she was a millionaire and exploiter — that she was devouring other men's lives and sucking the blood of the workers.

Here there lay a heap of letters read through and laid aside already.   They were all begging letters. They were from people who were hungry, drunken, dragged down by large families, sick, degraded, despised. . . . Anna Akimovna had already noted on each letter, three roubles to be paid to one, five **to** another; these letters would go the same day to the office, and next the distribution of assistance would take place, or, as the clerks used to say, the beasts would be fed.

They would distribute also in small sums four hundred and seventy roubles — the interest on a sum bequeathed by the late Akim Ivanovitch for the relief of the poor and needy. There would be a hideous crush. From the gates to the doors of the office there would stretch a long file of strange people with brutal faces, in rags, numb with cold, hungry and already drunk, in husky voices calling down blessings upon Anna Akimovna, their benefactress, and her parents: those at the back would press upon those in front, and those in front would abuse them with bad language. The clerk would get tired of the noise, the swearing, and the sing-song whining and blessing; would fly out and give some one a box on the ear to the delight of all. And her own people, the factory hands, who received nothing at Christmas but their wages, and had already spent every farthing of it, would stand in the middle of the yard, looking on and laughing — some enviously, others ironically.

" Merchants, and still more their wives, are fonder of beggars than they are of their own workpeople," thought Anna Akimovna. " It's always so."

Her eye fell upon the roll of money. It would

be nice to distribute that hateful, useless money among the workpeople tomorrow, but it did not do to give the workpeople anything for nothing, or they would demand it again next time.   And what would be the good of fifteen hundred roubles when there were eighteen hundred workmen in the factory besides their wives and children?   Or she might, perhaps, pick out one of the writers of those begging letters — some luckless man who had long ago lost all hope of anything better, and give him the fifteen hundred.   The money would come upon the poor creature like a thunder-clap, and perhaps for the first time in his life he would feel happy.   This idea struck Anna Akimovna as original and amusing, and it fascinated her.   She took one letter at random out of the pile and read it.   Some petty official called Tchalikov had long been out of a situation, was ill, and living in Gushtchin's Buildings; his wife was in consumption, and he had five little girls.   Anna Akimovna knew well the four-storeyed house, Gushtchin's Buildings, in which Tchalikov lived.   Oh, it was a horrid, foul, unhealthy house!

" Well, I will give it to that Tchalikov," she decided.   " I won't send it; I had better take it myself to prevent unnecessary talk.   Yes," she reflected, as she put the fifteen hundred roubles in her pocket, " and I'll have a look at them, and perhaps I can do something for the little girls."

She felt light-hearted; she rang the bell and ordered the horses to be brought round.

When she got into the sledge it was past six o'clock in the evening. The windows in all the blocks of buildings were brightly lighted up, and that made the huge courtyard seem very dark: at the gates, and at the far end of the yard near the warehouses and the workpeople's barracks, electric lamps were gleaming.

Anna Akimovna disliked and feared those huge dark buildings, warehouses, and barracks where the workmen lived. She had only once been in the main building since her father's death. The high ceilings with iron girders; the multitude of huge, rapidly turning wheels, connecting straps and levers; the shrill hissing; the clank of steel; the rattle of the trolleys; the harsh puffing of steam; the faces — pale, crimson, or black with coal-dust; the shirts soaked with sweat; the gleam of steel, of copper, and of fire; the smell of oil and coal; and the draught, at times very hot and at times very cold — gave her an impression of hell. It seemed to her as though the wheels, the levers, and the hot hissing cylinders were trying to tear themselves away from their fastenings to crush the men, while the men, not hearing one another, ran about with anxious faces, and busied themselves about the machines, trying to stop their terrible movement. They showed Anna

Akimovna something and respectfully explained it to her. She remembered how in the forge a piece of red-hot iron was pulled out of the furnace; and how an old man with a strap round his head, and another, a young man in a blue shirt with a chain on his breast, and an angry face, probably one of the foremen, struck the piece of iron with hammers; and how the golden sparks had been scattered in all directions; and how, a little afterwards, they had dragged out a huge piece of sheet-iron with a clang. The old man had stood erect and smiled, while the young man had wiped his face with his sleeve and explained something to her. And she remembered, too, how in another department an old man with one eye had been filing a piece of iron, and how the iron filings were scattered about; and how a red-haired man in black spectacles, with holes in his shirt, had been working at a lathe, making something out of a piece of steel: the lathe roared and hissed and squeaked, and Anna Akimovna felt sick at the sound, and it seemed as though they were boring into her ears. She looked, listened, did not understand, smiled graciously, and felt ashamed. To get hundreds of thousands of roubles from a business which one does not understand and cannot like — how strange it is!

And she had not once been in the workpeople's barracks. There, she was told, it was damp; there were bugs, debauchery, anarchy. It was an astonishing thing: a thousand roubles were spent annually on keeping the barracks in good order, yet, if she were to believe the anonymous letters, the condition of the workpeople was growing worse and worse every year.

"There was more order in my father's day," thought Anna Akimovna, as she drove out of the yard, "because he had been a workman himself. I know nothing about it and only do silly things."

She felt depressed again, and was no longer glad that she had come, and the thought of the lucky man upon whom fifteen hundred roubles would drop from heaven no longer struck her as original and amusing. To go to some Tchalikov or other, when at home a business worth a million was gradually going to pieces and being ruined, and the workpeople in the barracks were living worse than convicts, meant doing something silly and cheating her conscience. Along the highroad and across the fields near it, workpeople from the neighbouring cotton and paper factories were walking towards the lights of the town. There was the sound of talk and laughter in the frosty air. Anna Akimovna looked at the women and young people, and she suddenly felt a longing for a plain rough life among a crowd. She recalled vividly that far-away time when she used to be called Anyutka, when she was a little girl and used to lie under the same quilt with her mother, while a washerwoman who lodged with them used to wash clothes in the next room; while through the thin walls there came from the neighbouring flats sounds of laughter, swearing, children's crying, the accordion, and the whirr of carpenters' lathes and sewing-machines; while her father, Akim Ivanovitch, who was clever at almost every craft, would be soldering something near the stove, or drawing or planing, taking no notice whatever of the noise and stuffiness. And she longed to wash, to iron, to run to the shop and the tavern as she used to do every day when she lived with her mother. She ought to have been a work-girl and not the factory owner! Her big house with its chandeliers and pictures; her footman Mishenka, with his glossy moustache and swallow-tail coat; the devout and dignified Varvarushka, and smooth-tongued Agafyushka; and the young people of both sexes who came almost every day to ask her for money, and with whom she always for some reason felt guilty; and the clerks, the doctors, and the ladies who were charitable at her expense, who flattered her and secretly despised her for her humble origin — how wearisome and alien it all was to her!

Here was the railway crossing and the city gate; then came houses alternating with kitchen gardens; and at last the broad street where stood the renowned Gushtchin's Buildings. The street, usually quiet, was now on Christmas Eve full of life and movement. The eating-houses and beer-shops were noisy. If some one who did not belong to that quarter but lived in the centre of the town had driven through the street now, he would have noticed nothing but dirty, drunken, and abusive people; but Anna Akimovna, who had lived in those parts all her life, was constantly recognizing in the crowd her own father or mother or uncle. Her father was a soft fluid character, a little fantastical, frivolous, and irresponsible. He did not care for money, respectability, or power; he used to say that a working man had no time to keep the holy-days and go to church; and if it had not been for his wife, he would probably never have gone to confession, taken the sacrament or kept the fasts. While her uncle, Ivan Ivanovitch, on the contrary, was like flint; in everything relating to religion, politics, and morality, he was harsh and relentless, and kept a strict watch, not only over himself, but also over all his servants and acquaintances. God forbid that one should go into his room without crossing oneself before the ikon! The luxurious mansion in which Anna Akimovna now lived he had always kept locked up, and only opened it on great holidays for important visitors, while he lived himself in the office, in a little room covered with ikons. He had leanings towards the Old Believers, and was continually entertaining priests and bishops of the old ritual, though he had

been christened, and married, and had buried his
wife in accordance with the Orthodox rites.   He
disliked Akim, his only brother and his heir, for his
frivolity, which he called simpleness and folly, and
for his indifference to religion.   He treated him as
an inferior, kept him in the position of a workman,
paid him sixteen roubles a month.   Akim addressed
his brother with formal respect, and on the days of
asking forgiveness, he and his wife and daughter
bowed down to the ground before him.   But three
years before his death Ivan Ivanovitch had drawn
closer to his brother, forgave his shortcomings, and
ordered him to get a governess for Anyutka.

There was a dark, deep, evil-smelling archway under Gushtchin's Buildings; there was a sound of men
coughing near the walls.   Leaving the sledge in the
street, Anna Akimovna went in at the gate and there
inquired how to get to No. 46 to see a clerk called
Tchalikov.   She was directed to the furthest door
on the right in the third story.   And in the courtyard and near the outer door, and even on the stairs,
there was still the same loathsome smell as under the
archway.   In Anna Akimovna's childhood, when her
father was a simple workman, she used to live in a
building like that, and afterwards, when their circumstances were different, she had often visited them
in the character of a Lady Bountiful.   The narrow

stone staircase with its steep dirty steps, with landings at every story; the greasy swinging lanterns; the stench; the troughs, pots, and rags on the landings near the doors,— all this had been familiar to her long ago. . . . One door was open, and within could be seen Jewish tailors in caps, sewing. Anna Akimovna met people on the stairs, but it never entered her head that people might be rude to her. She was no more afraid of peasants or workpeople, drunk or sober, than of her acquaintances of the educated class.

There was no entry at No. 46; the door opened straight into the kitchen. As a rule the dwellings of workmen and mechanics smell of varnish, tar, hides, smoke, according to the occupation of the tenant; the dwellings of persons of noble or official class who have come to poverty may be known by a peculiar rancid, sour smell. This disgusting smell enveloped Anna Akimovna on all sides, and as yet she was only on the threshold. A man in a black coat, no doubt Tchalikov himself, was sitting in a corner at the table with his back to the door, and with him were five little girls. The eldest, a broad-faced thin girl with a comb in her hair, looked about fifteen, while the youngest, a chubby child with hair that stood up like a hedge-hog, was not more than three. All the six were eating. Near the stove stood a very thin little woman with a yellow face, far gone in pregnancy. She was wearing a skirt and a white blouse, and had an oven fork in her hand.

"I did not expect you to be so disobedient, Liza," the man was saying reproachfully. "Fie, fie, for shame! Do you want papa to whip you — eh?"

Seeing an unknown lady in the doorway, the thin woman started, and put down the fork.

"Vassily Nikititch!" she cried, after a pause, in a hollow voice, as though she could not believe her eyes.

The man looked round and jumped up. He was a flat-chested, bony man with narrow shoulders and sunken temples. His eyes were small and hollow with dark rings round them, he had a wide mouth, and a long nose like a bird's beak — a little bit bent to the right. His beard was parted in the middle, his moustache was shaven, and this made him look more like a hired footman than a government clerk.

"Does Mr. Tchalikov live here?" asked Anna Akimovna.

"Yes, madam," Tchalikov answered severely, but immediately recognizing Anna Akimovna, he cried: "Anna Akimovna!" and all at once he gasped and clasped his hands as though in terrible alarm. "Benefactress!"

With a moan he ran to her, grunting inarticulately

as though he were paralyzed — there was cabbage on his beard and he smelt of vodka — pressed his forehead to her muff, and seemed as though he were in a swoon.

"Your hand, your holy hand!" he brought out breathlessly. "It's a dream, a glorious dream! Children, awaken me!"

He turned towards the table and said in a sobbing voice, shaking his fists:

"Providence has heard us! Our saviour, our angel, has come! We are saved! Children, down on your knees! on your knees!"

MadameTchalikov and the little girls, except the youngest one, began for some reason rapidly clearing the table.

"You wrote that your wife was very ill," said Anna Akimovna, and she felt ashamed and annoyed. "I am not going to give them the fifteen hundred," she thought.

"Here she is, my wife," said Tchalikov in a thin feminine voice, as though his tears had gone to his head. "Here she is, unhappy creature! With one foot in the grave! But we do not complain, madam. Better death than such a life. Better die, unhappy woman!"

"Why is he playing these antics?" thought Anna Akimovna with annoyance. "One can see at once he is used to dealing with merchants."

"Speak to me like a human being," she said.   "I don't care for farces."

"Yes, madam; five bereaved children round their mother's coffin with funeral candles — that's a farce?   Eh?" said Tchalikov bitterly, and turned away.

"Hold your tongue," whispered his wife, and she pulled at his sleeve.   "The place has not been tidied up, madam," she said, addressing Anna Akimovna; "please excuse it . . . you know what it is where there are children.   A crowded hearth, but harmony."

"I am not going to give them the fifteen hundred," Anna Akimovna thought again.

And to escape as soon as possible from these people and from the sour smell, she brought out her purse and made up her mind to leave them twenty-five roubles, not more; but she suddenly felt ashamed that she had come so far and disturbed people for so little.

"If you give me paper and ink, I will write at once to a doctor who is a friend of mine to come and see you," she said, flushing red.   "He is a very good doctor.   And I will leave you some money for medicine."

Madame Tchalikov was hastening to wipe the table.

"It's messy here!   What are you doing?" hissed

Tchalikov, looking at her wrathfully.   " Take her
to the lodger's room!   I make bold to ask you,
madam, to step into the lodger's room," he said,
addressing Anna Akimovna.   " It's clean there."

" Osip Ilyitch told us not to go into his room! "
said one of the little girls, sternly.

But they had already led Anna Akimovna out of
the kitchen, through a narrow passage room between
two bedsteads: it was evident from the arrangement
of the beds that in one two slept lengthwise, and in
the other three slept across the bed.   In the lodger's
room, that came next, it really was clean.   A neat-
looking bed with a red woollen quilt, a pillow in a
white pillow-case, even a slipper for the watch, a
table covered with a hempen cloth and on it, an ink-
stand of milky-looking glass, pens, paper, photographs in frames — everything as it ought to be; and
another table for rough work, on which lay tidily
arranged a watchmaker's tools and watches taken
to pieces.   On the walls hung hammers, pliers, awls,
chisels, nippers, and so on, and there were three
hanging clocks which were ticking; one was a big
clock with thick weights, such as one sees in eating-
houses.

As she sat down to write the letter, Anna Akimovna saw facing her on the table the photographs
of her father and of herself.   That surprised
her.

" Who lives here with you ? " she asked.

" Our lodger, madam, Pimenov. He works in your factory."

" Oh, I thought he must be a watchmaker."

" He repairs watches privately, in his leisure hours. He is an amateur."

After a brief silence during which nothing could be heard but the ticking of the clocks and the scratching of the pen on the paper, Tchalikov heaved a sigh and said ironically, with indignation:

" It's a true saying: gentle birth and a grade in the service won't put a coat on your back. A cockade in your cap and a noble title, but nothing to eat. To my thinking, if any one of humble class helps the poor he is much more of a gentleman than any Tchalikov who has sunk into poverty and vice."

To flatter Anna Akimovna, he uttered a few more disparaging phrases about his gentle birth, and it was evident that he was humbling himself because he considered himself superior to her. Meanwhile she had finished her letter and had sealed it up. The letter would be thrown away and the money would not be spent on medicine — that she knew, but she put twenty-five roubles on the table all the same, and after a moment's thought, added two more red notes. She saw the wasted, yellow hand of Madame Tchalikov, like the claw of a hen, dart out and clutch the money tight.

"You have graciously given this for medicine," said Tchalikov in a quivering voice, "but hold out a helping hand to me also . . . and the children!" he added with a sob. "My unhappy children! I am not afraid for myself; it is for my daughters I fear! It's the hydra of vice that I fear!"

Trying to open her purse, the catch of which had gone wrong, Anna Akimovna was confused and turned red. She felt ashamed that people should be standing before her, looking at her hands and waiting, and most likely at the bottom of their hearts laughing at her. At that instant some one came into the kitchen and stamped his feet, knocking the snow off.

"The lodger has come in," said Madame Tchalikov.

Anna Akimovna grew even more confused. She did not want any one from the factory to find her in this ridiculous position. As ill-luck would have it, the lodger came in at the very moment when, having broken the catch at last, she was giving Tchalikov some notes, and Tchalikov, grunting as though he were paraylzed, was feeling about with his lips where he could kiss her. In the lodger she recognized the workman who had once clanked the sheet-iron before her in the forge, and had explained things to her. Evidently he had come in straight from the factory; his face looked dark and grimy, and on one cheek near his nose was a smudge of soot. His hands were perfectly black, and his unbelted shirt shone with oil and grease. He was a man of thirty, of medium height, with black hair and broad shoulders, and a look of great physical strength. At the first glance Anna Akimovna perceived that he must be a foreman, who must be receiving at least thirty-five roubles a month, and a stern, loud-voiced man who struck the workmen in the face; all this was evident from his manner of standing, from the attitude he involuntarily assumed at once on seeing a lady in his room, and most of all from the fact that he did not wear top-boots, that he had breast pockets, and a pointed, picturesquely clipped beard. Her father, Akim Ivanovitch, had been the brother of the factory owner, and yet he had been afraid of foremen like this lodger and had tried to win their favour.

"Excuse me for having come in here in your absence," said Anna Akimovna.

The workman looked at her in surprise, smiled in confusion and did not speak.

"You must speak a little louder, madam . . ." said Tchalikov softly. "When Mr. Pimenov comes home from the factory in the evenings he is a little hard of hearing."

But Anna Akimovna was by now relieved that there was nothing more for her to do here; she nodded to them and went rapidly out of the room. Pimenov went to see her out.

"Have you been long in our employment?" she asked in a loud voice, without turning to him.

"From nine years old. I entered the factory in your uncle's time."

"That's a long while! My uncle and my father knew all the workpeople, and I know hardly any of them. I had seen you before, but I did not know your name was Pimenov."

Anna Akimovna felt a desire to justify herself before him, to pretend that she had just given the money not seriously, but as a joke.

"Oh, this poverty," she sighed. "We give charity on holidays and working days, and still there is no sense in it. I believe it is useless to help such people as this Tchalikov."

"Of course it is useless," he agreed. "However much you give him, he will drink it all away. And now the husband and wife will be snatching it from one another and fighting all night," he added with a laugh.

"Yes, one must admit that our philanthropy is useless, boring, and absurd. But still, you must agree, one can't sit with one's hand in one's lap; one must do something. What's to be done with the Tchalikovs, for instance?"

She turned to Pimenov and stopped, expecting an answer from him; he, too, stopped and slowly, without speaking, shrugged his shoulders. Obviously he knew what to do with the Tchalikovs, but the treatment would have been so coarse and inhuman that he did not venture to put it into words. And the Tchalikovs were to him so utterly uninteresting and worthless, that a moment later he had forgotten them; looking into Anna Akimovna's eyes, he smiled with pleasure, and his face wore an expression as though he were dreaming about something very pleasant. Only, now standing close to him, Anna Akimovna saw from his face, and especially from his eyes, how exhausted and sleepy he was.

" Here, I ought to give him the fifteen hundred roubles! " she thought, but for some reason this idea seemed to her incongruous and insulting to Pimenov.

" I am sure you are aching all over after your work, and you come to the door with me," she said as they went down the stairs. " Go home."

But he did not catch her words. When they came out into the street, he ran on ahead, unfastened the cover of the sledge, and helping Anna Akimovna in, said:

" I wish you a happy Christmas! "

II

CHRISTMAS MORNING

"They have left off ringing ever so long! It's dreadful; you won't be there before the service is over! Get up!"

"Two horses are racing, racing . . ." said Anna Akimovna, and she woke up; before her, candle in hand, stood her maid, red-haired Masha. "Well, what is it?"

"Service is over already," said Masha with despair. "I have called you three times! Sleep till evening for me, but you told me yourself to call you!"

Anna Akimovna raised herself on her elbow and glanced towards the window. It was still quite dark outside, and only the lower edge of the window-frame was white with snow. She could hear a low, mellow chime of bells; it was not the parish church, but somewhere further away. The watch on the little table showed three minutes past six.

"Very well, Masha. . . . In three minutes . . ." said Anna Akimovna in an imploring voice, and she snuggled under the bed-clothes.

She imagined the snow at the front door, the sledge, the dark sky, the crowd in the church, and

the smell of juniper, and she felt dread at the
thought; but all the same, she made up her mind
that she would get up at once and go to early service.
And while she was warm in bed and struggling with
sleep — which seems, as though to spite one, particularly sweet when one ought to get up — and while
she had visions of an immense garden on a mountain
and then Gushtchin's Buildings, she was worried all
the time by the thought that she ought to get up that
very minute and go to church.

But when she got up it was quite light, and it
turned out to be half-past nine.   There had been a
heavy fall of snow in the night; the trees were
clothed in white, and the air was particularly light,
transparent, and tender, so that when Anna Akimovna looked out of the window her first impulse was
to draw a deep, deep breath.   And when she had
washed, a relic of far-away childish feelings — joy
that today was Christmas — suddenly stirred within
her; after that she felt light-hearted, free and pure
in soul, as though her soul, too, had been washed or
plunged in the white snow.   Masha came in, dressed
up and tightly laced, and wished her a happy Christmas; then she spent a long time combing her mistress's hair and helping her to dress.   The fragrance
and feeling of the new, gorgeous, splendid dress, its
faint rustle, and the smell of fresh scent, excited
Anna Akimovna.

"Well, it's Christmas," she said gaily to Masha. "Now we will try our fortunes."

"Last year, I was to marry an old man. It turned up three times the same."

"Well, God is merciful."

"Well, Anna Akimovna, what I think is, rather than neither one thing nor the other, I'd marry an old man," said Masha mournfully, and she heaved a sigh. "I am turned twenty; it's no joke."

Every one in the house knew that red-haired Masha was in love with Mishenka, the footman, and this genuine, passionate, hopeless love had already lasted three years.

"Come, don't talk nonsense," Anna Akimovna consoled her. "I am going on for thirty, but I am still meaning to marry a young man."

While his mistress was dressing, Mishenka, in a new swallow-tail and polished boots, walked about the hall and drawing-room and waited for her to come out, to wish her a happy Christmas. He had a peculiar walk, stepping softly and delicately; looking at his feet, his hands, and the bend of his head, it might be imagined that he was not simply walking, but learning to dance the first figure of a quadrille. In spite of his fine velvety moustache and handsome, rather flashy appearance, he was steady, prudent, and devout as an old man. He said his prayers, bowing down to the ground, and liked burning incense in his room.   He respected people of wealth and rank and had a reverence for them; he despised poor people, and all who came to ask favours of any kind, with all the strength of his cleanly flunkey soul. Under his starched shirt he wore a flannel, winter and summer alike, being very careful of his health; his ears were plugged with cotton-wool.

When Anna Akimovna crossed the hall with Masha, he bent his head downwards a little and said in his agreeable, honeyed voice:

"I have the honour to congratulate you, Anna Akimovna, on the most solemn feast of the birth of our Lord."

Anna Akimovna gave him five roubles, while poor Masha was numb with ecstasy.   His holiday get-up, his attitude, his voice, and what he said, impressed her by their beauty and elegance; as she followed her mistress she could think of nothing, could see nothing, she could only smile, first blissfully and then bitterly.   The upper story of the house was called the best or visitors' half, while the name of the business part — old people's or simply women's part — was given to the rooms on the lower story where Aunt Tatyana Ivanovna kept house.   In the upper part the gentry and educated visitors were entertained; in the lower story, simpler folk and the aunt's personal friends.   Handsome,   plump,   and   healthy,   still young and fresh, and feeling she had on a magnifi-

cent dress which seemed to her to diffuse a sort of
radiance all about her, Anna Akimovna went down
to the lower story. Here she was met with re-
proaches for forgetting God now that she was so
highly educated, for sleeping too late for the service,
and for not coming downstairs to break the fast, and
they all clasped their hands and exclaimed with perfect sincerity that she was lovely, wonderful; and she
believed it, laughed, kissed them, gave one a rouble,
another three or five according to their position.
She liked being downstairs. Wherever one looked
there were shrines, ikons, little lamps, portraits of
ecclesiastical   personages — the   place   smelt   of
monks; there was a rattle of knives in the kitchen,
and already a smell of something savoury, exceedingly appetizing, was pervading all the rooms. The
yellow-painted floors shone, and from the doors
narrow rugs with bright blue stripes ran like little
paths to the ikon corner, and the sunshine was simply
pouring in at the windows.

In the dining-room some old women, strangers,
were sitting; in Varvarushka's room, too, there were
old women, and with them a deaf and dumb girl, who
seemed abashed about something and kept saying,
" Bli, bli! . . ." Two skinny-looking little girls
who had been brought out of the orphanage for
Christmas came up to kiss Anna Akimovna's hand,
and stood before her transfixed with admiration of

her splendid dress; she noticed that one of the girls squinted, and in the midst of her light-hearted holiday mood she felt a sick pang at her heart at the thought that young men would despise the girl, and that she would never marry.   In the cook Agafya's room, five huge peasants in new shirts were sitting round the samovar; these were not workmen from the factory, but relations of the cook.   Seeing Anna Akimovna, all the peasants jumped up from their seats, and from regard for decorum, ceased munching, though their mouths were full.   The cook Stepan, in a white cap, with a knife in his hand, came into the room and gave her his greetings; porters in high felt boots came in, and they, too, offered their greetings.   The water-carrier peeped in with icicles on his beard, but did not venture to come in.

Anna Akimovna walked through the rooms followed by her retinue — the aunt, Varvarushka, Nikandrovna, the sewing-maid Marfa Petrovna, and the downstairs Masha.   Varvarushka — a tall, thin, slender woman, taller than any one in the house, dressed all in black, smelling of cypress and coffee — crossed herself in each room before the ikon, bowing down from the waist.   And whenever one looked at her one was reminded that she had already prepared her shroud and that lottery tickets were hidden away by her in the same box.

"Anyutinka, be merciful at Christmas," she said,

opening the door into the kitchen. "Forgive him, bless the man! Have done with it!"

The coachman Panteley, who had been dismissed for drunkenness in November, was on his knees in the middle of the kitchen. He was a good-natured man, but he used to be unruly when he was drunk, and could not go to sleep, but persisted in wandering about the buildings and shouting in a threatening voice, "I know all about it!" Now from his beefy and bloated face and from his bloodshot eyes it could be seen that he had been drinking continually from November till Christmas.

"Forgive me, Anna Akimovna," he brought out in a hoarse voice, striking his forehead on the floor and showing his bull-like neck.

"It was Auntie dismissed you; ask her."

"What about auntie?" said her aunt, walking into the kitchen, breathing heavily; she was very stout, and on her bosom one might have stood a tray of teacups and a samovar. "What about auntie now? You are mistress here, give your own orders; though these rascals might be all dead for all I care. Come, get up, you hog!" she shouted at Panteley, losing patience. "Get out of my sight! It's the last time I forgive you, but if you transgress again — don't ask for mercy!"

Then they went into the dining-room to coffee. But they had hardly sat down, when the downstairs

Masha rushed headlong in, saying with horror, "The singers!" And ran back again. They heard some one blowing his nose, a low bass cough, and footsteps that sounded like horses' iron-shod hoofs tramping about the entry near the hall. For half a minute all was hushed. . . . The singers burst out so suddenly and loudly that every one started. While they were singing, the priest from the almshouses with the deacon and the sexton arrived. Putting on the stole, the priest slowly said that when they were ringing for matins it was snowing and not cold, but that the frost was sharper towards morning, God bless it! and now there must be twenty degrees of frost.

"Many people maintain, though, that winter is healthier than summer," said the deacon; then immediately assumed an austere expression and chanted after the priest. "Thy Birth, O Christ our Lord. . . ."

Soon the priest from the workmen's hospital came with the deacon, then the Sisters from the hospital, children from the orphanage, and then singing could be heard almost uninterruptedly. They sang, had lunch, and went away.

About twenty men from the factory came to offer their Christmas greetings. They were only the foremen, mechanicians, and their assistants, the pattern-makers, the accountant, and so on — all of good appearance, in new black coats. They were all first-rate men, as it were picked men; each one knew his value — that is, knew that if he lost his berth to-day, people would be glad to take him on at another factory. Evidently they liked Auntie, as they behaved freely in her presence and even smoked, and when they had all trooped in to have something to eat, the accountant put his arm round her immense waist. They were free-and-easy, perhaps, partly also because Varvarushka, who under the old masters had wielded great power and had kept watch over the morals of the clerks, had now no authority whatever in the house; and perhaps because many of them still remembered the time when Auntie Tatyana Ivanovna, whose brothers kept a strict hand over her, had been dressed like a simple peasant woman like Agafya, and when Anna Akimovna used to run about the yard near the factory buildings and every one used to call her Anyutya.

The foremen ate, talked, and kept looking with amazement at Anna Akimovna, how she had grown up and how handsome she had become! But this elegant girl, educated by governesses and teachers, was a stranger to them; they could not understand her, and they instinctively kept closer to " Auntie," who called them by their names, continually pressed them to eat and drink, and, clinking glasses with them, had already drunk two wineglasses of rowanberry wine with them.   Anna Akimovna was always afraid of their thinking her proud, an upstart, or a crow in peacock's feathers; and now while the foremen were crowding round the food, she did not leave the dining-room, but took part in the conversation.   She asked Pimenov, her acquaintance of the previous day:

" Why have you so many clocks in your room? "

" I mend clocks," he answered.   " I take the work up between times, on holidays, or when I can't sleep."

" So if my watch goes wrong I can bring it to you to be repaired? " Anna Akimovna asked, laughing.

" To be sure, I will do it with pleasure," said Pimenov, and there was an expression of tender devotion in his face, when, not herself knowing why, she unfastened her magnificent watch from its chain and handed it to him; he looked at it in silence and gave it back.   " To be sure, I will do it with pleasure," he repeated.   " I don't mend watches now.   My eyes are weak, and the doctors have forbidden me to do fine work.   But for you I can make an exception."

" Doctors talk nonsense," said the accountant. They all laughed.   " Don't you believe them," he went on, flattered by the laughing; " last year a tooth flew out of a cylinder and hit old Kalmykov

such a crack on the head that you could see his
brains, and the doctor said he would die; but he is
alive and working to this day, only he has taken
to stammering since that mishap."

" Doctors do talk nonsense, they do, but not so
much," sighed Auntie. " Pyotr Andreyitch, poor
dear, lost his sight. Just like you, he used to work
day in day out at the factory near the hot furnace,
and he went blind. The eyes don't like heat. But
what are we talking about? " she said, rousing herself. " Come and have a drink. My best wishes
for Christmas, my dears. I never drink with any
one else, but I drink with you, sinful woman as I
am. Please God! "

Anna Akimovna fancied that after yesterday Pimenov despised her as a philanthropist, but was
fascinated by her as a woman. She looked at him
and thought that he behaved very charmingly and
was nicely dressed. It is true that the sleeves of
his coat were not quite long enough, and the coat
itself seemed short-waisted, and his trousers were
not wide and fashionable, but his tie was tied carelessly and with taste and was not as gaudy as the
others'. And he seemed to be a good-natured man,
for he ate submissively whatever Auntie put on his
plate. She remembered how black he had been the
day before, and how sleepy, and the thought of it for
some reason touched her.

When the men were preparing to go, Anna Akimovna put out her hand to Pimenov. She wanted
to ask him to come in sometimes to see her, without ceremony, but she did not know how to — her
tongue would not obey her; and that they might not
think she was attracted by Pimenov, she shook hands
with his companions, too.

Then the boys from the school of which she was
a patroness came. They all had their heads closely
cropped and all wore grey blouses of the same pat-
tern. The teacher — a tall, beardless young man
with patches of red on his face — was visibly agitated as he formed the boys into rows; the boys
sang in tune, but with harsh, disagreeable voices.
The manager of the factory, Nazaritch, a bald,
sharp-eyed Old Believer, could never get on with
the teachers, but the one who was now anxiously
waving his hands he despised and hated, though
he could not have said why. He behaved rudely
and condescendingly to the young man, kept back
his salary, meddled with the teaching, and had finally
tried to dislodge him by appointing, a fortnight before Christmas, as porter to the school a drunken
peasant, a distant relation of his wife's, who dis-
obeyed the teacher and said rude things to him before the boys.

Anna Akimovna was aware of all this, but she
could be of no help, for she was afraid of Nazaritch

herself. Now she wanted at least to be very nice to the schoolmaster, to tell him she was very much pleased with him; but when after the singing he began apologizing for something in great confusion, and Auntie began to address him familiarly as she drew him without ceremony to the table, she felt, for some reason, bored and awkward, and giving orders that the children should be given sweets, went upstairs.

"In reality there is something cruel in these Christmas customs," she said a little while afterwards, as it were to herself, looking out of window at the boys, who were flocking from the house to the gates and shivering with cold, putting their coats on as they ran. "At Christmas one wants to rest, to sit at home with one's own people, and the poor boys, the teacher, and the clerks and foremen, are obliged for some reason to go through the frost, then to offer their greetings, show their respect, be put to confusion . . ."

Mishenka, who was standing at the door of the drawing-room and overheard this, said:

"It has not come from us, and it will not end with us. Of course, I am not an educated man, Anna Akimovna, but I do understand that the poor must always respect the rich. It is well said, 'God marks the rogue.' In prisons, night refuges, and pot-houses you never see any but the poor, while

decent people, you may notice, are always rich.   It
has been said of the rich, ' Deep calls to deep.' "

" You always express yourself so tediously and in-
comprehensibly," said Anna Akimovna, and she
walked to the other end of the big drawing-room.

It was only just past eleven.   The stillness of the
big room, only broken by the singing that floated up
from below, made her yawn.   The bronzes, the
albums, and the pictures on the walls, representing
a ship at sea, cows in a meadow, and views of the
Rhine, were so absolutely stale that her eyes simply
glided over them without observing them.   The
holiday mood was already growing tedious.   As before, Anna Akimovna felt that she was beautiful,
good-natured, and wonderful, but now it seemed to
her that that was of no use to any one; it seemed to
her that she did not know for whom and for what
she had put on this expensive dress, too, and, as always happened on all holidays, she began to be
fretted by loneliness and the persistent thought that
her beauty, her health, and her wealth, were a mere
cheat, since she was not wanted, was of no use to
any one, and nobody loved her.   She walked through
all the rooms, humming and looking out of window;
stopping in the drawing-room, she could not resist
beginning to talk to Mishenka.

" I don't know what you think of yourself,

Misha," she said, and heaved a sigh. " Really, God might punish you for it."

" What do you mean? "

" You know what I mean. Excuse my meddling in your affairs. But it seems you are spoiling your own life out of obstinacy. You'll admit that it is high time you got married, and she is an excellent and deserving girl. You will never find any one better. She's a beauty, clever, gentle, and devoted. . . . And her appearance! . . . If she belonged to our circle or a higher one, people would be falling in love with her for her red hair alone. See how beautifully her hair goes with her complexion. Oh, goodness! You don't understand anything, and don't know what you want," Anna Akimovna said bitterly, and tears came into her eyes. " Poor girl, I am so sorry for her! I know you want a wife with money, but I have told you already I will give Masha a dowry."

Mishenka could not picture his future spouse in his imagination except as a tall, plump, substantial, pious woman, stepping like a peacock, and, for some reason, with a long shawl over her shoulders; while Masha was thin, slender, tightly laced, and walked with little steps, and, worst of all, she was too fascinating and at times extremely attractive to Mishenka, and that, in his opinion, was incongruous with matrimony and only in keeping with loose behaviour. When Anna Akimovna had promised to give Masha a dowry, he had hesitated for a time; but once a poor student in a brown overcoat over his uniform, coming with a letter for Anna Akimovna, was fascinated by Masha, and could not resist embracing her near the hat-stand, and she had uttered a faint shriek; Mishenka, standing on the stairs above, had seen this, and from that time had begun to cherish a feeling of disgust for Masha.   A poor student! Who knows, if she had been embraced by a rich student or an officer the consequences might have been different.

"Why don't you wish it?" Anna Akimovna asked.   "What more do you want?"

Mishenka was silent and looked at the arm-chair fixedly, and raised his eyebrows.

"Do you love some one else?"

Silence.   The red-haired Masha came in with letters and visiting cards on a tray.   Guessing that they were talking about her, she blushed to tears.

"The postmen have come," she muttered.   "And there is a clerk called Tchalikov waiting below.   He says you told him to come to-day for something."

"What insolence!" said Anna Akimovna, moved to anger.   "I gave him no orders.   Tell him to take himself off; say I am not at home!"

A ring was heard.   It was the priests from her

parish. They were always shown into the aristocratic part of the house — that is, upstairs. After
the priests, Nazaritch, the manager of the factory,
came to pay his visit, and then the factory doctor;
then Mishenka announced the inspector of the ele-
mentary schools. Visitors kept arriving.

When there was a moment free, Anna Akimovna
sat down in a deep arm-chair in the drawing-room,
and shutting her eyes, thought that her loneliness was
quite natural because she had not married and never
would marry. . . . But that was not her fault.
Fate itself had flung her out of the simple working-
class surroundings in which, if she could trust her
memory, she had felt so snug and at home, into these
immense rooms, where she could never think what
to do with herself, and could not understand why so
many people kept passing before her eyes. What
was happening now seemed to her trivial, useless,
since it did not and could not give her happiness for
one minute.

" If I could fall in love," she thought, stretching; the very thought of this sent a rush of warmth
to her heart. " And if I could escape from the
factory . . ." she mused, imagining how the weight
of those factory buildings, barracks, and schools
would roll off her conscience, roll off her mind. . . .
Then she remembered her father, and thought if
he had lived longer he would certainly have married

her to a working man — to Pimenov, for instance. He would have told her to marry, and that would have been all about it.   And it would have been a good thing; then the factory would have passed into capable hands.

She pictured his curly head, his bold profile, his delicate, ironical lips and the strength, the tremendous strength, in his shoulders, in his arms, in his chest, and the tenderness with which he had looked at her watch that day.

"Well," she said, "it would have been all right. . . . I would have married him."

"Anna Akimovna," said Mishenka, coming noiselessly into the drawing-room.

"How you frightened me!" she said, trembling all over.   "What do you want?"

"Anna Akimovna," he said, laying his hand on his heart and raising his eyebrows, "you are my mistress and my benefactress, and no one but you can tell me what I ought to do about marriage, for you are as good as a mother to me. . . . But kindly forbid them to laugh and jeer at me downstairs.   They won't let me pass without it."

"How do they jeer at you?"

"They call me Mashenka's Mishenka."

"Pooh, what nonsense!" cried Anna Akimovna indignantly.   "How stupid you all are!   What a stupid you are, Misha! How sick I am of you! I can't bear the sight of you."

III

DINNER

Just as the year before, the last to pay her visits were Krylin, an actual civil councillor, and Lysevitch, a well-known barrister. It was already dark when they arrived. Krylin, a man of sixty, with a wide mouth and with grey whiskers close to his ears, with a face like a lynx, was wearing a uniform with an Anna ribbon, and white trousers. He held Anna Akimovna's hand in both of his for a long while, looked intently in her face, moved his lips, and at last said, drawling upon one note:

" I used to respect your uncle . . . and your father, and enjoyed the privilege of their friendship. Now I feel it an agreeable duty, as you see, to present my Christmas wishes to their honoured heiress . . . in spite of my infirmities and the distance I have to come. . . . And I am very glad to see you in good health."

The lawyer Lysevitch, a tall, handsome fair man, with a slight sprinkling of grey on his temples and beard, was distinguished by exceptionally elegant manners; he walked with a swaying step, bowed as it were reluctantly, and shrugged his shoulders as he talked, and all this with an indolent grace, like a spoiled horse fresh from the stable. He was well fed, extremely healthy, and very well off; on one occasion he had won forty thousand roubles, but concealed the fact from his friends. He was fond of good fare, especially cheese, truffles, and grated radish with hemp oil; while in Paris he had eaten, so he said, baked but unwashed guts. He spoke smoothly, fluently, without hesitation, and only occasionally, for the sake of effect, permitted himself to hesitate and snap his fingers as if picking up a word. He had long ceased to believe in anything he had to say in the law courts, or perhaps he did believe in it, but attached no kind of significance to it; it had all so long been familiar, stale, ordinary. . . . He believed in nothing but what was original and unusual. A copy-book moral in an original form would move him to tears. Both his notebooks were filled with extraordinary expressions which he had read in various authors; and when he needed to look up any expression, he would search nervously in both books, and usually failed to find it. Anna Akimovna's father had in a good-humoured moment ostentatiously appointed him legal adviser in matters concerning the factory, and had assigned him a salary of twelve thousand roubles. The legal business of the factory had been confined to two or three trivial actions for recovering debts, which Lysevitch handed to his assistants.

Anna Akimovna knew that he had nothing to do at the factory, but she could not dismiss him — she had not the moral courage; and besides, she was used to him. He used to call himself her legal adviser, and his salary, which he invariably sent for on the first of the month punctually, he used to call " stern prose." Anna Akimovna knew that when, after her father's death, the timber of her forest was sold for railway sleepers, Lysevitch had made more than fifteen thousand out of the transaction, and had shared it with Nazaritch. When first she found out they had cheated her she had wept bitterly, but afterwards she had grown used to it.

Wishing her a happy Christmas, and kissing both her hands, he looked her up and down, and frowned.

" You mustn't," he said with genuine disappointment. · " I have told you, my dear, you mustn't! "

" What do you mean, Viktor Nikolaitch? "

" I have told you you mustn't get fat. All your family have an unfortunate tendency to grow fat. You mustn't," he repeated in an imploring voice, and kissed her hand. " You are so handsome! You are so splendid! Here, your Excellency, let me introduce the one woman in the world whom I have ever seriously loved."

" There is nothing surprising in that.   To know
Anna Akimovna at your age and not to be in love
with her, that would be impossible."

" I adore her," the lawyer continued with perfect
sincerity, but with his usual indolent grace.   " I love
her, but not because I am a man and she is a woman.
When I am with her I always feel as though she be-
longs to some third sex, and I to a fourth, and we
float away together into the domain of the subtlest
shades, and there we blend into the spectrum.   Le-
conte de Lisle defines such relations better than any
one.   He has a superb passage, a marvellous passage. . . ."

Lysevitch rummaged in one notebook, then in the
other, and, not finding the quotation, subsided.
They began talking of the weather, of the opera, of
the arrival, expected shortly, of Duse.   Anna Akimovna remembered that the year before Lysevitch
and, she fancied, Krylin had dined with her, and
now when they were getting ready to go away, she
began with perfect sincerity pointing out to them in
an imploring voice that as they had no more visits
to pay, they ought to remain to dinner with her.
After some hesitation the visitors agreed.

In addition to the family dinner, consisting of
cabbage soup, sucking pig, goose with apples, and
so on, a so-called " French " or " chef's " dinner

used to be prepared in the kitchen on great holidays, in case any visitor in the upper story wanted a meal. When they heard the clatter of crockery in the dining-room, Lysevitch began to betray a noticeable excitement; he rubbed his hands, shrugged his shoulders, screwed up his eyes, and described with feeling what dinners her father and uncle used to give at one time, and a marvellous *matelote* of turbots the cook here could make: it was not a *matelote*, but a veritable revelation! He was already gloating over the dinner, already eating it in imagination and enjoying it. When Anna Akimovna took his arm and led him to the dining-room, he tossed off a glass of vodka and put a piece of salmon in his mouth; he positively purred with pleasure. He munched loudly, disgustingly, emitting sounds from his nose, while his eyes grew oily and rapacious.

The *hors d'œuvres* were superb; among other things, there were fresh white mushrooms stewed in cream, and *sauce provençale* made of fried oysters and crayfish, strongly flavoured with some bitter pickles. The dinner, consisting of elaborate holiday dishes, was excellent, and so were the wines. Mishenka waited at table with enthusiasm. When he laid some new dish on the table and lifted the shining cover, or poured out the wine, he did it with the solemnity of a professor of black magic, and, looking at his face and his movements suggesting the first figure of a quadrille, the lawyer thought several times, " What a fool! "

After the third course Lysevitch said, turning to Anna Akimovna:

" The *fin de siècle* woman — I mean when she is young, and of course wealthy — must be independent, clever, elegant, intellectual, bold, and a little depraved.   Depraved within limits, a little; for excess, you know, is wearisome.   You ought not to vegetate, my dear; you ought not to live like every one else, but to get the full savour of life, and a slight flavour of depravity is the sauce of life. Revel among flowers of intoxicating fragrance, breathe the perfume of musk, eat hashish, and best of all, love, love, love. . . .   To begin with, in your place I would set up seven lovers — one for each day of the week; and one I would call Monday, one Tuesday, the third Wednesday, and so on, so that each might know his day."

This conversation troubled Anna Akimovna; she ate nothing and only drank a glass of wine.

" Let me speak at last," she said.   " For myself personally, I can't conceive of love without family life.   I am lonely, lonely as the moon in the sky, and a waning moon, too; and whatever you may say, I am convinced, I feel that this waning can only be restored by love in its ordinary sense.   It seems to me that such love would define my duties, my work, make clear my conception of life. I want from love peace of soul, tranquillity; I want the very opposite of musk, and spiritualism, and *fin de siècle* . . . in short "— she grew embarrassed —" a husband and children."

" You want to be married? Well, you can do that, too," Lysevitch assented. " You ought to have all experiences: marriage, and jealousy, and the sweetness of the first infidelity, and even children. . . . But make haste and live — make haste, my dear: time is passing; it won't wait."

" Yes, I'll go and get married ! " she said, looking angrily at his well-fed, satisfied face. " I will marry in the simplest, most ordinary way and be radiant with happiness. And, would you believe it, I will marry some plain working man, some mechanic or draughtsman."

" There is no harm in that, either. The Duchess Josiana loved Gwinplin, and that was permissible for her because she was a grand duchess. Everything is permissible for you, too, because you are an exceptional woman: if, my dear, you want to love a negro or an Arab, don't scruple; send for a negro. Don't deny yourself anything. You ought to be as bold as your desires; don't fall short of them."

" Can it be so hard to understand me ? " Anna

Akimovna asked with amazement, and her eyes were bright with tears. " Understand, I have an immense business on my hands — two thousand workmen, for whom I must answer before God. The men who work for me grow blind and deaf. I am afraid to go on like this; I am afraid! I am wretched, and you have the cruelty to talk to me of negroes and . . . and you smile! " Anna Akimovna brought her fist down on the table. " To go on living the life I am living now, or to marry some one as idle and incompetent as myself, would be a crime. I can't go on living like this," she said hotly, " I cannot! "

" How handsome she is! " said Lysevitch, fascinated by her. " My God, how handsome she is! But why are you angry, my dear? Perhaps I am wrong; but surely you don't imagine that if, for the sake of ideas for which I have the deepest respect, you renounce the joys of life and lead a dreary existence, your workmen will be any the better for it? Not a scrap! No, frivolity, frivolity! " he said decisively. " It's essential for you; it's your duty to be frivolous and depraved! Ponder that, my dear, ponder it."

Anna Akimovna was glad she had spoken out, and her spirits rose. She was pleased she had spoken so well, and that her ideas were so fine and just, and she was already convinced that if Pimenov, for instance, loved her, she would marry him with pleasure.

Mishenka began to pour out champagne.

"You make me angry, Viktor Nikolaitch," she said, clinking glasses with the lawyer. "It seems to me you give advice and know nothing of life yourself. According to you, if a man be a mechanic or a draughtsman, he is bound to be a peasant and an ignoramus! But they are the cleverest people! Extraordinary people!"

"Your uncle and father . . . I knew them and respected them . . ." Krylin said, pausing for emphasis (he had been sitting upright as a post, and had been eating steadily the whole time), "were people of considerable intelligence and . . . of lofty spiritual qualities."

"Oh, to be sure, we know all about their qualities," the lawyer muttered, and asked permission to smoke.

When dinner was over Krylin was led away for a nap. Lysevitch finished his cigar, and, staggering from repletion, followed Anna Akimovna into her study. Cosy corners with photographs and fans on the walls, and the inevitable pink or pale blue lanterns in the middle of the ceiling, he did not like, as the expression of an insipid and unoriginal character; besides, the memory of certain of his love affairs of which he was now ashamed was associated with such lanterns. Anna Akimovna's study with its bare walls and tasteless furniture pleased him exceedingly. It was snug and comfortable for him to sit on a Turkish divan and look at Anna Akimovna, who usually sat on the rug before the fire, clasping her knees and looking into the fire and thinking of something; and at such moments it seemed to him that her peasant Old Believer blood was stirring within her.

Every time after dinner when coffee and liqueurs were handed, he grew livelier and began telling her various bits of literary gossip. He spoke with eloquence and inspiration, and was carried away by his own stories; and she listened to him and thought every time that for such enjoyment it was worth paying not only twelve thousand, but three times that sum, and forgave him everything she disliked in him. He sometimes told her the story of some tale or novel he had been reading, and then two or three hours passed unnoticed like a minute. Now he began rather dolefully in a failing voice with his eyes shut.

" It's ages, my dear, since I have read anything," he said when she asked him to tell her something. " Though I do sometimes read Jules Verne."

" I was expecting you to tell me something new."

" H'm! . . . new," Lysevitch muttered sleepily, and he settled himself further back in the corner of the sofa. " None of the new literature, my dear, is any use for you or me. Of course, it is bound to be such as it is, and to refuse to recognize it is to refuse to recognize — would mean refusing to recognize the natural order of things, and I do recognize it, but . . ." Lysevitch seemed to have fallen asleep. But a minute later his voice was heard again:

" All the new literature moans and howls like the autumn wind in the chimney. 'Ah, unhappy wretch! Ah, your life may be likened to a prison! Ah, how damp and dark it is in your prison! Ah, you will certainly come to ruin, and there is no chance of escape for you!' That's very fine, but I should prefer a literature that would tell us how to escape from prison. Of all contemporary writers, how-ever, I prefer Maupassant." Lysevitch opened his eyes. " A fine writer, a perfect writer! " Lysevitch shifted in his seat. " A wonderful artist! A ter-rible, prodigious, supernatural artist! " Lysevitch got up from the sofa and raised his right arm. " Maupassant! " he said rapturously. " My dear, read Maupassant! one page of his gives you more than all the riches of the earth! Every line is a new horizon. The softest, tenderest impulses of the soul alternate with violent tempestuous sensa-tions; your soul, as though under the weight of forty thousand atmospheres, is transformed into the most

insignificant little bit of some great thing of an undefined rosy hue which I fancy, if one could put it
on one's tongue, would yield a pungent, voluptuous
taste.   What a fury of transitions, of motives, of
melodies!   You rest peacefully on the lilies and the
roses, and suddenly a thought — a terrible, splendid, irresistible thought — swoops down upon you
like a locomotive, and bathes you in hot steam and
deafens you with its whistle.   Read Maupassant,
dear girl; I insist on it."

Lysevitch waved his arms and paced from corner to corner in violent excitement.

"Yes, it is inconceivable," he pronounced, as
though in despair; "his last thing overwhelmed
me, intoxicated me!   But I am afraid you will not
care for it.   To be carried away by it you must
savour it, slowly suck the juice from each line, drink
it in. . . . You must drink it in! . . ."

After a long introduction, containing many words
such as dæmonic sensuality, a network of the most
delicate nerves, simoom, crystal, and so on, he began at last telling the story of the novel.   He did
not tell the story so whimsically, but told it in minute
detail, quoting from memory whole descriptions and
conversations; the characters of the novel fascinated
him, and to describe them he threw himself into attitudes, changed the expression of his face and voice
like a real actor.   He laughed with delight at one

moment in a deep bass, and at another, on a high shrill note, clasped his hands and clutched at his head with an expression which suggested that it was just going to burst. Anna Akimovna listened enthralled, though she had already read the novel, and it seemed to her ever so much finer and more subtle in the lawyer's version than in the book itself. He drew her attention to various subtleties, and emphasized the felicitous expressions and the profound thoughts, but she saw in it, only life, life, life and herself, as though she had been a character in the novel. Her spirits rose, and she, too, laughing and clasping her hands, thought that she could not go on living such a life, that there was no need to have a wretched life when one might have a splendid one. She remembered her words and thoughts at dinner, and was proud of them; and when Pimenov suddenly rose up in her imagination, she felt happy and longed for him to love her.

When he had finished the story, Lysevitch sat down on the sofa, exhausted.

" How splendid you are! How handsome!" he began, a little while afterwards in a faint voice as if he were ill. " I am happy near you, dear girl, but why am I forty-two instead of thirty? Your tastes and mine do not coincide: you ought to be depraved, and I have long passed that phase, and want a love as delicate and immaterial as a ray of sunshine —

that is, from the point of view of a woman of your age, I am of no earthly use."

In his own words, he loved Turgenev, the singer of virginal love and purity, of youth, and of the melancholy Russian landscape; but he loved virginal love, not from knowledge but from hearsay, as something abstract, existing outside real life. Now he assured himself that he loved Anna Akimovna platonically, ideally, though he did not know what those words meant.   But he felt comfortable, snug, warm.   Anna Akimovna seemed to him enchanting, original, and he imagined that the pleasant sensation that was aroused in him by these surroundings was the very thing that was called platonic love.

He laid his cheek on her hand and said in the tone commonly used in coaxing little children:

" My precious, why have you punished me? "

" How?   When? "

" I have had no Christmas present from you."

Anna Akimovna had never heard before of their sending a Christmas box to the lawyer, and now she was at a loss how much to give him.   But she must give him something, for he was expecting it, though he looked at her with eyes full of love.

" I suppose Nazaritch forgot it," she said, " but it is not too late to set it right."

She suddenly remembered the fifteen hundred she had received the day before, which was now lying in the toilet drawer in her bedroom. And when she brought that ungrateful money and gave it to the lawyer, and he put it in his coat pocket with indolent grace, the whole incident passed off charmingly and naturally. The sudden reminder of a Christmas box and this fifteen hundred was not unbecoming in Lysevitch.

" Merci," he said, and kissed her finger.

Krylin came in with blissful, sleepy face, but without his decorations.

Lysevitch and he stayed a little longer and drank a glass of tea each, and began to get ready to go. Anna Akimovna was a little embarrassed. . . . She had utterly forgotten in what department Krylin served, and whether she had to give him money or not; and if she had to, whether to give it now or send it afterwards in an envelope.

" Where does he serve? " she whispered to Lysevitch.

" Goodness knows," muttered Lysevitch, yawning.

She reflected that if Krylin used to visit her father and her uncle and respected them, it was probably not for nothing: apparently he had been charitable at their expense, serving in some charitable institution. As she said good-bye she slipped three hundred roubles into his hand; he seemed taken aback, and looked at her for a minute in silence with his pewtery eyes, but then seemed to understand and said:

" The receipt, honoured Anna Akimovna, you can only receive on the New Year."

Lysevitch had become utterly limp and heavy, and he staggered when Mishenka put on his overcoat.

As he went downstairs he looked like a man in the last stage of exhaustion, and it was evident that he would drop asleep as soon as he got into his sledge.

" Your Excellency," he said languidly to Krylin, stopping in the middle of the staircase, " has it ever happened to you to experience a feeling as though some unseen force were drawing you out longer and longer?   You are drawn out and turn into the finest wire.   Subjectively this finds expression in a curious voluptuous feeling which is impossibe to compare with anything."

Anna Akimovna, standing at the top of the stairs, saw each of them give Mishenka a note.

" Good-bye!   Come again! " she called to them, and ran into her bedroom.

She quickly threw off her dress, that she was weary of already, put on a dressing-gown, and ran downstairs; and as she ran downstairs she laughed and thumped with her feet like a school-boy; she had a great desire for mischief.

IV

EVENING

Auntie, in a loose print blouse, Varvarushka
and two old women, were sitting in the dining-
room having supper. A big piece of salt meat, a
ham, and various savouries, were lying on the table
before them, and clouds of steam were rising from
the meat, which looked particularly fat and appetizing. Wine was not served on the lower story,
but they made up for it with a great number of
spirits and home-made liqueurs. Agafyushka, the
fat, white-skinned, well-fed cook, was standing with
her arms crossed in the doorway and talking to the
old women, and the dishes were being handed by
the downstairs Masha, a dark girl with a crimson
ribbon in her hair. The old women had had enough
to eat before the morning was over, and an hour
before supper had had tea and buns, and so they
were now eating with effort — as it were, from a
sense of duty.

"Oh, my girl!" sighed Auntie, as Anna Akimovna ran into the dining-room and sat down beside her. "You've frightened me to death!"

Every one in the house was pleased when Anna
Akimovna was in good spirits and played pranks;
this always reminded them that the old men were

dead and that the old women had no authority in the house, and any one could do as he liked without any fear of being sharply called to account for it. Only the two old women glanced askance at Anna Akimovna with amazement: she was humming, and it was a sin to sing at table.

"Our mistress, our beauty, our picture," Agafyushka began chanting with sugary sweetness. "Our precious jewel! The people, the people that have come to-day to look at our queen. Lord have mercy upon us! Generals, and officers and gentlemen. . . . I kept looking out of window and counting and counting till I gave it up."

"I'd as soon they did not come at all," said Auntie; she looked sadly at her niece and added: "They only waste the time for my poor orphan girl."

Anna Akimovna felt hungry, as she had eaten nothing since the morning. They poured her out some very bitter liqueur; she drank it off, and tasted the salt meat with mustard, and thought it extraordinarily nice. Then the downstairs Masha brought in the turkey, the pickled apples and the gooseberries. And that pleased her, too. There was only one thing that was disagreeable: there was a draught of hot air from the tiled stove; it was stiflingly close and every one's cheeks were burning. After supper the cloth was taken off and plates of peppermint biscuits, walnuts, and raisins were brought in.

"You sit down, too . . . no need to stand there!" said Auntie to the cook.

Agafyushka sighed and sat down to the table; Masha set a wineglass of liqueur before her, too, and Anna Akimovna began to feel as though Agafyushka's white neck were giving out heat like the stove. They were all talking of how difficult it was nowadays to get married, and saying that in old days, if men did not court beauty, they paid attention to money, but now there was no making out what they wanted; and while hunchbacks and cripples used to be left old maids, nowadays men would not have even the beautiful and wealthy. Auntie began to set this down to immorality, and said that people had no fear of God, but she suddenly remembered that Ivan Ivanitch, her brother, and Varvarushka — both people of holy life — had feared God, but all the same had had children on the sly, and had sent them to the Foundling Asylum. She pulled herself up and changed the conversation, telling them about a suitor she had once had, a factory hand, and how she had loved him, but her brothers had forced her to marry a widower, an ikon-painter, who, thank God, had died two years after. The downstairs Masha sat down to the table, too, and told them with a mysterious air that for the last week some unknown man with a black moustache, in a great-coat with an astrachan collar, had made his appearance every morning in the yard, had stared at the windows of the big house, and had gone on further — to the buildings; the man was all right, nice-looking. . . .

All this conversation made Anna Akimovna suddenly long to be married — long intensely, painfully; she felt as though she would give half her life and all her fortune only to know that upstairs there was a man who was closer to her than any one in the world, that he loved her warmly and was missing her; and the thought of such closeness, ecstatic and inexpressible in words, troubled her soul.   And the instinct of youth and health flattered her with lying assurances that the real poetry of life was not over but still to come, and she believed it, and leaning back in her chair (her hair fell down as she did so), she began laughing, and, looking at her, the others laughed, too.   And it was a long time before this causeless laughter died down in the dining-room.

She was informed that the Stinging Beetle had come.   This was a pilgrim woman called Pasha or Spiridonovna — a thin little woman of fifty, in a black dress with a white kerchief, with keen eyes, sharp nose, and a sharp chin; she had sly, viperish eyes and she looked as though she could see right

through every one. Her lips were shaped like a
heart. Her viperishness and hostility to every one
had earned her the nickname of the Stinging Beetle.

Going into the dining-room without looking at
any one, she made for the ikons and chanted in a
high voice " Thy Holy Birth," then she sang " The
Virgin today gives birth to the Son," then " Christ
is born," then she turned round and bent a piercing
gaze upon all of them.

" A happy Christmas," she said, and she kissed
Anna Akimovna on the shoulder. " It's all I could
do, all I could do to get to you, my kind friends."
She kissed Auntie on the shoulder. " I should have
come to you this morning, but I went in to some good
people to rest on the way. ' Stay, Spiridonovna,
stay,' they said, and I did not notice that evening
was coming on."

As she did not eat meat, they gave her salmon
and caviare. She ate looking from under her eye-
lids at the company, and drank three glasses of
vodka. When she had finished she said a prayer
and bowed down to Anna Akimovna's feet.

They began to play a game of " kings," as they
had done the year before, and the year before
that, and all the servants in both stories crowded
in at the doors to watch the game. Anna Akimovna
fancied she caught a glimpse once or twice of Mishenka, with a patronizing smile on his face, among

the crowd of peasant men and women. The first
to be king was Stinging Beetle, and Anna Akimovna
as the soldier paid her tribute; and then Auntie was
king and Anna Akimovna was peasant, which excited general delight, and Agafyushka was prince,
and was quite abashed with pleasure. Another
game was got up at the other end of the table —
played by the two Mashas, Varvarushka, and the
sewing-maid Marfa Ptrovna, who was waked on
purpose to play " kings," and whose face looked
cross and sleepy.

While they were playing they talked of men,
and of how difficult it was to get a good husband
nowadays, and which state was to be preferred —
that of an old maid or a widow.

" You are a handsome, healthy, sturdy lass," said
Stinging Beetle to Anna Akimovna. " But I can't
make out for whose sake you are holding back."

" What's to be done if nobody will have me? "

" Or maybe you have taken a vow to remain
a maid? " Stinging Beetle went on, as though she
did not hear. " Well, that's a good deed. . . . Remain one," she repeated, looking intently and ma-
liciously at her cards. " All right, my dear, remain
one. . . . Yes . . . only maids, these saintly maids,
are not all alike." She heaved a sigh and played the
king. " Oh, no, my girl, they are not all alike!
Some really watch over themselves like nuns, and

butter would not melt in their mouths; and if such
a one does sin in an hour of weakness, she is worried
to death, poor thing! so it would be a sin to condemn
her.   While others will go dressed in black and sew
their shroud, and yet love rich old men on the sly.
Yes, y-es, my canary birds, some hussies will bewitch
an old man and rule over him, my doves, rule over
him and turn his head; and when they've saved up
money and lottery tickets enough, they will bewitch
him to his death."

Varvarushka's only response to these hints was
to heave a sigh and look towards the ikons.   There
was an expression of Christian meekness on her
countenance.

" I know a maid like that, my bitterest enemy,"
Stinging Beetle went on, looking round at every one
in triumph; " she is always sighing, too, and looking at the ikons, the she-devil.   When she used to
rule in a certain old man's house, if one went to
her she would give one a crust, and bid one bow
down to the ikons while she would sing: ' In conception Thou dost abide a Virgin . . .!'   On holidays she will give one a bite, and on working days
she will reproach one for it.   But nowadays I will
make merry over her!   I will make as merry as I
please, my jewel."

Varvarushka glanced at the ikons again and
crossed herself.

" But no one will have me, Spiridonovna," said
Anna Akimovna to change the conversation.
" What's to be done? "

" It's your own fault.   You keep waiting for
highly educated gentlemen, but you ought to marry
one of your own sort, a merchant."

" We don't want a merchant," said Auntie, all
in a flutter.   " Queen of Heaven, preserve us!   A
gentleman will spend your money, but then he will
be kind to you, you poor little fool.   But a merchant
will be so strict that you won't feel at home in your
own house.   You'll be wanting to fondle him and
he will be counting his money, and when you sit down
to meals with him, he'll grudge you every mouthful,
though it's your own, the lout! . . . Marry a gentleman."

They all talked at once, loudly interrupting one
another, and Auntie tapped on the table with the
nutcrackers and said, flushed and angry:

" We won't have a merchant; we won't have one!
If you choose a merchant I shall go to an almshouse."

" Sh . . . Sh! . . . Hush! " cried Stinging Beetle; when all were silent she screwed up one eye and
said: " Do you know what, Annushka, my bir-
die . . .?   There is no need for you to get married really like every one else.   You're rich and
free, you are your own mistress; but yet, my child,
it doesn't seem the right thing for you to be an old

maid. I'll find you, you know, some trumpery and simple-witted man. You'll marry him for appearances and then have your fling, bonny lass! You can hand him five thousand or ten maybe, and pack him off where he came from, and you will be mistress in your own house — you can love whom you like and no one can say anything to you. And then you can love your highly educated gentleman. You'll have a jolly time!" Stinging Beetle snapped her fingers and gave a whistle.

"It's sinful," said Auntie.

"Oh, sinful," laughed Stinging Beetle. "She is educated, she understands. To cut some one's throat or bewitch an old man — that's a sin, that's true; but to love some charming young friend is not a sin at all. And what is there in it, really? There's no sin in it at all! The old pilgrim women have invented all that to make fools of simple folk. I, too, say everywhere it's a sin; I don't know myself why it's a sin." Stinging Beetle emptied her glass and cleared her throat. "Have your fling, bonny lass," this time evidently addressing herself. "For thirty years, wenches, I have thought of nothing but sins and been afraid, but now I see I have wasted my time, I've let it slip by like a ninny! Ah, I have been a fool, a fool!" She sighed. "A woman's time is short and every day is precious. You are handsome, Annushka, and very rich; but as

soon as thirty-five or forty strikes for you your time
is up.   Don't listen to any one, my girl; live, have
your fling till you are forty, and then you will have
time to pray forgiveness — there will be plenty of
time to bow down and to sew your shroud.   A candle to God and a poker to the devil!   You can do
both at once!   Well, how is it to be?   Will you
make some little man happy?"

"I will," laughed Anna Akimovna.   "I don't
care now; I would marry a working man."

"Well, that would do all right!   Oh, what a
fine fellow you would choose then!"   Stinging
Beetle screwed up her eyes and shook her head.
"O — o — oh!"

"I tell her myself," said Auntie, "it's no good
waiting for a gentleman, so she had better marry,
not a gentleman, but some one humbler; anyway
we should have a man in the house to look after
things.   And there are lots of good men.   She
might have some one out of the factory.   They
are all sober, steady men. . . ."

"I should think so," Stinging Beetle agreed.
"They are capital fellows.   If you like, Aunt, I
will make a match for her with Vassily Lebedin-
sky?"

"Oh, Vasya's legs are so long," said Auntie seriously.   "He is so lanky.   He has no looks."

There was laughter in the crowd by the door.

"Well, Pimenov? Would you like to marry Pimenov?" Stinging Beetle asked Anna Akimovna.

"Very good. Make a match for me with Pimenov."

"Really?"

"Yes, do!" Anna Akimovna said resolutely, and she struck her fist on the table. "On my honour, I will marry him."

"Really?"

Anna Akimovna suddenly felt ashamed that her cheeks were burning and that every one was looking at her; she flung the cards together on the table and ran out of the room. As she ran up the stairs and, reaching the upper story, sat down to the piano in the drawing-room, a murmur of sound reached her from below like the roar of the sea; most likely they were talking of her and of Pimenov, and perhaps Stinging Beetle was taking advantage of her absence to insult Varvarushka and was putting no check on her language.

The lamp in the big room was the only light burning in the upper story, and it sent a glimmer through the door into the dark drawing-room. It was between nine and ten, not later. Anna Akimovna played a waltz, then another, then a third; she went on playing without stopping. She looked into the dark corner beyond the piano, smiled, and inwardly called to it, and the idea occurred to her that she might drive off to the town to see some one, Lysevitch for instance, and tell him what was passing in her heart.   She wanted to talk without ceasing, to laugh, to play the fool, but the dark corner was sullenly silent, and all round in all the rooms of the upper story it was still and desolate.

She was fond of sentimental songs, but she had a harsh, untrained voice, and so she only played the accompaniment and sang hardly audibly, just above her breath.   She sang in a whisper one song after another, for the most part about love, separation, and frustrated hopes, and she imagined how she would hold out her hands to him and say with entreaty, with tears, " Pimenov, take this burden from me! "   And then, just as though her sins had been forgiven, there would be joy and comfort in her soul, and perhaps a free, happy life would begin.   In an anguish of anticipation she leant over the keys, with a passionate longing for the change in her life to come at once without delay, and was terrified at the thought that her old life would go on for some time   longer.   Then   she   played   again   and   sang hardly above her breath, and all was stillness about her.   There was no noise coming from downstairs now, they must have gone to bed.   It had struck ten some time before.   A long, solitary, wearisome night was approaching.

Anna Akimovna walked through all the rooms,

lay down for a while on the sofa, and read in her study the letters that had come that evening; there were twelve letters of Christmas greetings and three anonymous letters. In one of them some workman complained in a horrible, almost illegible handwriting that Lenten oil sold in the factory shop was rancid and smelt of paraffin; in another, some one respectfully informed her that over a purchase of iron Nazaritch had lately taken a bribe of a thousand roubles from some one; in a third she was abused for her inhumanity.

The excitement of Christmas was passing off, and to keep it up Anna Akimovna sat down at the piano again and softly played one of the new waltzes, then she remembered how cleverly and creditably she had spoken at dinner today. She looked round at the dark windows, at the walls with the pictures, at the faint light that came from the big room, and all at once she began suddenly crying, and she felt vexed that she was so lonely, and that she had no one to talk to and consult. To cheer herself she tried to picture Pimenov in her imagination, but it was unsuccessful.

It struck twelve. Mishenka, no longer wearing his swallowtail but in his reefer jacket, came in, and without speaking lighted two candles; then he went out and returned a minute later with a cup of tea on a tray.

" What are you laughing at? " she asked, noticing
a smile on his face.

" I was downstairs and heard the jokes you were
making about Pimenov . . ." he said, and put his
hand before his laughing mouth. " If he were sat
down to dinner today with Viktor Nikolaevitch and
the general, he'd have died of fright."   Mishenka's
shoulders were shaking with laughter. " He doesn't
know even how to hold his fork, I bet."

The footman's laughter and words, his reefer
jacket and moustache, gave Anna Akimovna a feeling of uncleanness.   She shut her eyes to avoid seeing him, and, against her own will, imagined Pimenov
dining with Lysevitch and Krylin, and his timid, unintellectual figure seemed to her pitiful and helpless,
and she felt repelled by it.   And only now, for the
first time in the whole day, she realized clearly that
all she had said and thought about Pimenov and marrying a workman was nonsense, folly, and wilful-
ness.   To convince herself of the opposite, to overcome her repulsion, she tried to recall what she had
said at dinner, but now she could not see anything
in it: shame at her own thoughts and actions, and
the fear that she had said something improper during the day, and disgust at her own lack of spirit,
overwhelmed her completely.   She took up a candle
and, as rapidly as if some one were pursuing her,
ran downstairs, woke Spiridonovna, and began as-

suring her she had been joking. Then she went to her bedroom. Red-haired Masha, who was dozing in an arm-chair near the bed, jumped up and began shaking up the pillows. Her face was exhausted and sleepy, and her magnificent hair had fallen on one side.

" Tchalikov came again this evening," she said, yawning, " but I did not dare to announce him; he was very drunk. He says he will come again tomorrow."

" What does he want with me? " said Anna Akimovna, and she flung her comb on the floor. " I won't see him, I won't."

She made up her mind she had no one left in life but this Tchalikov, that he would never leave off persecuting her, and would remind her every day how uninteresting and absurd her life was. So all she was fit for was to help the poor. Oh, how stupid it was!

She lay down without undressing, and sobbed with shame and depression: what seemed to her most vexatious and stupid of all was that her dreams that day about Pimenov had been right, lofty, honourable, but at the same time she felt that Lysevitch and even Krylin were nearer to her than Pimenov and all the workpeople taken together. She thought that if the long day she had just spent could have been represented in a picture, all that

had been bad and vulgar — as, for instance, the
dinner, the lawyer's talk, the game of " kings "—
would have been true, while her dreams and talk
about Pimenov would have stood out from the whole
as something false, as out of drawing; and she
thought, too, that it was too late to dream of happiness, that everything was over for her, and it was
impossible to go back to the life when she had slept
under the same quilt with her mother, or to devise
some new special sort of life.

Red-haired Masha was kneeling before the bed,
gazing at her in mournful perplexity; then she, too,
began crying, and laid her face against her mistress's arm, and without words it was clear why she
was so wretched.

" We are fools! " said Anna Akimovna, laughing and crying.   " We are fools!   Oh, what fools
we are! "

1894

A PROBLEM

A PROBLEM

THE strictest measures were taken that the Uskovs' family secret might not leak out and become
generally known. Half of the servants were sent
off to the theatre or the circus; the other half were
sitting in the kitchen and not allowed to leave it.
Orders were given that no one was to be admitted.
The wife of the Colonel, her sister, and the governess, though they had been initiated into the secret,
kept up a pretence of knowing nothing; they sat in
the dining-room and did not show themselves in the
drawing-room or the hall.

Sasha Uskov, the young man of twenty-five who
was the cause of all the commotion, had arrived
some time before, and by the advice of kind-hearted
Ivan Markovitch, his uncle, who was taking his part,
he sat meekly in the hall by the door leading to the
study, and prepared himself to make an open, candid explanation.

The other side of the door, in the study, a family
council was being held. The subject under discussion was an exceedingly disagreeable and delicate
one. Sasha Uskov had cashed at one of the banks

a false promissory note, and it had become due for payment three days before, and now his two paternal uncles and Ivan Markovitch, the brother of his dead mother, were deciding the question whether they should pay the money and save the family honour, or wash their hands of it and leave the case to go for trial.

To outsiders who have no personal interest in the matter such questions seem simple; for those who are so unfortunate as to have to decide them in earnest they are extremely difficult. The uncles had been talking for a long time, but the problem seemed no nearer decision.

" My friends ! " said the uncle who was a colonel, and there was a note of exhaustion and bitterness in his voice. " Who says that family honour is a mere convention? I don't say that at all. I am only warning you against a false view; I am pointing out the possibility of an unpardonable mistake. How can you fail to see it? I am not speaking Chinese; I am speaking Russian ! "

" My dear fellow, we do understand," Ivan Markovitch protested mildly.

" How can you understand if you say that I don't believe in family honour? I repeat once more : fa-mil-y ho-nour fal-sely un-der-stood is a prejudice ! Falsely understood ! That's what I say : whatever may be the motives for screening a scoundrel, who-

ever he may be, and helping him to escape punish-
ment, it is contrary to law and unworthy of a gentleman. It's not saving the family honour; it's civic
cowardice! Take the army, for instance. . . . The
honour of the army is more precious to us than any
other honour, yet we don't screen our guilty members, but condemn them. And does the honour of
the army suffer in consequence? Quite the opposite!"

The other paternal uncle, an official in the Treasury, a taciturn, dull-witted, and rheumatic man, sat
silent, or spoke only of the fact that the Uskovs'
name would get into the newspapers if the case went
for trial. His opinion was that the case ought to
be hushed up from the first and not become public
property; but, apart from publicity in the newspapers, he advanced no other argument in support of
this opinion.

The maternal uncle, kind-hearted Ivan Markovitch, spoke smoothly, softly, and with a tremor in
his voice. He began with saying that youth has
its rights and its peculiar temptations. Which of
us has not been young, and who has not been led
astray? To say nothing of ordinary mortals, even
great men have not escaped errors and mistakes in
their youth. Take, for instance, the biography of
great writers. Did not every one of them gamble,
drink, and draw down upon himself the anger of

right-thinking people in his young days? If Sasha's
error bordered upon crime, they must remember that
Sasha had received practically no education; he had
been expelled from the high school in the fifth class;
he had lost his parents in early childhood, and so
had been left at the tenderest age without guidance
and good, benevolent influences. He was nervous,
excitable, had no firm ground under his feet, and,
above all, he had been unlucky. Even if he were
guilty, anyway he deserved indulgence and the sym-
pathy of all compassionate souls. He ought, of
course, to be punished, but he was punished as it
was by his conscience and the agonies he was en-
during now while awaiting the sentence of his relations. The comparison with the army made by the
Colonel was delightful, and did credit to his lofty
intelligence; his appeal to their feeling of public
duty spoke for the chivalry of his soul, but they
must not forget that in each individual the citizen
is closely linked with the Christian. . . .

" Shall we be false to civic duty," Ivan Markovitch exclaimed passionately, " if instead of punish-
ing an erring boy we hold out to him a helping
hand? "

Ivan Markovitch talked further of family honour.
He had not the honour to belong to the Uskov family himself, but he knew their distinguished family
went back to the thirteenth century; he did not forget

for a minute, either, that his precious, beloved sister
had been the wife of one of the representatives of
that name. In short, the family was dear to him
for many reasons, and he refused to admit the idea
that, for the sake of a paltry fifteen hundred roubles,
a blot should be cast on the escutcheon that was beyond all price. If all the motives he had brought
forward were not sufficiently convincing, he, Ivan
Markovitch, in conclusion, begged his listeners to
ask themselves what was meant by crime? Crime
is an immoral act founded upon ill-will. But is the
will of man free? Philosophy has not yet given a
positive answer to that question. Different views
were held by the learned. The latest school of Lombroso, for instance, denies the freedom of the will,
and considers every crime as the product of the
purely anatomical peculiarities of the individual.

" Ivan Markovitch," said the Colonel, in a voice
of entreaty, " we are talking seriously about an important matter, and you bring in Lombroso, you
clever fellow. Think a little, what are you saying
all this for? Can you imagine that all your thun-
derings and rhetoric will furnish an answer to the
question? "

Sasha Uskov sat at the door and listened. He
felt neither terror, shame, nor depression, but only
weariness and inward emptiness. It seemed to him
that it made absolutely no difference to him whether

they forgave him or not; he had come here to hear
his sentence and to explain himself simply because
kind-hearted Ivan Markovitch had begged him to
do so.   He was not afraid of the future.   It made
no difference to him where he was: here in the hall,
in prison, or in Siberia.

"If Siberia, then let it be Siberia, damn it all!"

He was sick of life and found it insufferably hard.
He was inextricably involved in debt; he had not
a farthing in his pocket; his family had become detestable to him; he would have to part from his
friends and his women sooner or later, as they had
begun to be too contemptuous of his sponging on
them.   The future looked black.

Sasha was indifferent, and was only disturbed by
one circumstance; the other side of the door they
were calling him a scoundrel and a criminal.   Every
minute he was on the point of jumping up, bursting
into the study and shouting in answer to the detestable metallic voice of the Colonel:

"You are lying!"

"Criminal" is a dreadful word — that is what
murderers, thieves, robbers are; in fact, wicked and
morally hopeless people.   And Sasha was very far
from being all that. . . . It was true he owed a
great deal and did not pay his debts.   But debt is
not a crime, and it is unusual for a man not to be

in debt. The Colonel and Ivan Markovitch were both in debt. . . .

" What have I done wrong besides? " Sasha wondered.

He had discounted a forged note. But all the young men he knew did the same. Handrikov and Von Burst always forged IOU's from their parents or friends when their allowances were not paid at the regular time, and then when they got their money from home they redeemed them before they became due. Sasha had done the same, but had not redeemed the IOU because he had not got the money which Handrikov had promised to lend him. He was not to blame; it was the fault of circumstances. It was true that the use of another person's signature was considered reprehensible; but, still, it was not a crime but a generally accepted dodge, an ugly formality which injured no one and was quite harmless, for in forging the Colonel's signature Sasha had had no intention of causing anybody damage or loss.

" No, it doesn't mean that I am a criminal . . ." thought Sasha. " And it's not in my character to bring myself to commit a crime. I am soft, emotional. . . . When I have the money I help the poor. . . ."

Sasha was musing after this fashion while they went on talking the other side of the door.

"But, my friends, this is endless," the Colonel declared, getting excited. "Suppose we were to forgive him and pay the money. You know he would not give up leading a dissipated life, squandering money, making debts, going to our tailors and ordering suits in our names! Can you guarantee that this will be his last prank? As far as I am concerned, I have no faith whatever in his reforming!"

The official of the Treasury muttered something in reply; after him Ivan Markovitch began talking blandly and suavely again. The Colonel moved his chair impatiently and drowned the other's words with his detestable metallic voice. At last the door opened and Ivan Markovitch came out of the study; there were patches of red on his lean shaven face.

"Come along," he said, taking Sasha by the hand. "Come and speak frankly from your heart. Without pride, my dear boy, humbly and from your heart."

Sasha went into the study. The official of the Treasury was sitting down; the Colonel was standing before the table with one hand in his pocket and one knee on a chair. It was smoky and stifling in the study. Sasha did not look at the official or the Colonel; he felt suddenly ashamed and uncomfortable. He looked uneasily at Ivan Markovitch and muttered:

"I'll pay it . . . I'll give it back. . . ."

"What did you expect when you discounted the IOU?" he heard a metallic voice.

"I . . . Handrikov promised to lend me the money before now."

Sasha could say no more. He went out of the study and sat down again on the chair near the door. He would have been glad to go away altogether at once, but he was choking with hatred and he awfully wanted to remain, to tear the Colonel to pieces, to say something rude to him. He sat trying to think of something violent and effective to say to his hated uncle, and at that moment a woman's figure, shrouded in the twilight, appeared at the drawing-room door. It was the Colonel's wife. She beckoned Sasha to her, and, wringing her hands, said, weeping:

"*Alexandre,* I know you don't like me, but . . . listen to me; listen, I beg you. . . . But, my dear, how can this have happened? Why, it's awful, awful! For goodness' sake, beg them, defend yourself, entreat them."

Sasha looked at her quivering shoulders, at the big tears that were rolling down her cheeks, heard behind his back the hollow, nervous voices of worried and exhausted people, and shrugged his shoulders. He had not in the least expected that his aristocratic relations would raise such a tempest over a paltry fifteen hundred roubles! He could not understand her tears nor the quiver of their voices.

An hour later he heard that the Colonel was getting the best of it; the uncles were finally inclining to let the case go for trial.

"The matter's settled," said the Colonel, sighing. "Enough."

After this decision all the uncles, even the emphatic Colonel, became noticeably depressed. A silence followed.

"Merciful Heavens!" sighed Ivan Markovitch. "My poor sister!"

And he began saying in a subdued voice that most likely his sister, Sasha's mother, was present unseen in the study at that moment. He felt in his soul how the unhappy, saintly woman was weeping, grieving, and begging for her boy. For the sake of her peace beyond the grave, they ought to spare Sasha.

The sound of a muffled sob was heard. Ivan Markovitch was weeping and muttering something which it was impossible to catch through the door. The Colonel got up and paced from corner to corner. The long conversation began over again.

But then the clock in the drawing-room struck two. The family council was over. To avoid seeing the person who had moved him to such wrath, the Colonel went from the study, not into the hall, but into the vestibule. . . . Ivan Markovitch came out into the hall. . . . He was agitated and rubbing his hands joyfully. His tear-stained eyes looked good-humoured and his mouth was twisted into a smile.

"Capital," he said to Sasha. "Thank God! You can go home, my dear, and sleep tranquilly. We have decided to pay the sum, but on condition that you repent and come with me tomorrow into the country and set to work."

A minute later Ivan Markovitch and Sasha in their great-coats and caps were going down the stairs. The uncle was muttering something edifying. Sasha did not listen, but felt as though some uneasy weight were gradually slipping off his shoulders. They had forgiven him; he was free! A gust of joy sprang up within him and sent a sweet chill to his heart. He longed to breathe, to move swiftly, to live! Glancing at the street lamps and the black sky, he remembered that Von Burst was celebrating his name-day that evening at the "Bear," and again a rush of joy flooded his soul. . . .

"I am going!" he decided.

But then he remembered he had not a farthing, that the companions he was going to would despise him at once for his empty pockets. He must get hold of some money, come what may!

"Uncle, lend me a hundred roubles," he said to Ivan Markovitch.

His uncle, surprised, looked into his face and backed against a lamp-post.

"Give it to me," said Sasha, shifting impatiently from one foot to the other and beginning to pant. "Uncle, I entreat you, give me a hundred roubles."

His face worked; he trembled, and seemed on the point of attacking his uncle. . . .

"Won't you?" he kept asking, seeing that his uncle was still amazed and did not understand. "Listen.   If you don't, I'll give myself up tomorrow!   I won't let you pay the IOU!   I'll present another false note tomorrow!"

Petrified, muttering something incoherent in his horror, Ivan Markovitch took a hundred-rouble note out of his pocket-book and gave it to Sasha.   The young man took it and walked rapidly away from him. . . .

Taking a sledge, Sasha grew calmer, and felt a rush of joy within him again.   The "rights of youth" of which kind-hearted Ivan Markovitch had spoken at the family council woke up and asserted themselves.   Sasha pictured the drinking-party before him, and, among the bottles, the women, and his friends, the thought flashed through his mind:

"Now I see that I am a criminal; yes, I am a criminal."

1891

THE KISS

THE KISS

At eight o'clock on the evening of the twentieth of May all the six batteries of the N—— Reserve Artillery Brigade halted for the night in the village of Myestetchki on their way to camp. When the general commotion was at its height, while some officers were busily occupied around the guns, while others, gathered together in the square near the church enclosure, were listening to the quartermasters, a man in civilian dress, riding a strange horse, came into sight round the church. The little dun-coloured horse with a good neck and a short tail came, moving not straight forward, but as it were sideways, with a sort of dance step, as though it were being lashed about the legs. When he reached the officers the man on the horse took off his hat and said:

"His Excellency Lieutenant-General von Rabbek invites the gentlemen to drink tea with him this minute. . . ."

The horse turned, danced, and retired sideways; the messenger raised his hat once more, and in an instant disappeared with his strange horse behind the church.

"What the devil does it mean?" grumbled some of the officers, dispersing to their quarters. "One is sleepy, and here this Von Rabbek with his tea! We know what tea means."

The officers of all the six batteries remembered vividly an incident of the previous year, when during manœuvres they, together with the officers of a Cossack regiment, were in the same way invited to tea by a count who had an estate in the neighbourhood and was a retired army officer: the hospitable and genial count made much of them, fed them, and gave them drink, refused to let them go to their quarters in the village and made them stay the night. All that, of course, was very nice — nothing better could be desired, but the worst of it was, the old army officer was so carried away by the pleasure of the young men's company that till sunrise he was telling the officers anecdotes of his glorious past, taking them over the house, showing them expensive pictures, old engravings, rare guns, reading them autograph letters from great people, while the weary and exhausted officers looked and listened, longing for their beds and yawning in their sleeves; when at last their host let them go, it was too late for sleep.

Might not this Von Rabbek be just such another? Whether he were or not, there was no help for it. The officers changed their uniforms, brushed themselves, and went all together in search of the gentleman's house. In the square by the church they were told they could get to His Excellency's by the lower path — going down behind the church to the river, going along the bank to the garden, and there an avenue would taken them to the house; or by the upper way — straight from the church by the road which, half a mile from the village, led right up to His Excellency's granaries. The officers decided to go by the upper way.

"What Von Rabbek is it?" they wondered on the way. "Surely not the one who was in command of the N—— cavalry division at Plevna?"

"No, that was not Von Rabbek, but simply Rabbe and no 'von.'"

"What lovely weather!"

At the first of the granaries the road divided in two: one branch went straight on and vanished in the evening darkness, the other led to the owner's house on the right. The officers turned to the right and began to speak more softly. . . . On both sides of the road stretched stone granaries with red roofs, heavy and sullen-looking, very much like barracks of a district town. Ahead of them gleamed the windows of the manor-house.

"A good omen, gentlemen," said one of the officers. "Our setter is the foremost of all; no doubt he scents game ahead of us! . . ."

Lieutenant Lobytko, who was walking in front, a tall and stalwart fellow, though entirely without moustache (he was over five-and-twenty, yet for some reason there was no sign of hair on his round, well-fed face), renowned in the brigade for his peculiar faculty for divining the presence of women at a distance, turned round and said:

" Yes, there must be women here; I feel that by instinct."

On the threshold the officers were met by Von Rabbek himself, a comely-looking man of sixty in civilian dress. Shaking hands with his guests, he said that he was very glad and happy to see them, but begged them earnestly for God's sake to excuse him for not asking them to stay the night; two sisters with their children, some brothers, and some neighbours, had come on a visit to him, so that he had not one spare room left.

The General shook hands with every one, made his apologies, and smiled, but it was evident by his face that he was by no means so delighted as their last year's count, and that he had invited the officers simply because, in his opinion, it was a social obligation to do so. And the officers themselves, as they walked up the softly carpeted stairs, as they listened to him, felt that they had been invited to this house simply because it would have been awkward not to invite them; and at the sight of the footmen,

who hastened to light the lamps in the entrance below and in the anteroom above, they began to feel
as though they had brought uneasiness and discomfort into the house with them.   In a house in which
two sisters and their children, brothers, and neighbours were gathered together, probably on account
of some family festivity, or event, how could the
presence of nineteen unknown officers possibly be
welcome?

At the entrance to the drawing-room the officers
were met by a tall, graceful old lady with black
eyebrows and a long face, very much like the Empress Eugénie.   Smiling graciously and majestically,
she said she was glad and happy to see her guests,
and apologized that her husband and she were on
this occasion unable to invite *messieurs les officiers*
to stay the night.   From her beautiful majestic
smile, which instantly vanished from her face every
time she turned away from her guests, it was evident that she had seen numbers of officers in her day,
that she was in no humour for them now, and if she
invited them to her house and apologized for not
doing more, it was only because her breeding and
position in society required it of her.

When the officers went into the big dining-room,
there were about a dozen people, men and ladies,
young and old, sitting at tea at the end of a long
table.   A group of men was dimly visible behind

their chairs, wrapped in a haze of cigar smoke; and in the midst of them stood a lanky young man with red whiskers, talking loudly, with a lisp, in English. Through a door beyond the group could be seen a light room with pale blue furniture.

"Gentlemen, there are so many of you that it is impossible to introduce you all!" said the General in a loud voice, trying to sound very cheerful. "Make each other's acquaintance, gentlemen, without any ceremony!"

The officers — some with very serious and even stern faces, others with forced smiles, and all feeling extremely awkward — somehow made their bows and sat down to tea.

The most ill at ease of them all was Ryabovitch — a little officer in spectacles, with sloping shoulders, and whiskers like a lynx's. While some of his comrades assumed a serious expression, while others wore forced smiles, his face, his lynx-like whiskers, and spectacles seemed to say: "I am the shyest, most modest, and most undistinguished officer in the whole brigade!" At first, on going into the room and sitting down to the table, he could not fix his attention on any one face or object. The faces, the dresses, the cut-glass decanters of brandy, the steam from the glasses, the moulded cornices — all blended in one general impression that inspired in Ryabovitch alarm and a desire to hide his head. Like a lecturer making his first appearance before the public, he saw everything that was before his eyes, but apparently only had a dim understanding of it (among physiologists this condition, when the subject sees but does not understand, is called psychical blindness). After a little while, growing accustomed to his surroundings, Ryabovitch saw clearly and began to observe. As a shy man, unused to society, what struck him first was that in which he had always been deficient — namely, the extraordinary boldness of his new acquaintances. Von Rabbek, his wife, two elderly ladies, a young lady in a lilac dress, and the young man with the red whiskers, who was, it appeared, a younger son of Von Rabbek, very cleverly, as though they had rehearsed it beforehand, took seats between the officers, and at once got up a heated discussion in which the visitors could not help taking part. The lilac young lady hotly asserted that the artillery had a much better time than the cavalry and the infantry, while Von Rabbek and the elderly ladies maintained the opposite. A brisk interchange of talk followed. Ryabovitch watched the lilac young lady who argued so hotly about what was unfamiliar and utterly uninteresting to her, and watched artificial smiles come and go on her face.

Von Rabbek and his family skilfully drew the officers into the discussion, and meanwhile kept a sharp lookout over their glasses and mouths, to see whether all of them were drinking, whether all had enough sugar, why some one was not eating cakes or not drinking brandy. And the longer Ryabovitch watched and listened, the more he was attracted by this insincere but splendidly disciplined family.

After tea the officers went into the drawing-room. Lieutenant Lobytko's instinct had not deceived him. There were a great number of girls and young married ladies. The "setter" lieutenant was soon standing by a very young, fair girl in a black dress, and, bending down to her jauntily, as though leaning on an unseen sword, smiled and shrugged his shoulders coquettishly. He probably talked very interesting nonsense, for the fair girl looked at his well-fed face condescendingly and asked indifferently, "Really?" And from that uninterested "Really?" the setter, had he been intelligent, might have concluded that she would never call him to heel.

The piano struck up; the melancholy strains of a valse floated out of the wide open windows, and every one, for some reason, remembered that it was spring, a May evening. Every one was conscious of the fragrance of roses, of lilac, and of the young leaves of the poplar. Ryabovitch, in whom the brandy he had drunk made itself felt, under the influence of the music stole a glance towards the win-

dow, smiled, and began watching the movements of
the women, and it seemed to him that the smell of
roses, of poplars, and lilac came not from the garden, but from the ladies' faces and dresses.

Von Rabbek's son invited a scraggy-looking young
lady to dance, and waltzed round the room twice
with her.   Lobytko, gliding over the parquet floor,
flew up to the lilac young lady and whirled her away.
Dancing began. . . . Ryabovitch stood near the
door among those who were not dancing and looked
on.   He had never once danced in his whole life,
and he had never once in his life put his arm round
the waist of a respectable woman.   He was highly
delighted that a man should in the sight of all take
a girl he did not know round the waist and offer her
his shoulder to put her hand on, but he could not
imagine himself in the position of such a man.
There were times when he envied the boldness and
swagger of his companions and was inwardly
wretched; the consciousness that he was timid, that
he was round-shouldered and uninteresting, that
he had a long waist and lynx-like whiskers, had
deeply mortified him, but with years he had grown
used to this feeling, and now, looking at his comrades dancing or loudly talking, he no longer envied
them, but only felt touched and mournful.

When the quadrille began, young Von Rabbek
came up to those who were not dancing and invited

two officers to have a game at billiards.   The officers accepted and went with him out of the drawing-
room.   Ryabovitch, having nothing to do and wishing to take part in the general movement, slouched
after them.   From the big drawing-room they went
into the little drawing-room, then into a narrow corridor with a glass roof, and thence into a room in
which on their entrance three sleepy-looking footmen
jumped up quickly from the sofa.   At last, after
passing through a long succession of rooms, young
Von Rabbek and the officers came into a small room
where there was a billiard-table.   They began to
play.

Ryabovitch, who had never played any game but
cards, stood near the billiard-table and looked indifferently at the players, while they in unbuttoned
coats, with cues in their hands, stepped about, made
puns, and kept shouting out unintelligible words.

The players took no notice of him, and only now
and then one of them, shoving him with his elbow
or accidentally touching him with the end of his cue,
would turn round and say "Pardon!"   Before the
first game was over he was weary of it, and began
to feel he was not wanted and in the way. . . . He
felt disposed to return to the drawing-room, and he
went out.

On his way back he met with a little adventure.
When he had gone half-way he noticed he had taken

a wrong turning. He distinctly remembered that he ought to meet three sleepy footmen on his way, but he had passed five or six rooms, and those sleepy figures seemed to have vanished into the earth. Noticing his mistake, he walked back a little way and turned to the right; he found himself in a little dark room which he had not seen on his way to the billiard-room. After standing there a little while, he resolutely opened the first door that met his eyes and walked into an absolutely dark room. Straight in front could be seen the crack in the doorway through which there was a gleam of vivid light; from the other side of the door came the muffled sound of a melancholy mazurka. Here, too, as in the drawing-room, the windows were wide open and there was a smell of poplars, lilac and roses. . . .

Ryabovitch stood still in hesitation. . . . At that moment, to his surprise, he heard hurried footsteps and the rustling of a dress, a breathless feminine voice whispered " At last! " And two soft, fragrant, unmistakably feminine arms were clasped about his neck; a warm cheek was pressed to his cheek, and simultaneously there was the sound of a kiss. But at once the bestower of the kiss uttered a faint shriek and skipped back from him, as it seemed to Ryabovitch, with aversion. He, too, almost shrieked and rushed towards the gleam of light at the door. . . .

When he went back into the drawing-room his heart was beating and his hands were trembling so noticeably that he made haste to hide them behind his back.   At first he was tormented by shame and dread that the whole drawing-room knew that he had just been kissed and embraced by a woman. He shrank into himself and looked uneasily about him, but as he became convinced that people were dancing and talking as calmly as ever, he gave himself up entirely to the new sensation which he had never experienced before in his life.   Something strange was happening to him. . . . His neck, round which soft, fragrant arms had so lately been clasped, seemed to him to be anointed with oil; on his left cheek near his moustache where the unknown had kissed him there was a faint chilly tingling sensation as from peppermint drops, and the more he rubbed the place the more distinct was the chilly sensation; all over, from head to foot, he was full of a strange new feeling which grew stronger and stronger. . . . He wanted to dance, to talk, to run into the garden, to laugh aloud. . . . He quite forgot that he was round-shouldered and uninteresting, that he had lynx-like whiskers and an " undistinguished appearance " (that was how his appearance had been described by some ladies whose conversation he had accidentally overheard).   When Von Rabbek's wife happened to pass by him, he gave her such a broad and friendly smile that she stood still and looked at him inquiringly.

"I like your house immensely!" he said, setting his spectacles straight.

The General's wife smiled and said that the house had belonged to her father; then she asked whether his parents were living, whether he had long been in the army, why he was so thin, and so on. . . . After receiving answers to her questions, she went on, and after his conversation with her his smiles were more friendly than ever, and he thought he was surrounded by splendid people. . . .

At supper Ryabovitch ate mechanically everything offered him, drank, and without listening to anything, tried to understand what had just happened to him. . . . The adventure was of a mysterious and romantic character, but it was not difficult to explain it. No doubt some girl or young married lady had arranged a tryst with some one in the dark room; had waited a long time, and being nervous and excited had taken Ryabovitch for her hero; this was the more probable as Ryabovitch had stood still hesitating in the dark room, so that he, too, had seemed like a person expecting something. . . . This was how Ryabovitch explained to himself the kiss he had received.

"And who is she?" he wondered, looking round at the women's faces. "She must be young, for

elderly ladies don't give rendezvous.   That she was
a lady, one could tell by the rustle of her dress, her
perfume, her voice. . . ."

His eyes rested on the lilac young lady, and he
thought her very attractive; she had beautiful shoulders and arms, a clever face, and a delightful voice.
Ryabovitch, looking at her, hoped that she and no
one else was his unknown. . . . But she laughed
somehow artificially and wrinkled up her long nose,
which seemed to him to make her look old.   Then
he turned his eyes upon the fair girl in a black dress.
She was younger, simpler, and more genuine, had
a charming brow, and drank very daintily out of her
wineglass.   Ryabovitch now hoped that it was she.
But soon he began to think her face flat, and fixed
his eyes upon the one next her.

" It's difficult to guess," he thought, musing.   " If
one takes the shoulders and arms of the lilac one
only, adds the brow of the fair one and the eyes of
the one on the left of Lobytko, then . . ."

He made a combination of these things in his mind
and so formed the image of the girl who had kissed
him, the image that he wanted her to have, but could
not find at the table. . . .

After supper, replete and exhilarated, the officers
began to take leave and say thank you.   Von Rabbek and his wife began again apologizing that they
could not ask them to stay the night.

"Very, very glad to have met you, gentlemen," said Von Rabbek, and this time sincerely (probably because people are far more sincere and good-humoured at speeding their parting guests than on meeting them). "Delighted. I hope you will come on your way back! Don't stand on ceremony! Where are you going? Do you want to go by the upper way? No, go across the garden; it's nearer here by the lower way."

The officers went out into the garden. After the bright light and the noise the garden seemed very dark and quiet. They walked in silence all the way to the gate. They were a little drunk, pleased, and in good spirits, but the darkness and silence made them thoughtful for a minute. Probably the same idea occurred to each one of them as to Ryabovitch: would there ever come a time for them when, like Von Rabbek, they would have a large house, a family, a garden — when they, too, would be able to welcome people, even though insincerely, feed them, make them drunk and contented?

Going out of the garden gate, they all began talking at once and laughing loudly about nothing. They were walking now along the little path that led down to the river, and then ran along the water's edge, winding round the bushes on the bank, the pools, and the willows that overhung the water.

The bank and the path were scarcely visible, and the other bank was entirely plunged in darkness. Stars were reflected here and there on the dark water; they quivered and were broken up on the surface — and from that alone it could be seen that the river was flowing rapidly. It was still. Drowsy curlews cried plaintively on the further bank, and in one of the bushes on the nearest side a nightingale was trilling loudly, taking no notice of the crowd of officers. The officers stood round the bush, touched it, but the nightingale went on singing.

" What a fellow! " they exclaimed approvingly. " We stand beside him and he takes not a bit of notice! What a rascal! "

At the end of the way the path went uphill, and, skirting the church enclosure, turned into the road. Here the officers, tired with walking uphill, sat down and lighted their cigarettes. On the other side of the river a murky red fire came into sight, and having nothing better to do, they spent a long time in discussing whether it was a camp fire or a light in a window, or something else. . . . Ryabovitch, too, looked at the light, and he fancied that the light looked and winked at him, as though it knew about the kiss.

On reaching his quarters, Ryabovitch undressed as quickly as possible and got into bed. Lobytko and

Lieutenant Merzlyakov — a peaceable, silent fellow, who was considered in his own circle a highly educated officer, and was always, whenever it was possible, reading the " Vyestnik Evropi," which he carried about with him everywhere — were quartered in the same hut with Ryabovitch. Lobytko undressed, walked up and down the room for a long while with the air of a man who has not been satisfied, and sent his orderly for beer. Merzlyakov got into bed, put a candle by his pillow and plunged into reading the " Vyestnik Evropi."

" Who was she? " Ryabovitch wondered, looking at the smoky ceiling.

His neck still felt as though he had been anointed with oil, and there was still the chilly sensation near his mouth as though from peppermint drops. The shoulders and arms of the young lady in lilac, the brow and the truthful eyes of the fair girl in black, waists, dresses, and brooches, floated through his imagination. He tried to fix his attention on these images, but they danced about, broke up and flickered. When these images vanished altogether from the broad dark background which every man sees when he closes his eyes, he began to hear hurried footsteps, the rustle of skirts, the sound of a kiss and — an intense groundless joy took possession of him. . . . Abandoning himself to this joy, he heard the orderly return and announce that there was no beer. Lobytko was terribly indignant, and began pacing up and down again.

"Well, isn't he an idiot?" he kept saying, stopping first before Ryabovitch and then before Merzlyakov. "What a fool and a dummy a man must be not to get hold of any beer! Eh? Isn't he a scoundrel?"

"Of course you can't get beer here," said Merzlyakov, not removing his eyes from the "Vyestnik Evropi."

"Oh! Is that your opinion?" Lobytko persisted. "Lord have mercy upon us, if you dropped me on the moon I'd find you beer and women directly! I'll go and find some at once. . . . You may call me an impostor if I don't!"

He spent a long time in dressing and pulling on his high boots, then finished smoking his cigarette in silence and went out.

"Rabbek, Grabbek, Labbek," he muttered, stopping in the outer room. "I don't care to go alone, damn it all! Ryabovitch, wouldn't you like to go for a walk? Eh?"

Receiving no answer, he returned, slowly undressed and got into bed. Merzlyakov sighed, put the "Vyestnik Evropi" away, and put out the light.

"H'm! . . ." muttered Lobytko, lighting a cigarette in the dark.

Ryabovitch pulled the bed-clothes over his head, curled himself up in bed, and tried to gather together the floating images in his mind and to combine them into one whole. But nothing came of it. He soon fell asleep, and his last thought was that some one had caressed him and made him happy — that something extraordinary, foolish, but joyful and delightful, had come into his life. The thought did not leave him even in his sleep.

When he woke up the sensations of oil on his neck and the chill of peppermint about his lips had gone, but joy flooded his heart just as the day before. He looked enthusiastically at the window-frames, gilded by the light of the rising sun, and listened to the movement of the passers-by in the street. People were talking loudly close to the window. Lebedetsky, the commander of Ryabovitch's battery, who had only just overtaken the brigade, was talking to his sergeant at the top of his voice, being always accustomed to shout.

" What else? " shouted the commander.

" When they were shoeing yesterday, your high nobility, they drove a nail into Pigeon's hoof. The vet. put on clay and vinegar; they are leading him apart now. And also, your honour, Artemyev got drunk yesterday, and the lieutenant ordered him to be put in the limber of a spare gun-carriage."

The sergeant reported that Karpov had forgotten

the new cords for the trumpets and the rings for the tents, and that their honours, the officers, had spent the previous evening visiting General Von Rabbek. In the middle of this conversation the red-bearded face of Lebedetsky appeared in the window. He screwed up his short-sighted eyes, looking at the sleepy faces of the officers, and said good-morning to them.

" Is everything all right? " he asked.

" One of the horses has a sore neck from the new collar," answered Lobytko, yawning.

The commander sighed, thought a moment, and said in a loud voice:

" I am thinking of going to see Alexandra Yev-grafovna. I must call on her. Well, good-bye. I shall catch you up in the evening."

A quarter of an hour later the brigade set off on its way. When it was moving along the road by the granaries, Ryabovitch looked at the house on the right. The blinds were down in all the windows. Evidently the household was still asleep. The one who had kissed Ryabovitch the day before was asleep, too. He tried to imagine her asleep. The wide-open windows of the bedroom, the green branches peeping in, the morning freshness, the scent of the poplars, lilac, and roses, the bed, a chair, and on it the skirts that had rustled the day before, the little slippers, the little watch on the table — all this he pictured to himself clearly and distinctly, but the features of the face, the sweet sleepy smile, just what was characteristic and important, slipped through his imagination like quicksilver through the fingers. When he had ridden on half a mile, he looked back: the yellow church, the house, and the river, were all bathed in light; the river with its bright green banks, with the blue sky reflected in it and glints of silver in the sunshine here and there, was very beautiful. Ryabovitch gazed for the last time at Myestetchki, and he felt as sad as though he were parting with something very near and dear to him.

And before him on the road lay nothing but long familiar, uninteresting pictures. . . . To right and to left, fields of young rye and buckwheat with rooks hopping about in them. If one looked ahead, one saw dust and the backs of men's heads; if one looked back, one saw the same dust and faces. . . . Foremost of all marched four men with sabres — this was the vanguard. Next, behind, the crowd of singers, and behind them the trumpeters on horseback. The vanguard and the chorus of singers, like torch-bearers in a funeral procession, often forgot to keep the regulation distance and pushed a long way ahead. . . . Ryabovitch was with the first cannon of the fifth battery. He could see all the four batteries moving in front of him. For any one not a military man this long tedious procession of a moving brigade seems an intricate and unintelligible muddle; one cannot understand why there are so many people round one cannon, and why it is drawn by so many horses in such a strange network of harness, as though it really were so terrible and heavy. To Ryabovitch it was all perfectly comprehensible and therefore uninteresting. He had known for ever so long why at the head of each battery there rode a stalwart bombardier, and why he was called a bombardier; immediately behind this bombardier could be seen the horsemen of the first and then of the middle units. Ryabovitch knew that the horses on which they rode, those on the left, were called one name, while those on the right were called another — it was extremely uninteresting. Behind the horsemen came two shaft-horses. On one of them sat a rider with the dust of yesterday on his back and a clumsy and funny-looking piece of wood on his leg. Ryabovitch knew the object of this piece of wood, and did not think it funny. All the riders waved their whips mechanically and shouted from time to time. The cannon itself was ugly. On the fore part lay sacks of oats covered with canvas, and the cannon itself was hung all over with kettles, soldiers' knapsacks, bags, and looked like some small harmless animal surrounded for some unknown reason by men and horses. To the leeward of it marched six men, the gunners, swinging their arms. After the cannon there came again more bombardiers, riders, shaft-horses, and behind them another cannon, as ugly and unimpressive as the first. After the second followed a third, a fourth; near the fourth an officer, and so on. There were six batteries in all in the brigade, and four cannons in each battery. The procession covered half a mile; it ended in a string of wagons near which an extremely attractive creature — the ass, Magar, brought by a battery commander from Turkey — paced pensively with his long-eared head drooping.

Ryabovitch looked indifferently before and behind, at the backs of heads and at faces; at any other time he would have been half asleep, but now he was entirely absorbed in his new agreeable thoughts. At first when the brigade was setting off on the march he tried to persuade himself that the incident of the kiss could only be interesting as a mysterious little adventure, that it was in reality trivial, and to think of it seriously, to say the least of it, was stupid; but now he bade farewell to logic and gave himself up to dreams. . . . At one moment he imagined himself in Von Rabbek's drawing-room beside a girl who was like the young lady in lilac and the fair girl in black; then he would close his eyes and see himself with another, entirely unknown girl, whose features were very vague. In his imagination he talked, caressed her, leaned on her shoulder, pictured war, separation, then meeting again, supper with his wife, children. . . .

" Brakes on! " the word of command rang out every time they went downhill.

He, too, shouted " Brakes on! " and was afraid this shout would disturb his reverie and bring him back to reality. . . .

As they passed by some landowner's estate Ryabovitch looked over the fence into the garden.   A long avenue, straight as a ruler, strewn with yellow sand and bordered with young birch-trees, met his eyes. . . . With the eagerness of a man given up to dreaming, he pictured to himself little feminine feet tripping along yellow sand, and quite unexpectedly had a clear vision in his imagination of the girl who had kissed him and whom he had succeeded in picturing to himself the evening before at supper. This image remained in his brain and did not desert him again.

At midday there was a shout in the rear near the string of wagons:

" Easy!   Eyes to the left!   Officers! "

The general of the brigade drove by in a carriage with a pair of white horses.   He stopped near the second battery, and shouted something which no one understood.   Several officers, among them Ryabovitch, galloped up to them.

"Well?" asked the general, blinking his red eyes. "Are there any sick?"

Receiving an answer, the general, a little skinny man, chewed, thought for a moment and said, addressing one of the officers:

"One of your drivers of the third cannon has taken off his leg-guard and hung it on the fore part of the cannon, the rascal. Reprimand him."

He raised his eyes to Ryabovitch and went on:

"It seems to me your front strap is too long."

Making a few other tedious remarks, the general looked at Lobytko and grinned.

"You look very melancholy today, Lieutenant Lobytko," he said. "Are you pining for Madame Lopuhov? Eh? Gentlemen, he is pining for Madame Lopuhov."

The lady in question was a very stout and tall person who had long passed her fortieth year. The general, who had a predilection for solid ladies, whatever their ages, suspected a similar taste in his officers. The officers smiled respectfully. The general, delighted at having said something very amusing and biting, laughed loudly, touched his coachman's back, and saluted. The carriage rolled on. . . .

"All I am dreaming about now which seems to me so impossible and unearthly is really quite an ordinary thing," thought Ryabovitch, looking at the clouds of dust racing after the general's carriage. " It's all very ordinary, and every one goes through it. . . . That general, for instance, has once been in love; now he is married and has children. Captain Vahter, too, is married and beloved, though the nape of his neck is very red and ugly and he has no waist. . . . Salmanov is coarse and very Tatar, but he has had a love affair that has ended in marriage. . . . I am the same as every one else, and I, too, shall have the same experience as every one else, sooner or later. . . ."

And the thought that he was an ordinary person, and that his life was ordinary, delighted him and gave him courage. He pictured *her* and his happiness as he pleased, and put no rein on his imagination. . . .

When the brigade reached their halting-place in the evening, and the officers were resting in their tents, Ryabovitch, Merzlyakov, and Lobytko were sitting round a box having supper. Merzlyakov ate without haste, and, as he munched deliberately, read the " Vyestnik Evropi," which he held on his knees. Lobytko talked incessantly and kept filling up his glass with beer, and Ryabovitch, whose head was confused from dreaming all day long, drank and said nothing. After three glasses he got a little drunk, felt weak, and had an irresistible desire to impart his new sensations to his comrades.

" A strange thing happened to me at those Von Rabbeks'," he began, trying to put an indifferent and ironical tone into his voice. " You know I went into the billiard-room. . . ."

He began describing very minutely the incident of the kiss, and a moment later relapsed into silence. . . . In the course of that moment he had told everything, and it surprised him dreadfully to find how short a time it took him to tell it. He had imagined that he could have been telling the story of the kiss till next morning. Listening to him, Lobytko, who was a great liar and consequently believed no one, looked at him sceptically and laughed. Merzlyakov twitched his eyebrows and, without removing his eyes from the " Vyestnik Evropi," said:

" That's an odd thing! How strange! . . . throws herself on a man's neck, without addressing him by name. . . . She must be some sort of hysterical neurotic."

" Yes, she must," Ryabovitch agreed.

" A similar thing once happened to me," said Lobytko, assuming a scared expression. " I was going last year to Kovno. . . . I took a second-class ticket. The train was crammed, and it was impossible to sleep. I gave the guard half a rouble; he took my luggage and led me to another compartment. . . . I lay down and covered myself with a rug. . . . It was dark, you understand. Suddenly I felt some one touch me on the shoulder and breathe in my face. I made a movement with my hand and felt somebody's elbow. . . . I opened my eyes and only imagine — a woman. Black eyes, lips red as a prime salmon, nostrils breathing passionately — a bosom like a buffer. . . ."

"Excuse me," Merzlyakov interrupted calmly, "I understand about the bosom, but how could you see the lips if it was dark?"

Lobytko began trying to put himself right and laughing at Merzlyakov's unimaginativeness. It made Ryabovitch wince. He walked away from the box, got into bed, and vowed never to confide again.

Camp life began. . . . The days flowed by, one very much like another. All those days Ryabovitch felt, thought, and behaved as though he were in love. Every morning when his orderly handed him water to wash with, and he sluiced his head with cold water, he thought there was something warm and delightful in his life.

In the evenings when his comrades began talking of love and women, he would listen, and draw up closer; and he wore the expression of a soldier when he hears the description of a battle in which he has taken part. And on the evenings when the officers,

out on the spree with the setter — Lobytko — at
their head, made Don Juan excursions to the
"suburb," and Ryabovitch took part in such excursions, he always was sad, felt profoundly guilty, and
inwardly begged *her* forgiveness. . . . In hours of
leisure or on sleepless nights, when he felt moved
to recall his childhood, his father and mother —
everything near and dear, in fact, he invariably
thought of Myestetchki, the strange horse, Von
Rabbek, his wife who was like the Empress
Eugénie, the dark room, the crack of light at the
door. . . .

On the thirty-first of August he went back from the
camp, not with the whole brigade, but with only two
batteries of it. He was dreaming and excited all the
way, as though he were going back to his native
place. He had an intense longing to see again the
strange horse, the church, the insincere family of the
Von Rabbeks, the dark room. The "inner voice,"
which so often deceives lovers, whispered to him for
some reason that he would be sure to see her . . .
and he was tortured by the questions, How he should
meet her? What he would talk to her about?
Whether she had forgotten the kiss? If the worst
came to the worst, he thought, even if he did not
meet her, it would be a pleasure to him merely to
go through the dark room and recall the past. . . .

Towards evening there appeared on the horizon

the familiar church and white granaries.   Ryabovitch's heart beat. . . . He did not hear the officer
who was riding beside him and saying something to
him, he forgot everything, and looked eagerly at the
river shining in the distance, at the roof of the
house, at the dovecote round which the pigeons were
circling in the light of the setting sun.

When they reached the church and were listening
to the billeting orders, he expected every second that
a man on horseback would come round the church
enclosure and invite the officers to tea, but . . . the
billeting orders were read, the officers were in haste
to go on to the village, and the man on horseback did
not appear.

" Von Rabbek will hear at once from the peasants
that we have come and will send for us," thought
Ryabovitch, as he went into the hut, unable to understand why a comrade was lighting a candle and
why the orderlies were hurriedly setting samovars. . . .

A painful uneasiness took possession of him.   He
lay down, then got up and looked out of the window
to see whether the messenger were coming.   But
there was no sign of him.

He lay down again, but half an hour later he got
up, and, unable to restrain his uneasiness, went into
the street and strode towards the church.   It was
dark and deserted in the square near the church. . . .

Three soldiers were standing silent in a row where
the road began to go downhill. Seeing Ryabovitch,
they roused themselves and saluted. He returned
the salute and began to go down the familiar path.

On the further side of the river the whole sky was
flooded with crimson: the moon was rising; two
peasant women, talking loudly, were picking cabbage
in the kitchen garden; behind the kitchen garden
there were some dark huts. . . . And everything on
the near side of the river was just as it had been in
May: the path, the bushes, the willows overhanging
the water . . . but there was no sound of the brave
nightingale, and no scent of poplar and fresh grass.

Reaching the garden, Ryabovitch looked in at the
gate. The garden was dark and still. . . . He
could see nothing but the white stems of the nearest
birch-trees and a little bit of the avenue; all the rest
melted together into a dark blur. Ryabovitch
looked and listened eagerly, but after waiting for a
quarter of an hour without hearing a sound or catching a glimpse of a light, he trudged back. . . .

He went down to the river. The General's bath-
house and the bath-sheets on the rail of the little
bridge showed white before him. . . . He went on
to the bridge, stood a little, and, quite unnecessarily,
touched the sheets. They felt rough and cold. He
looked down at the water. . . . The river ran rapidly and with a faintly audible gurgle round the piles

of the bath-house.   The red moon was reflected near
the left bank; little ripples ran over the reflection,
stretching it out, breaking it into bits, and seemed
trying to carry it away. . . .

"How stupid, how stupid!" thought Ryabovitch,
looking at the running water.   "How unintelligent
it all is!"

Now that he expected nothing, the incident of the
kiss, his impatience, his vague hopes and disappointment, presented themselves in a clear light.   It no
longer seemed to him strange that he had not seen
the General's messenger, and that he would never see
the girl who had accidentally kissed him instead of
some one else; on the contrary, it would have been
strange if he had seen her. . . .

The water was running, he knew not where or
why, just as it did in May.   In May it had flowed
into the great river, from the great river into the
sea; then it had risen in vapour, turned into rain,
and perhaps the very same water was running now
before Ryabovitch's eyes again. . . . What for?
Why?

And the whole world, the whole of life, seemed
to Ryabovitch an unintelligible, aimless jest. . . .
And turning his eyes from the water and looking at
the sky, he remembered again how fate in the person
of an unknown woman had by chance caressed him,
he remembered his summer dreams and fancies, and

his life struck him as extraordinarily meagre, poverty-stricken, and colourless. . . .

When he went back to his hut he did not find one of his comrades. The orderly informed him that they had all gone to " General von Rabbek's, who had sent a messenger on horseback to invite them. . . ."

For an instant there was a flash of joy in Ryabovitch's heart, but he quenched it at once, got into bed, and in his wrath with his fate, as though to spite it, did not go to the General's.

1887

"ANNA ON THE NECK"

"ANNA ON THE NECK"

I

AFTER the wedding they had not even light refreshments; the happy pair simply drank a glass of champagne, changed into their travelling things, and drove to the station. Instead of a gay wedding ball and supper, instead of music and dancing, they went on a journey to pray at a shrine a hundred and fifty miles away. Many people commended this, saying that Modest Alexeitch was a man high up in the service and no longer young, and that a noisy wedding might not have seemed quite suitable; and music is apt to sound dreary when a government official of fifty-two marries a girl who is only just eighteen. People said, too, that Modest Alexeitch, being a man of principle, had arranged this visit to the monastery expressly in order to make his young bride realize that even in marriage he put religion and morality above everything.

The happy pair were seen off at the station. The crowd of relations and colleagues in the service stood, with glasses in their hands, waiting for the train to start to shout "Hurrah!" and the bride's

father, Pyotr Leontyitch, wearing a top-hat and the
uniform of a teacher, already drunk and very pale,
kept craning towards the window, glass in hand and
saying in an imploring voice:

" Anyuta!   Anya, Anya! one word! "

Anna bent out of the window to him, and he whispered something to her, enveloping her in a stale
smell of alcohol, blew into her ear — she could make
out nothing — and made the sign of the cross over
her face, her bosom, and her hands; meanwhile he
was breathing in gasps and tears were shining in his
eyes.   And the schoolboys, Anna's brothers, Petya
and Andrusha, pulled at his coat from behind, whispering in confusion:

" Father, hush! . . . Father, that's enough. . . ."

When the train started, Anna saw her father run
a little way after the train, staggering and spilling
his wine, and what a kind, guilty, pitiful face he had:

" Hurra — ah! " he shouted.

The happy pair were left alone.   Modest Alexeitch looked about the compartment, arranged their
things on the shelves, and sat down, smiling, opposite
his young wife.   He was an official of medium
height, rather stout and puffy, who looked exceedingly well nourished, with long whiskers and no
moustache.   His clean-shaven, round, sharply defined chin looked like the heel of a foot.   The most
characteristic point in his face was the absence of

moustache, the bare, freshly shaven place, which gradually passed into the fat cheeks, quivering like jelly. His deportment was dignified, his movements were deliberate, his manner was soft.

" I cannot help remembering now one circumstance," he said, smiling. " When, five years ago, Kosorotov received the order of St. Anna of the second grade, and went to thank His Excellency, His Excellency expressed himself as follows: ' So now you have three Annas: one in your buttonhole and two on your neck.' And it must be explained that at that time Kosorotov's wife, a quarrelsome and frivolous person, had just returned to him, and that her name was Anna. I trust that when I receive the Anna of the second grade His Excellency will not have occasion to say the same thing to me."

He smiled with his little eyes. And she, too, smiled, troubled at the thought that at any moment this man might kiss her with his thick damp lips, and that she had no right to prevent his doing so. The soft movements of his fat person frightened her; she felt both fear and disgust. He got up, without haste took off the order from his neck, took off his coat and waistcoat, and put on his dressing-gown.

" That's better," he said, sitting down beside Anna.

Anna remembered what agony the wedding had

been, when it had seemed to her that the priest, and the guests, and every one in church had been looking at her sorrowfully and asking why, why was she, such a sweet, nice girl, marrying such an elderly, uninteresting gentleman. Only that morning she was delighted that everything had been satisfactorily arranged, but at the time of the wedding, and now in the railway carriage, she felt cheated, guilty, and ridiculous. Here she had married a rich man and yet she had no money, her wedding-dress had been bought on credit, and when her father and brothers had been saying good-bye, she could see from their faces that they had not a farthing. Would they have any supper that day? And tomorrow? And for some reason it seemed to her that her father and the boys were sitting tonight hungry without her, and feeling the same misery as they had the day after their mother's funeral.

"Oh, how unhappy I am!" she thought. "Why am I so unhappy?"

With the awkwardness of a man with settled habits, unaccustomed to deal with women, Modest Alexeitch touched her on the waist and patted her on the shoulder, while she went on thinking about money, about her mother and her mother's death. When her mother died, her father, Pyotr Leontyitch, a teacher of drawing and writing in the high school, had taken to drink, impoverishment had followed,

the boys had not had boots or goloshes, their father
had been hauled up before the magistrate, the war-
rant officer had come and made an inventory of the
furniture. . . . What a disgrace! Anna had had
to look after her drunken father, darn her brothers'
stockings, go to market, and when she was compli-
mented on her youth, her beauty, and her elegant
manners, it seemed to her that every one was looking
at her cheap hat and the holes in her boots that were
inked over.   And at night there had been tears and
a haunting dread that her father would soon, very
soon, be dismissed from the school for his weakness,
and that he would not survive it, but would die, too,
like their mother.   But ladies of their acquaintance
had taken the matter in hand and looked about for a
good match for Anna.   This Modest Alexevitch,
who was neither young nor good-looking but had
money, was soon found.   He had a hundred thousand in the bank and the family estate, which he had
let on lease.   He was a man of principle and stood
well with His Excellency; it would be nothing to him,
so they told Anna, to get a note from His Excellency
to the directors of the high school, or even to the
Education Commissioner, to prevent Pyotr Leontyitch from being dismissed.

While she was recalling these details, she suddenly heard strains of music which floated in at the
window, together with the sound of voices.   The

train was stopping at a station.   In the crowd beyond the platform an accordion and a cheap squeaky fiddle were being briskly played, and the sound of a military band came from beyond the villas and the tall birches and poplars that lay bathed in the moonlight; there must have been a dance in the place. Summer visitors and townspeople, who used to come out here by train in fine weather for a breath of fresh air, were parading up and down on the platform. Among them was the wealthy owner of all the summer villas — a tall, stout, dark man called Artynov. He had prominent eyes and looked like an Armenian. He wore a strange costume; his shirt was unbuttoned, showing his chest; he wore high boots with spurs, and a black cloak hung from his shoulders and dragged on the ground like a train.   Two boarhounds followed him with their sharp noses to the ground.

Tears were still shining in Anna's eyes, but she was not thinking now of her mother, nor of money, nor of her marriage; but shaking hands with schoolboys and officers she knew, she laughed gaily and said quickly:

" How do you do?   How are you? "

She went out on to the platform between the carriages into the moonlight, and stood so that they could all see her in her new splendid dress and hat.

" Why are we stopping here? " she asked.

"This is a junction. They are waiting for the mail train to pass."

Seeing that Artynov was looking at her, she screwed up her eyes coquettishly and began talking aloud in French; and because her voice sounded so pleasant, and because she heard music and the moon was reflected in the pond, and because Artynov, the notorious Don Juan and spoiled child of fortune, was looking at her eagerly and with curiosity, and because every one was in good spirits — she suddenly felt joyful, and when the train started and the officers of her acquaintance saluted her, she was humming the polka the strains of which reached her from the military band playing beyond the trees; and she returned to her compartment feeling as though it had been proved to her at the station that she would certainly be happy in spite of everything.

The happy pair spent two days at the monastery, then went back to town. They lived in a rent-free flat. When Modest Alexevitch had gone to the office, Anna played the piano, or shed tears of depression, or lay down on a couch and read novels or looked through fashion papers. At dinner Modest Alexevitch ate a great deal and talked about politics, about appointments, transfers, and promotions in the service, about the necessity of hard work, and said that, family life not being a pleasure but a duty, if you took care of the kopecks the roubles would take care of themselves, and that he put religion and morality before everything else in the world. And holding his knife in his fist as though it were a sword, he would say:

"Every one ought to have his duties!"

And Anna listened to him, was frightened, and could not eat, and she usually got up from the table hungry. After dinner her husband lay down for a nap and snored loudly, while Anna went to see her own people. Her father and the boys looked at her in a peculiar way, as though just before she came in they had been blaming her for having married for money a tedious, wearisome man she did not love; her rustling skirts, her bracelets, and her general air of a married lady, offended them and made them uncomfortable. In her presence they felt a little embarrassed and did not know what to talk to her about; but yet they still loved her as before, and were not used to having dinner without her. She sat down with them to cabbage soup, porridge, and fried potatoes, smelling of mutton dripping. Pyotr Leontyitch filled his glass from the decanter with a trembling hand and drank it off hurriedly, greedily, with repulsion, then poured out a second glass and then a third. Petya and Andrusha, thin, pale boys with big eyes, would take the decanter and say desperately:

"You mustn't, father. . . . Enough, father. . . ."

And Anna, too, was troubled and entreated him to drink no more; and he would suddenly fly into a rage and beat the table with his fists:

" I won't allow any one to dictate to me!" he would shout. "Wretched boys! wretched girl! I'll turn you all out!"

But there was a note of weakness, of good-nature in his voice, and no one was afraid of him. After dinner he usually dressed in his best. Pale, with a cut on his chin from shaving, craning his thin neck, he would stand for half an hour before the glass, prinking, combing his hair, twisting his black moustache, sprinkling himself with scent, tying his cravat in a bow; then he would put on his gloves and his top-hat, and go off to give his private lessons. Or if it was a holiday he would stay at home and paint, or play the harmonium, which wheezed and growled; he would try to wrest from it pure harmonious sounds and would sing to it; or would storm at the boys:

" Wretches! Good-for-nothing boys! You have spoiled the instrument!"

In the evening Anna's husband played cards with his colleagues, who lived under the same roof in the government quarters. The wives of these gentlemen would come in — ugly, tastelessly dressed women, as coarse as cooks — and gossip would begin in the flat as tasteless and unattractive as the ladies themselves.   Sometimes Modest Alexevitch would take Anna to the theatre.   In the intervals he would never let her stir a step from his side, but walked about arm in arm with her through the corridors and the foyer.   When he bowed to some one, he immediately whispered to Anna: "A civil councillor . . . visits at His Excellency's"; or, "A man of means . . . has a house of his own."   When they passed the buffet Anna had a great longing for something sweet; she was fond of chocolate and apple cakes, but she had no money, and she did not like to ask her husband.   He would take a pear, pinch it with his fingers, and ask uncertainly:

"How much?"

"Twenty-five kopecks!"

"I say!" he would reply, and put it down; but as it was awkward to leave the buffet without buying anything, he would order some seltzer-water and drink the whole bottle himself, and tears would come into his eyes.   And Anna hated him at such times.

And suddenly flushing crimson, he would say to her rapidly:

"Bow to that old lady!"

"But I don't know her."

"No matter.   That's the wife of the director of the local treasury!   Bow, I tell you," he would grumble insistently.   "Your head won't drop off."

Anna bowed and her head certainly did not drop

off, but it was agonizing. She did everything her
husband wanted her to, and was furious with herself for having let him deceive her like the veriest
idiot. She had only married him for his money, and
yet she had less money now than before her marriage. In old days her father would sometimes give
her twenty kopecks, but now she had not a farthing.
To take money by stealth or ask for it, she could not;
she was afraid of her husband, she trembled before
him. She felt as though she had been afraid of him
for years. In her childhood the director of the
high school had always seemed the most impressive
and terrifying force in the world, sweeping down
like a thunderstorm or a steam-engine ready to crush
her; another similar force of which the whole family
talked, and of which they were for some reason
afraid, was His Excellency; then there were a dozen
others, less formidable, and among them the teachers
at the high school, with shaven upper lips, stern,
implacable; and now finally, there was Modest
Alexeitch, a man of principle, who even resembled
the director in the face. And in Anna's imagination all these forces blended together into one, and,
in the form of a terrible, huge white bear, menaced
the weak and erring such as her father. And she
was afraid to say anything in opposition to her husband, and gave a forced smile, and tried to make a
show of pleasure when she was coarsely caressed

and defiled by embraces that excited her terror.

Only once Pyotr Leontyitch had the temerity to ask for a loan of fifty roubles in order to pay some very irksome debt, but what an agony it had been!

"Very good; I'll give it to you," said Modest Alexeitch after a moment's thought; "but I warn you I won't help you again till you give up drinking. Such a failing is disgraceful in a man in the government service! I must remind you of the well-known fact that many capable people have been ruined by that passion, though they might possibly, with temperance, have risen in time to a very high position."

And long-winded phrases followed: "inasmuch as . . .," "following upon which proposition . . .," "in view of the aforesaid contention . . ."; and Pyotr Leontyitch was in agonies of humiliation and felt an intense craving for alcohol.

And when the boys came to visit Anna, generally in broken boots and threadbare trousers, they, too, had to listen to sermons.

"Every man ought to have his duties!" Modest Alexeitch would say to them.

And he did not give them money. But he did give Anna bracelets, rings, and brooches, saying that these things would come in useful for a rainy day. And he often unlocked her drawer and made an inspection to see whether they were all safe.

II

Meanwhile winter came on. Long before Christmas there was an announcement in the local papers that the usual winter ball would take place on the twenty-ninth of December in the Hall of Nobility. Every evening after cards Modest Alexeitch was excitedly whispering with his colleagues' wives and glancing at Anna, and then paced up and down the room for a long while, thinking. At last, late one evening, he stood still, facing Anna, and said:

"You ought to get yourself a ball dress. Do you understand? Only please consult Marya Grigoryevna and Natalya Kuzminishna."

And he gave her a hundred roubles. She took the money, but she did not consult any one when she ordered the ball dress; she spoke to no one but her father, and tried to imagine how her mother would have dressed for a ball. Her mother had always dressed in the latest fashion and had always taken trouble over Anna, dressing her elegantly like a doll, and had taught her to speak French and dance the mazurka superbly (she had been a governess for five years before her marriage). Like her mother, Anna could make a new dress out of an old one, clean gloves with benzine, hire jewels; and, like her mother, she knew how to screw up her eyes, lisp, assume graceful attitudes, fly into raptures when necessary, and throw a mournful and enigmatic look into her eyes. And from her father she had inherited the dark colour of her hair and eyes, her highly-strung nerves, and the habit of always making herself look her best.

When, half an hour before setting off for the ball, Modest Alexeitch went into her room without his coat on, to put his order round his neck before her pier-glass, dazzled by her beauty and the splendour of her fresh, ethereal dress, he combed his whiskers complacently and said:

"So that's what my wife can look like . . . so that's what you can look like! Anyuta!" he went on, dropping into a tone of solemnity, "I have made your fortune, and now I beg you to do something for mine. I beg you to get introduced to the wife of His Excellency! For God's sake, do! Through her I may get the post of senior reporting clerk!"

They went to the ball. They reached the Hall of Nobility, the entrance with the hall porter. They came to the vestibule with the hat-stands, the fur coats; footmen scurrying about, and ladies with low necks putting up their fans to screen themselves from the draughts. There was a smell of gas and of soldiers. When Anna, walking upstairs on her husband's arm, heard the music and saw herself full length in the looking-glass in the full glow of the lights, there was a rush of joy in her heart, and she

felt the same presentiment of happiness as in the
moonlight at the station. She walked in proudly,
confidently, for the first time feeling herself not a
girl but a lady, and unconsciously imitating her
mother in her walk and in her manner. And for the
first time in her life she felt rich and free. Even
her husband's presence did not oppress her, for as
she crossed the threshold of the hall she had guessed
instinctively that the proximity of an old husband did
not detract from her in the least, but, on the contrary, gave her that shade of piquant mystery that
is so attractive to men. The orchestra was already
playing and the dances had begun. After their flat
Anna was overwhelmed by the lights, the bright col-
ours, the music, the noise, and looking round the
room, thought, " Oh, how lovely! " She at once
distinguished in the crowd all her acquaintances,
every one she had met before at parties or on picnics
— all the officers, the teachers, the lawyers, the officials, the landowners, His Excellency, Artynov, and
the ladies of the highest standing, dressed up and
very *décolletées*, handsome and ugly, who had already taken up their positions in the stalls and pa-
vilions of the charity bazaar, to begin selling things
for the benefit of the poor. A huge officer in epau-
lettes — she had been introduced to him in Staro-
Kievsky Street when she was a schoolgirl, but now
she could not remember his name — seemed to

spring from out of the ground, begging her for a waltz, and she flew away from her husband, feeling as though she were floating away in a sailing-boat in a violent storm, while her husband was left far away on the shore.   She danced passionately, with fervour, a waltz, then a polka and a quadrille, being snatched by one partner as soon as she was left by another, dizzy with music and the noise, mixing Russian with French, lisping, laughing, and with no thought of her husband or anything else.   She excited great admiration among the men — that was evident, and indeed it could not have been otherwise; she was breathless with excitement, felt thirsty, and convulsively clutched her fan.   Pyotr Leontyitch, her father, in a crumpled dress-coat that smelt of benzine, came up to her, offering her a plate of pink ice.

" You are enchanting this evening," he said, looking at her rapturously, " and I have never so much regretted that you were in such a hurry to get married. . . . What was it for?   I know you did it for our sake, but . . ."   With a shaking hand he drew out a roll of notes and said: " I got the money for my lessons today, and can pay your husband what I owe him."

She put the plate back into his hand, and was pounced upon by some one and borne off to a distance.   She caught a glimpse over her partner's shoulder of her father gliding over the floor, putting his arm round a lady and whirling down the ball-room with her.

" How sweet he is when he is sober! " she thought.

She danced the mazurka with the same huge offi-cer; he moved gravely, as heavily as a dead carcase in a uniform, twitched his shoulders and his chest, stamped his feet very languidly — he felt fearfully disinclined to dance. She fluttered round him, pro-voking him by her beauty, her bare neck; her eyes glowed defiantly, her movements were passionate, while he became more and more indifferent, and held out his hands to her as graciously as a king.

" Bravo, bravo! " said people watching them.

But little by little the huge officer, too, broke out; he grew lively, excited, and, overcome by her fascination, was carried away and danced lightly, youthfully, while she merely moved her shoulders and looked slvly at him as though she were now the queen and he were her slave; and at that mo-ment it seemed to her that the whole room was looking at them, and that everybody was thrilled and envied them. The huge officer had hardly had time to thank her for the dance, when the crowd suddenly parted and the men drew themselves up in a strange way, with their hands at their sides. His Excellency, with two stars on his dress-coat, was

walking up to her.   Yes, His Excellency was walking straight towards her, for he was staring directly
at her with a sugary smile, while he licked his lips
as he always did when he saw a pretty woman.

"Delighted, delighted . . ." he began.   "I shall
order your husband to be clapped in a lock-up for
keeping such a treasure hidden from us till now.
I've come to you with a message from my wife," he
went on, offering her his arm.   "You must help
us. . . . M-m-yes. . . . We ought to give you the
prize for beauty as they do in America. . . .
M-m-yes. . . . The Americans. . . . My wife is
expecting you impatiently."

He led her to a stall and presented her to a middle-aged lady, the lower part of whose face was dis-
proportionately large, so that she looked as though
she were holding a big stone in her mouth.

"You must help us," she said through her nose
in a sing-song voice.   "All the pretty women are
working for our charity bazaar, and you are the
only one enjoying yourself.   Why won't you help
us?"

She went away, and Anna took her place by the
cups and the silver samovar.   She was soon doing
a lively trade.   Anna asked no less than a rouble
for a cup of tea, and made the huge officer drink
three cups.   Artynov, the rich man with prominent
eyes, who suffered from asthma, came up, too; he

was not dressed in the strange costume in which
Anna had seen him in the summer at the station, but
wore a dress-coat like every one else. Keeping his
eyes fixed on Anna, he drank a glass of champagne
and paid a hundred roubles for it, then drank some
tea and gave another hundred — all this without
saying a word, as he was short of breath through
asthma. . . . Anna invited purchasers and got
money out of them, firmly convinced by now that her
smiles and glances could not fail to afford these people great pleasure. She realized now that she was
created exclusively for this noisy, brilliant, laughing
life, with its music, its dancers, its adorers, and her
old terror of a force that was sweeping down upon
her and menacing to crush her seemed to her ridiculous: she was afraid of no one now, and only regretted that her mother could not be there to rejoice
at her success.

Pyotr Leontyitch, pale by now but still steady
on his legs, came up to the stall and asked for a
glass of brandy. Anna turned crimson, expecting
him to say something inappropriate (she was already ashamed of having such a poor and ordinary
father) ; but he emptied his glass, took ten roubles
out of his roll of notes, flung it down, and walked
away with dignity without uttering a word. A
little later she saw him dancing in the grand chain,
and by now he was staggering and kept shouting

something, to the great confusion of his partner;
and Anna remembered how at the ball three years
before he had staggered and shouted in the same
way, and it had ended in the police-sergeant's taking him home to bed, and next day the director had
threatened to dismiss him from his post.   How inappropriate that memory was!

When the samovars were put out in the stalls
and the exhausted ladies handed over their takings
to the middle-aged lady with the stone in her mouth,
Artynov took Anna on his arm to the hall where
supper was served to all who had assisted at the
bazaar.   There were some twenty people at supper,
not more, but it was very noisy.   His Excellency
proposed a toast:

" In this magnificent dining-room it will be appropriate to drink to the success of the cheap dining-
rooms, which are the object of today's bazaar."

The brigadier-general proposed the toast: " To
the power by which even the artillery is vanquished,"
and all the company clinked glasses with the ladies.
It was very, very gay.

When Anna was escorted home it was daylight
and the cooks were going to market.   Joyful, intoxicated, full of new sensations, exhausted, she
undressed, dropped into bed, and at once fell
asleep. . . .

It was past one in the afternoon when the serv-

ant waked her and announced that M. Artynov had
called. She dressed quickly and went down into
the drawing-room. Soon after Artynov, His Excellency called to thank her for her assistance in the
bazaar. With a sugary smile, chewing his lips, he
kissed her hand, and asking her permission to come
again, took his leave, while she remained standing
in the middle of the drawing-room, amazed, en-
chanted, unable to believe that this change in her
life, this marvellous change, had taken place so
quickly; and at that moment Modest Alexeitch
walked in . . . and he, too, stood before her now
with the same ingratiating, sugary, cringingly respectful expression which she was accustomed to see
on his face in the presence of the great and powerful;
and with rapture, with indignation, with contempt,
convinced that no harm would come to her from it,
she said, articulating distinctly each word:

" Be off, you blockhead! "

From this time forward Anna never had one day
free, as she was always taking part in picnics, expe-
ditions, performances. She returned home every
day after midnight, and went to bed on the floor in
the drawing-room, and afterwards used to tell every
one, touchingly, how she slept under flowers. She
needed a very great deal of money, but she was no
longer afraid of Modest Alexeitch, and spent his
money as though it were her own; and she did not

ask, did not demand it, simply sent him in the bills. "Give bearer two hundred roubles," or "Pay one hundred roubles at once."

At Easter Modest Alexeitch received the Anna of the second grade. When he went to offer his thanks, His Excellency put aside the paper he was reading and settled himself more comfortably in his chair.

"So now you have three Annas," he said, scrutinizing his white hands and pink nails —"one on your buttonhole and two on your neck."

Modest Alexeitch put two fingers to his lips as a precaution against laughing too loud and said:

"Now I have only to look forward to the arrival of a little Vladimir. I make bold to beg your Excellency to stand godfather."

He was alluding to Vladimir of the fourth grade, and was already imagining how he would tell everywhere the story of this pun, so happy in its readiness and audacity, and he wanted to say something equally happy, but His Excellency was buried again in his newspaper, and merely gave him a nod.

And Anna went on driving about with three horses, going out hunting with Artynov, playing in one-act dramas, going out to supper, and was more and more rarely with her own family; they dined now alone. Pyotr Leontyitch was drinking more heavily than ever; there was no money, and the harmonium had been sold long ago for debt.   The boys did not let him go out alone in the street now, but looked after him for fear he might fall down; and whenever they met Anna driving in Staro-Kievsky Street with a pair of horses and Artynov on the box instead of a coachman, Pyotr Leontyitch took off his top-hat, and was about to shout to her, but Petya and Andrusha took him by the arm, and said imploringly:

"You mustn't, father.   Hush, father!"

1895

THE TEACHER OF LITERATURE

7

THE TEACHER OF LITERATURE

I

THERE was the thud of horses' hoofs on the wooden floor; they brought out of the stable the black horse, Count Nulin; then the white, Giant; then his sister Maika. They were all magnificent, expensive horses. Old Shelestov saddled Giant and said, addressing his daughter Masha:

" Well, Marie Godefroi, come, get on! Hopla! "

Masha Shelestov was the youngest of the family; she was eighteen, but her family could not get used to thinking that she was not a little girl, and so they still called her Manya and Manyusa; and after there had been a circus in the town which she had eagerly visited, every one began to call her Marie Godefroi.

" Hop-la! " she cried, mounting Giant. Her sister Varya got on Maika, Nikitin on Count Nulin, the officers on their horses, and the long picturesque cavalcade, with the officers in white tunics and the ladies in their riding habits, moved at a walking pace out of the yard.

Nikitin noticed that when they were mounting

the horses and afterwards riding out into the street,
Masha for some reason paid attention to no one
but himself. She looked anxiously at him and at
Count Nulin and said:

"You must hold him all the time on the curb,
Sergey Vassilitch. Don't let him shy. He's pretending."

And either because her Giant was very friendly
with Count Nulin, or perhaps by chance, she rode
all the time beside Nikitin, as she had done the
day before, and the day before that. And he
looked at her graceful little figure sitting on the
proud white beast, at her delicate profile, at the
chimney-pot hat, which did not suit her at all and
made her look older than her age — looked at her
with joy, with tenderness, with rapture; listened to
her, taking in little of what she said, and thought:

"I promise on my honour, I swear to God, I
won't be afraid and I'll speak to her today."

It was seven o'clock in the evening — the time
when the scent of white acacia and lilac is so strong
that the air and the very trees seem heavy with the
fragrance. The band was already playing in the
town gardens. The horses made a resounding thud
on the pavement, on all sides there were sounds of
laughter, talk, and the banging of gates. The soldiers they met saluted the officers, the schoolboys
bowed to Nikitin, and all the people who were

hurrying to the gardens to hear the band were pleased at the sight of the party. And how warm it was! How soft-looking were the clouds scattered carelessly about the sky, how kindly and comforting the shadows of the poplars and the acacias, which stretched across the street and reached as far as the balconies and second stories of the houses on the other side.

They rode on out of the town and set off at a trot along the highroad. Here there was no scent of lilac and acacia, no music of the band, but there was the fragrance of the fields, there was the green of young rye and wheat, the marmots were squeaking, the rooks were cawing. Wherever one looked it was green, with only here and there black patches of bare ground, and far away to the left in the cemetery a white streak of apple-blossom.

They passed the slaughter-houses, then the brewery, and overtook a military band hastening to the suburban gardens.

" Polyansky has a very fine horse, I don't deny that," Masha said to Nikitin, with a glance towards the officer who was riding beside Varya. " But it has blemishes. That white patch on its left leg ought not to be there, and, look, it tosses its head. You can't train it not to now; it will toss its head till the end of its days."

Masha was as passionate a lover of horses as her

father.　She felt a pang when she saw other people
with fine horses, and was pleased when she saw de-
fects in them.　Nikitin knew nothing about horses;
it made absolutely no difference to him whether he
held his horse on the bridle or on the curb, whether
he trotted or galloped; he only felt that his position
was strained and unnatural, and that consequently
the officers who knew how to sit in their saddles
must please Masha more than he could.　And he
was jealous of the officers.

As they rode by the suburban gardens some one
suggested their going in and getting some seltzer-
water.　They went in.　There were no trees but
oaks in the gardens; they had only just come into
leaf, so that through the young foliage the whole
garden could still be seen with its platform, little
tables, and swings, and the crows' nests were visible,
looking like big hats.　The party dismounted near
a table and asked for seltzer-water.　People they
knew, walking about the garden, came up to them.
Among them the army doctor in high boots, and
the conductor of the band, waiting for the musicians.
The doctor must have taken Nikitin for a student,
for he asked:

" Have you come for the summer holidays? "

" No, I am here permanently," answered Nikitin.
" I am a teacher at the school."

" You don't say so? " said the doctor, with

surprise. "So young and already a teacher?"

"Young, indeed! My goodness, I'm twenty-six!"

"You have a beard and moustache, but yet one would never guess you were more than twenty-two or twenty-three. How young-looking you are!"

"What a beast!" thought Nikitin. "He, too, takes me for a whipper-snapper!"

He disliked it extremely when people referred to his youth, especially in the presence of women or the schoolboys. Ever since he had come to the town as a master in the school he had detested his own youthful appearance. The schoolboys were not afraid of him, old people called him "young man," ladies preferred dancing with him to listening to his long arguments, and he would have given a great deal to be ten years older.

From the garden they went on to the Shelestovs' farm. There they stopped at the gate and asked the bailiff's wife, Praskovya, to bring some new milk. Nobody drank the milk; they all looked at one another, laughed, and galloped back. As they rode back the band was playing in the suburban garden; the sun was setting behind the cemetery, and half the sky was crimson from the sunset.

Masha again rode beside Nikitin. He wanted to tell her how passionately he loved her, but he was afraid he would be overheard by the officers and Varya, and he was silent. Masha was silent, too, and he felt why she was silent and why she was riding beside him, and was so happy that the earth, the sky, the lights of the town, the black outline of the brewery — all blended for him into something very pleasant and comforting, and it seemed to him as though Count Nulin were stepping on air and would climb up into the crimson sky.

They arrived home. The samovar was already boiling on the table, old Shelestov was sitting with his friends, officials in the Circuit Court, and as usual he was criticizing something.

"It's loutishness!" he said. "Loutishness and nothing more. Yes!"

Since Nikitin had been in love with Masha, everything at the Shelestovs' pleased him: the house, the garden, and the evening tea, and the wickerwork chairs, and the old nurse, and even the word "loutishness," which the old man was fond of using. The only thing he did not like was the number of cats and dogs and the Egyptian pigeons, who moaned disconsolately in a big cage in the verandah. There were so many house-dogs and yard-dogs that he had only learnt to recognize two of them in the course of his acquaintance with the Shelestovs: Mushka and Som. Mushka was a little mangy dog with a shaggy face, spiteful and spoiled. She hated Nikitin: when she saw him she put her head on one side, showed her teeth, and began: "Rrr . . . nga-nga-nga . . . rrr . . .!" Then she would get under his chair, and when he would try to drive her away she would go off into piercing yaps, and the family would say: "Don't be frightened. She doesn't bite. She is a good dog."

Som was a tall black dog with long legs and a tail as hard as a stick. At dinner and tea he usually moved about under the table, and thumped on people's boots and on the legs of the table with his tail. He was a good-natured, stupid dog, but Nikitin could not endure him because he had the habit of putting his head on people's knees at dinner and messing their trousers with saliva. Nikitin had more than once tried to hit him on his head with a knife-handle, to flip him on the nose, had abused him, had complained of him, but nothing saved his trousers.

After their ride the tea, jam, rusks, and butter seemed very nice. They all drank their first glass in silence and with great relish; over the second they began an argument. It was always Varya who started the arguments at tea; she was good-looking, handsomer than Masha, and was considered the cleverest and most cultured person in the house, and she behaved with dignity and severity, as an eldest daughter should who has taken the place of her dead mother in the house. As the mistress of the house, she felt herself entitled to wear a dressing-gown in the presence of her guests, and to call the officers by their surnames; she looked on Masha as a little girl, and talked to her as though she were a school-mistress.   She used to speak of herself as an old maid — so she was certain she would marry.

Every conversation, even about the weather, she invariably turned into an argument.   She had a pas-sion for catching at words, pouncing on contradic-tions, quibbling over phrases.   You would begin talking to her, and she would stare at you and sud-denly interrupt: " Excuse me, excuse me, Petrov, the other day you said the very opposite! "

Or she would smile ironically and say: " I no-tice, though, you begin to advocate the principles of the secret police.   I congratulate you."

If you jested or made a pun, you would hear her voice at once: " That's stale," " That's pointless." If an officer ventured on a joke, she would make a contemptuous grimace and say, "An army joke! "

And she rolled the r so impressively that Mushka invariably answered from under a chair, " Rrr . . . nga-nga-nga . . . ! "

On this occasion at tea the argument began with Nikitin's mentioning the school examinations.

" Excuse me, Sergey Vassilitch," Varya inter-rupted him.   " You say it's difficult for the boys. And whose fault is that, let me ask you?   For in-stance, you set the boys in the eighth class an essay on 'Pushkin as a Psychologist.' To begin with, you shouldn't set such a difficult subject; and, secondly, Pushkin was not a psychologist. Shtchedrin now, or Dostoevsky let us say, is a different matter, but Pushkin is a great poet and nothing more."

"Shtchedrin is one thing, and Pushkin is another," Nikitin answered sulkily.

"I know you don't think much of Shtchedrin at the high school, but that's not the point. Tell me, in what sense is Pushkin a psychologist?"

"Why, do you mean to say he was not a psychologist? If you like, I'll give you examples."

And Nikitin recited several passages from "Onyegin" and then from "Boris Godunov."

"I see no psychology in that." Varya sighed. "The psychologist is the man who describes the recesses of the human soul, and that's fine poetry and nothing more."

"I know the sort of psychology you want," said Nikitin, offended. "You want some one to saw my finger with a blunt saw while I howl at the top of my voice — that's what you mean by psychology."

"That's poor! But still you haven't shown me in what sense Pushkin is a psychologist?"

When Nikitin had to argue against anything that seemed to him narrow, conventional, or something of that kind, he usually leaped up from his seat, clutched at his head with both hands, and began with a moan, running from one end of the room to another. And it was the same now: he jumped up, clutched his head in his hands, and with a moan walked round the table, then he sat down a little way off.

The officers took his part. Captain Polyansky began assuring Varya that Pushkin really was a psychologist, and to prove it quoted two lines from Lermontov; Lieutenant Gernet said that if Pushkin had not been a psychologist they would not have erected a monument to him in Moscow.

" That's loutishness! " was heard from the other end of the table. " I said as much to the governor: ' It's loutishness, your Excellency,' I said."

" I won't argue any more," cried Nikitin. " It's unending. . . . Enough! Ach, get away, you nasty dog! " he cried to Som, who laid his head and paw on his knee.

" Rrr . . . nga-nga-nga! " came from under the table.

" Admit that you are wrong! " cried Varya. " Own up! "

But some young ladies came in, and the argument dropped of itself. They all went into the drawing-room. Varya sat down at the piano and began playing dances. They danced first a waltz, then a polka, then a quadrille with a grand chain which

Captain Polyansky led through all the rooms, then a waltz again.

During the dancing the old men sat in the drawing-room, smoking and looking at the young people. Among them was Shebaldin, the director of the municipal bank, who was famed for his love of literature and dramatic art. He had founded the local Musical and Dramatic Society, and took part in the performances himself, confining himself, for some reason, to playing comic footmen or to reading in a sing-song voice " The Woman who was a Sinner." His nickname in the town was " the Mummy," as he was tall, very lean and scraggy, and always had a solemn air and a fixed, lustreless eye. He was so devoted to the dramatic art that he even shaved his moustache and beard, and this made him still more like a mummy.

After the grand chain, he shuffled up to Nikitin sideways, coughed, and said:

" I had the pleasure of being present during the argument at tea. I fully share your opinion. We are of one mind, and it would be a great pleasure to me to talk to you. Have you read Lessing on the dramatic art of Hamburg? "

" No, I haven't."

Shebaldin was horrified, and waved his hands as though he had burnt his fingers, and saying nothing more, staggered back from Nikitin. Shebaldin's appearance, his question, and his surprise, struck Nikitin as funny, but he thought none the less:

"It really is awkward.   I am a teacher of literature, and to this day I've not read Lessing.   I must read him."

Before supper the whole company, old and young, sat down to play "fate."   They took two packs of cards: one pack was dealt round to the company, the other was laid on the table face downwards.

"The one who has this card in his hand," old Shelestov began solemnly, lifting the top card of the second pack, "is fated to go into the nursery and kiss nurse."

The pleasure of kissing the nurse fell to the lot of Shebaldin.   They all crowded round him, took him to the nursery, and laughing and clapping their hands, made him kiss the nurse.   There was a great uproar and shouting.

"Not so ardently!" cried Shelestov with tears of laughter.   "Not so ardently!"

It was Nikitin's "fate" to hear the confessions of all.   He sat on a chair in the middle of the drawing-room.   A shawl was brought and put over his head.   The first who came to confess to him was Varya.

"I know your sins," Nikitin began, looking in the darkness at her stern profile.   "Tell me, madam, how do you explain your walking with Polyansky every day?   Oh, it's not for nothing she walks with an hussar! "

" That's poor," said Varya, and walked away.

Then under the shawl he saw the shine of big motionless eyes, caught the lines of a dear profile in the dark, together with a familiar, precious fragrance which reminded Nikitin of Masha's room.

" Marie Godefroi," he said, and did not know his own voice, it was so soft and tender, " what are your sins? "

Masha screwed up her eyes and put out the tip of her tongue at him, then she laughed and went away.   And a minute later she was standing in the middle of the room, clapping her hands and crying:

" Supper, supper, supper! "

And they all streamed into the dining-room.   At supper Varya had another argument, and this time with her father.   Polyansky ate stolidly, drank red wine, and described to Nikitin how once in a winter campaign he had stood all night up to his knees in a bog; the enemy was so near that they were not allowed to speak or smoke, the night was cold and dark, a piercing wind was blowing.   Nikitin listened and stole side-glances at Masha.   She was gazing at him immovably, without blinking, as though she was pondering something or was lost in a reverie. . . . It was pleasure and agony to him both at once.

" Why does she look at me like that? " was the

question that fretted him. " It's awkward.   People may notice it.   Oh, how young, how naïve she is ! "

The party broke up at midnight.   When Nikitin went out at the gate, a window opened on the first-floor, and Masha showed herself at it.

" Sergey Vassilitch ! " she called.

" What is it ? "

" I tell you what . . ." said Masha, evidently thinking of something to say.   " I tell you what. . . . Polyansky said he would come in a day or two with his camera and take us all.   We must meet here."

" Very well."

Masha vanished, the window was slammed, and some one immediately began playing the piano in the house.

" Well, it is a house ! " thought Nikitin while he crossed the street.   " A house in which there is no moaning except from Egyptian pigeons, and they only do it because they have no other means of expressing their joy ! "

But the Shelestovs were not the only festive household.   Nikitin had not gone two hundred paces before he heard the strains of a piano from another house.   A little further he met a peasant playing the balalaika at the gate.   In the gardens the band struck up a potpourri of Russian songs.

Nikitin lived nearly half a mile from the Shelestovs' in a flat of eight rooms at the rent of three hundred roubles a year, which he shared with his colleague Ippolit Ippolititch, a teacher of geography and history. When Nikitin went in this Ippolit Ippolititch, a snub-nosed, middle-aged man with a reddish beard, with a coarse, good-natured, unintellectual face like a workman's, was sitting at the table correcting his pupils' maps. He considered that the most important and necessary part of the study of geeography was the drawing of maps, and of the study of history the learning of dates: he would sit for nights together correcting in blue pencil the maps drawn by the boys and girls he taught, or making chronological tables.

"What a lovely day it has been!" said Nikitin, going in to him. "I wonder at you — how can you sit indoors?"

Ippolit Ippolititch was not a talkative person; he either remained silent or talked of things which everybody knew already. Now what he answered was:

"Yes, very fine weather. It's May now; we soon shall have real summer. And summer's a very different thing from winter. In the winter you have to heat the stoves, but in summer you can keep warm without. In summer you have your window open at night and still are warm, and in winter you are cold even with the double frames in."

Nikitin had not sat at the table for more than one minute before he was bored.

" Good-night ! " he said, getting up and yawning. " I wanted to tell you something romantic concerning myself, but you are — geography ! If one talks to you of love, you will ask one at once, ' What was the date of the Battle of Kalka ? ' Confound you, with your battles and your capes in Siberia ! "

" What are you cross about ? "

" Why, it is vexatious ! "

And vexed that he had not spoken to Masha, and that he had no one to talk to of his love, he went to his study and lay down upon the sofa. It was dark and still in the study. Lying gazing into the darkness, Nikitin for some reason began thinking how in two or three years he would go to Petersburg, how Masha would see him off at the station and would cry; in Petersburg he would get a long letter from her in which she would entreat him to come home as quickly as possible. And he would write to her. . . . He would begin his letter like that: " My dear little rat ! "

" Yes, my dear little rat ! " he said, and he laughed.

He was lying in an uncomfortable position. He put his arms under his head and put his left leg over the back of the sofa.   He felt more comfortable. Meanwhile a pale light was more and more perceptible at the windows, sleepy cocks crowed in the yard.   Nikitin went on thinking how he would come back from Petersburg, how Masha would meet him at the station, and with a shriek of delight would fling herself on his neck; or, better still, he would cheat her and come home by stealth late at night: the cook would open the door, then he would go on tiptoe to the bedroom, undress noiselessly, and jump into bed!   And she would wake up and be overjoyed.

It was beginning to get quite light.   By now there were no windows, no study.   On the steps of the brewery by which they had ridden that day Masha was sitting, saying something.   Then she took Nikitin by the arm and went with him to the suburban garden.   There he saw the oaks and the crows' nests like hats.   One of the nests rocked; out of it peeped Shebaldin, shouting loudly: " You have not read Lessing! "

Nikitin shuddered all over and opened his eyes. Ippolit Ippolititch was standing before the sofa, and throwing back his head, was putting on his cravat.

" Get up; it's time for school," he said.   " You shouldn't sleep in your clothes; it spoils your clothes. You should sleep in your bed, undressed."

And as usual he began slowly and emphatically saying what everybody knew.

Nikitin's first lesson was on Russian language in the second class.   When at nine o'clock punctually he went into the classroom, he saw written on the blackboard two large letters — *M. S.*   That, no doubt, meant Masha Shelestov.

" They've scented it out already, the rascals . . ." thought Nikitin.   " How is it they know everything? "

The second lesson was in the fifth class.   And there two letters, *M. S.*, were written on the blackboard; and when he went out of the classroom at the end of the lesson, he heard the shout behind him as though from a theatre gallery:

" Hurrah for Masha Shelestov! "

His head was heavy from sleeping in his clothes, his limbs were weighted down with inertia.   The boys, who were expecting every day to break up before the examinations, did nothing, were restless, and so bored that they got into mischief.   Nikitin, too, was restless, did not notice their pranks, and was continually going to the window.   He could see the street brilliantly lighted up with the sun; above the houses the blue limpid sky, the birds, and far, far away, beyond the gardens and the houses, vast indefinite distance, the forests in the blue haze, the smoke from a passing train. . . .

Here two officers in white tunics, playing with their whips, passed in the street in the shade of the acacias. Here a lot of Jews, with grey beards, and caps on, drove past in a waggonette. . . . The governess walked by with the director's granddaughter. Som ran by in the company of two other dogs. . . . And then Varya, wearing a simple grey dress and red stockings, carrying the " Vyestnik Evropi " in her hand, passed by. She must have been to the town library. . . .

And it would be a long time before lessons were over at three o'clock! And after school he could not go home nor to the Shelestovs', but must go to give a lesson at Wolf's. This Wolf, a wealthy Jew who had turned Lutheran, did not send his children to the high school, but had them taught at home by the high-school masters, and paid five roubles a lesson.

He was bored, bored, bored.

At three o'clock he went to Wolf's and spent there, as it seemed to him, an eternity. He left there at five o'clock, and before seven he had to be at the high school again to a meeting of the masters — to draw up the plan for the *viva voce* examination of the fourth and sixth classes.

When late in the evening he left the high school and went to the Shelestovs', his heart was beating and his face was flushed. A month before, even a week before, he had, every time that he made up his mind to speak to her, prepared a whole speech, with an introduction and a conclusion. Now he had not one word ready; everything was in a muddle in his head, and all he knew was that today he would *certainly* declare himself, and that it was utterly impossible to wait any longer.

"I will ask her to come to the garden," he thought; "we'll walk about a little and I'll speak."

There was not a soul in the hall; he went into the dining-room and then into the drawing-room. . . . There was no one there either. He could hear Varya arguing with some one upstairs and the clink of the dressmaker's scissors in the nursery.

There was a little room in the house which had three names: the little room, the passage room, and the dark room. There was a big cupboard in it where they kept medicines, gunpowder, and their hunting gear. Leading from this room to the first floor was a narrow wooden staircase where cats were always asleep. There were two doors in it — one leading to the nursery, one to the drawing-room. When Nikitin went into this room to go upstairs, the door from the nursery opened and shut with such a bang that it made the stairs and the cupboard tremble; Masha, in a dark dress, ran in with a piece of blue material in her hand, and, not noticing Nikitin, darted towards the stairs.

"Stay . . ." said Nikitin, stopping her. 'Good-evening, Godefroi. . . . Allow me. . . ."

He gasped, he did not know what to say; with one hand he held her hand and with the other the blue material. And she was half frightened, half surprised, and looked at him with big eyes.

"Allow me . . ." Nikitin went on, afraid she would go away. "There's something I must say to you. . . . Only . . . it's inconvenient here. I cannot, I am incapable. . . . Understand, Godefroi, I can't — that's all. . . ."

The blue material slipped on to the floor, and Nikitin took Masha by the other hand. She turned pale, moved her lips, then stepped back from Nikitin and found herself in the corner between the wall and the cupboard.

"On my honour, I assure you . . ." he said softly. "Masha, on my honour. . . ."

She threw back her head and he kissed her lips, and that the kiss might last longer he put his fingers to her cheeks; and it somehow happened that he found himself in the corner between the cupboard and the wall, and she put her arms round his neck and pressed her head against his chin.

Then they both ran into the garden. The Shelestovs had a garden of nine acres. There were about twenty old maples and lime-trees in it; there was one fir-tree, and all the rest were fruit-trees: cherries, apples, pears, horse-chestnuts, silvery olive-trees. . . . There were heaps of flowers, too.

Nikitin and Masha ran along the avenues in silence, laughed, asked each other from time to time disconnected questions which they did not answer. A crescent moon was shining over the garden, and drowsy tulips and irises were stretching up from the dark grass in its faint light, as though entreating for words of love for them, too.

When Nikitin and Masha went back to the house, the officers and the young ladies were already assembled and dancing the mazurka. Again Polyansky led the grand chain through all the rooms, again after dancing they played " fate." Before supper, when the visitors had gone into the dining-room, Masha, left alone with Nikitin, pressed close to him and said:

" You must speak to papa and Varya yourself; I am ashamed."

After supper he talked to the old father. After listening to him, Shelestov thought a little and said:

" I am very grateful for the honour you do me and my daughter, but let me speak to you as a friend. I will speak to you, not as a father, but as one gentleman to another. Tell me, why do you want to be married so young? Only peasants are married so young, and that, of course, is loutishness. But why should you? Where's the satisfaction of putting on the fetters at your age? "

"I am not young!" said Nikitin, offended. "I am in my twenty-seventh year."

"Papa, the farrier has come!" cried Varya from the other room.

And the conversation broke off. Varya, Masha, and Polyansky saw Nikitin home. When they reached his gate, Varya said:

"Why is it your mysterious Metropolit Metropolititch never shows himself anywhere? He might come and see us."

The mysterious Ippolit Ippolititch was sitting on his bed, taking off his trousers, when Nikitin went in to him.

"Don't go to bed, my dear fellow," said Nikitin breathlessly. "Stop a minute; don't go to bed!"

Ippolit Ippolititch put on his trousers hurriedly and asked in a flutter:

"What is it?"

"I am going to be married."

Nikitin sat down beside his companion, and looking at him wonderingly, as though surprised at himself, said:

"Only fancy, I am going to be married! To Masha Shelestov! I made an offer today."

"Well? She seems a good sort of girl. Only she is very young."

"Yes, she is young," sighed Nikitin, and shrugged

his shoulders with a careworn air. "Very, very young!"

"She was my pupil at the high school. I know her. She wasn't bad at geography, but she was no good at history. And she was inattentive in class, too."

Nikitin for some reason felt suddenly sorry for his companion, and longed to say something kind and comforting to him.

"My dear fellow, why don't you get married?" he asked. "Why don't you marry Varya, for instance? She is a splendid, first-rate girl! It's true she is very fond of arguing, but a heart . . . what a heart! She was just asking about you. Marry her, my dear boy! Eh?"

He knew perfectly well that Varya would not marry this dull, snub-nosed man, but still persuaded him to marry her — why?

"Marriage is a serious step," said Ippolit Ippolititch after a moment's thought. "One has to look at it all round and weigh things thoroughly; it's not to be done rashly. Prudence is always a good thing, and especially in marriage, when a man, ceasing to be a bachelor, begins a new life."

And he talked of what every one has known for ages. Nikitin did not stay to listen, said goodnight, and went to his own room. He undressed quickly and quickly got into bed, in order to be able to think the sooner of his happiness, of Masha, of the future; he smiled, then suddenly recalled that he had not read Lessing.

"I must read him," he thought. "Though, after all, why should I? Bother him!"

And exhausted by his happiness, he fell asleep at once and went on smiling till the morning.

He dreamed of the thud of horses' hoofs on a wooden floor; he dreamed of the black horse Count Nulin, then of the white Giant and its sister Maika, being led out of the stable.

II

"It was very crowded and noisy in the church, and once some one cried out, and the head priest, who was marrying Masha and me, looked through his spectacles at the crowd, and said severely: 'Don't move about the church, and don't make a noise, but stand quietly and pray. You should have the fear of God in your hearts.'

"My best men were two of my colleagues, and Masha's best men were Captain Polyansky and Lieutenant Gernet. The bishop's choir sang superbly. The sputtering of the candles, the brilliant light, the gorgeous dresses, the officers, the numbers of gay, happy faces, and a special ethereal look in Masha, everything together — the surround-

260 The Party and Other Stories

ings and the words of the wedding prayers — moved me to tears and filled me with triumph. I thought how my life had blossomed, how poetically it was shaping itself! Two years ago I was still a student, I was living in cheap furnished rooms, without money, without relations, and, as I fancied then, with nothing to look forward to. Now I am a teacher in the high school in one of the best provincial towns, with a secure income, loved, spoiled. It is for my sake, I thought, this crowd is collected, for my sake three candelabra have been lighted, the deacon is booming, the choir is doing its best; and it's for my sake that this young creature, whom I soon shall call my wife, is so young, so elegant, and so joyful. I recalled our first meetings, our rides into the country, my declaration of love and the weather, which, as though expressly, was so exquisitely fine all the summer; and the happiness which at one time in my old rooms seemed to me possible only in novels and stories, I was now experiencing in reality — I was now, as it were, holding it in my hands.

"After the ceremony they all crowded in disorder round Masha and me, expressed their genuine pleasure, congratulated us and wished us joy. The brigadier-general, an old man of seventy, confined himself to congratulating Masha, and said to her in a squeaky, aged voice, so loud that it could be heard all over the church:

" ' I hope that even after you are married you may remain the rose you are now, my dear.'

" The officers, the director, and all the teachers smiled from politeness, and I was conscious of an agreeable artificial smile on my face, too. Dear Ippolit Ippolititch, the teacher of history and geography, who always says what every one has heard before, pressed my hand warmly and said with feeling:

" ' Hitherto you have been unmarried and have lived alone, and now you are married and no longer single.'

" From the church we went to a two-storied house which I am receiving as part of the dowry. Besides that house Masha is bringing me twenty thousand roubles, as well as a piece of waste land with a shanty on it, where I am told there are numbers of hens and ducks which are not looked after and are turning wild. When I got home from the church, I stretched myself at full length on the low sofa in my new study and began to smoke; I felt snug, cosy, and comfortable, as I never had in my life before. And meanwhile the wedding party were shouting ' Hurrah! ' while a wretched band in the hall played flourishes and all sorts of trash.

Varya, Masha's sister, ran into the study with a wineglass in her hand, and with a queer, strained expression, as though her mouth were full of water; apparently she had meant to go on further, but she suddenly burst out laughing and sobbing, and the wineglass crashed on the floor.   We took her by the arms and led her away.

"'Nobody can understand!' she muttered afterwards, lying on the old nurse's bed in a back room. 'Nobody, nobody!   My God, nobody can understand!'

"But every one understood very well that she was four years older than her sister Masha, and still unmarried, and that she was crying, not from envy, but from the melancholy consciousness that her time was passing, and perhaps had passed.   When they danced the quadrille, she was back in the drawing-room with a tear-stained and heavily powdered face, and I saw Captain Polyansky holding a plate of ice before her while she ate it with a spoon.

"It is past five o'clock in the morning.   I took up my diary to describe my complete and perfect happiness, and thought I would write a good six pages, and read it tomorrow to Masha; but, strange to say, everything is muddled in my head and as misty as a dream, and I can remember vividly nothing but that episode with Varya, and I want to write, 'Poor Varya!'   I could go on sitting here and writing 'Poor Varya!' By the way, the trees have begun rustling; it will rain. The crows are cawing, and my Masha, who has just gone to sleep, has for some reason a sorrowful face."

For a long while afterwards Nikitin did not write his diary. At the beginning of August he had the school examinations, and after the fifteenth the classes began. As a rule he set off for school before nine in the morning, and before ten o'clock he was looking at his watch and pining for his Masha and his new house. In the lower forms he would set some boy to dictate, and while the boys were writing, would sit in the window with his eyes shut, dreaming; whether he dreamed of the future or recalled the past, everything seemed to him equally delightful, like a fairy tale. In the senior classes they were reading aloud Gogol or Pushkin's prose works, and that made him sleepy; people, trees, fields, horses, rose before his imagination, and he would say with a sigh, as though fascinated by the author:

"How lovely!"

At the midday recess Masha used to send him lunch in a snow-white napkin, and he would eat it slowly, with pauses, to prolong the enjoyment of it; and Ippolit Ippolititch, whose lunch as a rule consisted of nothing but bread, looked at him with respect and envy, and gave expression to some familiar fact, such as:

" Men cannot live without food."

After school Nikitin went straight to give his private lessons, and when at last by six o'clock he got home, he felt excited and anxious, as though he had been away for a year. He would run upstairs breathless, find Masha, throw his arms round her, and kiss her and swear that he loved her, that he could not live without her, declare that he had missed her fearfully, and ask her in trepidation how she was and why she looked so depressed. Then they would dine together. After dinner he would lie on the sofa in his study and smoke, while she sat beside him and talked in a low voice.

His happiest days now were Sundays and holidays, when he was at home from morning till evenine. On those days he took part in the naïve but extraordinarily pleasant life which reminded him of a pastoral idyl. He was never weary of watching how his sensible and practical Masha was arranging her nest, and anxious to show that he was of some use in the house, he would do something useless — for instance, bring the chaise out of the stable and look at it from every side. Masha had installed a regular dairy with three cows, and in her cellar she had many jugs of milk and pots of sour cream, and she kept it all for butter. Sometimes, by way of a joke, Nikitin would ask her for a glass of milk, and she would be quite upset because it was against her rules; but he would laugh and throw his arms round her, saying:

"There, there; I was joking, my darling! I was joking!"

Or he would laugh at her strictness when, finding in the cupboard some stale bit of cheese or sausage as hard as a stone, she would say seriously:

"They will eat that in the kitchen."

He would observe that such a scrap was only fit for a mousetrap, and she would reply warmly that men knew nothing about housekeeping, and that it was just the same to the servants if you were to send down a hundredweight of savouries to the kitchen. He would agree, and embrace her enthusiastically. Everything that was just in what she said seemed to him extraordinary and amazing; and what did not fit in with his convictions seemed to him naïve and touching.

Sometimes he was in a philosophical mood, and he would begin to discuss some abstract subject while she listened and looked at his face with curiosity.

"I am immensely happy with you, my joy," he used to say, playing with her fingers or plaiting and unplaiting her hair. "But I don't look upon this happiness of mine as something that has come to me by chance, as though it had dropped from heaven. This happiness is a perfectly natural, consistent, logical consequence.   I believe that man is the creator of his own happiness, and now I am enjoying just what I have myself created.   Yes, I speak without false modesty: I have created this happiness myself and I have a right to it.   You know my past.   My unhappy childhood, without father or mother; my depressing youth, poverty — all this was a struggle, all this was the path by which I made my way to happiness. . . ."

In October the school sustained a heavy loss: Ippolit Ippolititch was taken ill with erysipelas on the head and died.   For two days before his death he was unconscious and delirious, but even in his delirium he said nothing that was not perfectly well known to every one.

"The Volga flows into the Caspian Sea. . . . Horses eat oats and hay. . . ."

There were no lessons at the high school on the day of his funeral.   His colleagues and pupils were the coffin-bearers, and the school choir sang all the way to the grave the anthem "Holy God."   Three priests, two deacons, all his pupils and the staff of the boys' high school, and the bishop's choir in their best kaftans, took part in the procession. And passers-by who met the solemn procession, crossed themselves and said:

"God grant us all such a death."

Returning home from the cemetery much moved,

Nikitin got out his diary from the table and wrote:
"We have just consigned to the tomb Ippolit
Ippolititch Ryzhitsky. Peace to your ashes, modest worker! Masha, Varya, and all the women at
the funeral, wept from genuine feeling, perhaps because they knew this uninteresting, humble man had
never been loved by a woman. I wanted to say a
warm word at my colleague's grave, but I was
warned that this might displease the director, as he
did not like our poor friend. I believe that this is
the first day since my marriage that my heart has
been heavy."

There was no other event of note in the scholastic
year.

The winter was mild, with wet snow and no frost;
on Epiphany Eve, for instance, the wind howled all
night as though it were autumn, and water trickled
off the roofs; and in the morning, at the ceremony of
the blessing of the water, the police allowed no one
to go on the river, because they said the ice was
swelling up and looked dark. But in spite of bad
weather Nikitin's life was as happy as in summer.
And, indeed, he acquired another source of pleasure;
he learned to play *vint*. Only one thing troubled
him, moved him to anger, and seemed to prevent him
from being perfectly happy: the cats and dogs which
formed part of his wife's dowry. The rooms,
especially in the morning, always smelt like a

menagerie, and nothing could destroy the odour; the cats frequently fought with the dogs. The spiteful beast Mushka was fed a dozen times a day; she still refused to recognize Nikitin and growled at him: "Rrr . . . nga-nga-nga!"

One night in Lent he was returning home from the club where he had been playing cards. It was dark, raining, and muddy. Nikitin had an unpleasant feeling at the bottom of his heart and could not account for it. He did not know whether it was because he had lost twelve roubles at cards, or whether because one of the players, when they were settling up, had said that of course Nikitin had pots of money, with obvious reference to his wife's portion. He did not regret the twelve roubles, and there was nothing offensive in what had been said; but, still, there was the unpleasant feeling. He did not even feel a desire to go home.

"Foo, how horrid!" he said, standing still at a lamp-post.

It occurred to him that he did not regret the twelve roubles because he got them for nothing. If he had been a working man he would have known the value of every farthing, and would not have been so careless whether he lost or won. And his good-fortune had all, he reflected, come to him by chance, for nothing, and really was as superfluous for him as medicine for the healthy. If, like the vast majority of people, he had been harassed by anxiety for his daily bread, had been struggling for existence, if his back and chest had ached from work, then supper, a warm snug home, and domestic happiness, would have been the necessity, the compensation, the crown of his life; as it was, all this had a strange, indefinite significance for him.

"Foo, how horrid!" he repeated, knowing perfectly well that these reflections were in themselves a bad sign.

When he got home Masha wes in bed: she was breathing evenly and smiling, and was evidently sleeping with great enjoyment. Near her the white cat lay curled up, purring. While Nikitin lit the candle and lighted his cigarette, Masha woke up and greedily drank a glass of water.

"I ate too many sweets," she said, and laughed. "Have you been home?" she asked after a pause.

"No."

Nikitin knew already that Captain Polyansky, on whom Varya had been building great hopes of late, was being transferred to one of the western provinces, and was already making his farewell visits in the town, and so it was depressing at his father-in-law's.

"Varya looked in this evening," said Masha, sitting up. "She did not say anything, but one could see from her face how wretched she is, poor darling!

I can't bear Polyansky.   He is fat and bloated, and
when he walks or dances his cheeks shake. . . . He
is not a man I would choose.   But, still, I did think
he was a decent person."

" I think he is a decent person now," said Nikitin.

" Then why has he treated Varya so badly? "

" Why badly? " asked Nikitin, beginning to feel
irritation against the white cat, who was stretching
and arching its back.   " As far as I know, he has
made no proposal and has given her no promises."

" Then why was he so often at the house?   If he
didn't mean to marry her, he oughtn't to have come."

Nikitin put out the candle and got into bed.   But
he felt disinclined to lie down and to sleep.   He felt
as though his head were immense and empty as a
barn, and that new, peculiar thoughts were wandering about in it like tall shadows.   He thought that,
apart from the soft light of the ikon lamp, that
beamed upon their quiet domestic happiness, that
apart from this little world in which he and this cat
lived so peacefully and happily, there was another
world. . . . And he had a passionate, poignant
longing to be in that other world, to work himself at
some factory or big workshop, to address big audi-
ences, to write, to publish, to raise a stir, to exhaust
himself, to suffer. . . . He wanted something that
would engross him till he forgot himself, ceased to
care for the personal happiness which yielded him

only sensations so monotonous. And suddenly there rose vividly before his imagination the figure of Shebaldin with his clean-shaven face, saying to him with horror: "You haven't even read Lessing! You are quite behind the times! How you have gone to seed!"

Masha woke up and again drank some water. He glanced at her neck, at her plump shoulders and throat, and remembered the word the brigadier-general had used in church —" rose."

" Rose," he muttered, and laughed.

His laugh was answered by a sleepy growl from Mushka under the bed: " Rrr . . . nga-nga-nga . . . !"

A heavy anger sank like a cold weight on his heart, and he felt tempted to say something rude to Masha, and even to jump up and hit her; his heart began throbbing.

" So then," he asked, restraining himself, " since I went to your house, I was bound in duty to marry you?"

" Of course. You know that very well."

" That's nice." And a minute later he repeated: " That's nice."

To relieve the throbbing of his heart, and to avoid saying too much, Nikitin went to his study and lay down on the sofa, without a pillow; then he lay on the floor on the carpet.

" What nonsense it is ! " he said to reassure himself. " You are a teacher, you are working in the noblest of callings. . . . What need have you of any other world? What rubbish ! "

But almost immediately he told himself with conviction that he was not a real teacher, but simply a government employé, as commonplace and mediocre as the Czech who taught Greek. He had never had a vocation for teaching, he knew nothing of the theory of teaching, and never had been interested in the subject; he did not know how to treat children; he did not understand the significance of what he taught, and perhaps did not teach the right things. Poor Ippolit Ippolititch had been frankly stupid, and all the boys, as well as his colleagues, knew what he was and what to expect from him; but he, Nikitin, like the Czech, knew how to conceal his stupidity and cleverly deceived every one by pretending that, thank God, his teaching was a success. These new ideas frightened Nikitin; he rejected them, called them stupid, and believed that all this was due to his nerves, that he would laugh at himself.

And he did, in fact, by the morning laugh at himself and call himself an old woman; but it was clear to him that his peace of mind was lost, perhaps, for ever, and that in that little two-story house happiness was henceforth impossible for him. He realized that the illusion had evaporated, and that a new life of unrest and clear sight was beginning which was incompatible with peace and personal happiness.

Next day, which was Sunday, he was at the school chapel, and there met his colleagues and the director. It seemed to him that they were entirely preoccupied with concealing their ignorance and discontent with life, and he, too, to conceal his uneasiness, smiled affably and talked of trivialities. Then he went to the station and saw the mail train come in and go out, and it was agreeable to him to be alone and not to have to talk to any one.

At home he found Varya and his father-in-law, who had come to dinner. Varya's eyes were red with crying, and she complained of a headache, while Shelestov ate a great deal, saying that young men nowadays were unreliable, and that there was very little gentlemanly feeling among them.

" It's loutishness! " he said. " I shall tell him so to his face: ' It's loutishness, sir,' I shall say."

Nikitin smiled affably and helped Masha to look after their guests, but after dinner he went to his study and shut the door.

The March sun was shining brightly in at the windows and shedding its warm rays on the table. It was only the twentieth of the month, but already the cabmen were driving with wheels, and the starlings were noisy in the garden. It was just the weather in which Masha would come in, put one arm

round his neck, tell him the horses were saddled or
the chaise was at the door, and ask him what she
should put on to keep warm.   Spring was beginning
as exquisitely as last spring, and it promised the same
joys. . . . But Nikitin was thinking that it would be
nice to take a holiday and go to Moscow, and stay
at his old lodgings there.   In the next room they
were drinking coffee and talking of Captain Polyansky, while he tried not to listen and wrote in his
diary: "Where am I, my God?   I am surrounded
by vulgarity and vulgarity.   Wearisome, insignificant people, pots of sour cream, jugs of milk, cock-
roaches, stupid women. . . . There is nothing more
terrible, mortifying, and distressing than vulgarity.
I must escape from here, I must escape today, or I
shall go out of my mind!"

1889

NOT WANTED

NOT WANTED

Between six and seven o'clock on a July evening, a crowd of summer visitors — mostly fathers of families — burdened with parcels, portfolios, and ladies' hat-boxes, was trailing along from the little station of Helkovo, in the direction of the summer villas. They all looked exhausted, hungry, and ill-humoured, as though the sun were not shining and the grass were not green for them.

Trudging along among the others was Pavel Matveyitch Zaikin, a member of the Circuit Court, a tall, stooping man, in a cheap cotton dust-coat and with a cockade on his faded cap. He was perspiring, red in the face, and gloomy. . . .

" Do you come out to your holiday home every day? " said a summer visitor, in ginger-coloured trousers, addressing him.

" No, not every day," Zaikin answered sullenly. " My wife and son are staying here all the while, and I come down two or three times a week. I haven't time to come every day; besides, it is expensive."

" You're right there; it is expensive," sighed he

of the ginger trousers.   " In town you can't walk to
the station, you have to take a cab; and then, the
ticket costs forty-two kopecks; you buy a paper for
the journey; one is tempted to drink a glass of vodka.
It's all petty expenditure not worth considering, but,
mind you, in the course of the summer it will run up
to some two hundred roubles.   Of course, to be in
the lap of Nature is worth any money — I don't dis-
pute it . . . idyllic and all the rest of it; but of
course, with the salary an official gets, as you know
yourself, every farthing has to be considered.   If
you waste a halfpenny you lie awake all night. . . .
Yes . . . I receive, my dear sir — I haven't the
honour of knowing your name — I receive a salary
of very nearly two thousand roubles a year.   I am
a civil councillor, I smoke second-rate tobacco, and
I haven't a rouble to spare to buy Vichy water, pre-
scribed me by the doctor for gall-stones."

" It's altogether abominable," said Zaikin after a
brief silence.   " I maintain, sir, that summer holidays are the invention of the devil and of woman.
The devil was actuated in the present instance by
malice, woman by excessive frivolity.   Mercy on
us, it is not life at all; it is hard labour, it is hell!
It's hot and stifling, you can hardly breathe, and you
wander about like a lost soul and can find no refuge.
In town there is no furniture, no servants . . .
everything has been carried off to the villa: you eat

what you can get; you go without your tea because
there is no one to heat the samovar; you can't wash
yourself; and when you come down here into this
'lap of Nature' you have to walk, if you please,
through the dust and heat. . . . Phew! Are you
married?"

"Yes . . . three children," sighs Ginger Trousers.

"It's abominable altogether. . . . It's a wonder
we are still alive."

At last the summer visitors reached their destina-
tion. Zaikin said good-bye to Ginger Trousers and
went into his villa. He found a death-like silence in
the house. He could hear nothing but the buzzing
of the gnats, and the prayer for help of a fly destined
for the dinner of a spider. The windows were hung
with muslin curtains, through which the faded flowers of the geraniums showed red. On the unpainted
wooden walls near the oleographs flies were slum-
bering. There was not a soul in the passage, the
kitchen, or the dining-room. In the room which
was called indifferently the parlour or the drawing-
room, Zaikin found his son Petya, a little boy of six.
Petya was sitting at the table, and breathing loudly
with his lower lip stuck out, was engaged in cutting
out the figure of a knave of diamonds from a card.

"Oh, that's you, father!" he said, without turning round. "Good-evening."

"Good-evening. . . . And where is mother?"

" Mother? She is gone with Olga Kirillovna to a rehearsal of the play. The day after tomorrow they will have a performance. And they will take me, too. . . . And will you go? "

" H'm! . . . When is she coming back? "

" She said she would be back in the evening."

" And where is Natalya? "

" Mamma took Natalya with her to help her dress for the performance, and Akulina has gone to the wood to get mushrooms. Father, why is it that when gnats bite you their stomachs get red? "

" I don't know. . . . Because they suck blood. So there is no one in the house, then? "

" No one; I am all alone in the house."

Zaikin sat down in an easy-chair, and for a moment gazed blankly at the window.

" Who is going to get our dinner? " he asked.

" They haven't cooked any dinner today, father. Mamma thought you were not coming today, and did not order any dinner. She is going to have dinner with Olga Kirillovna at the rehearsal."

" Oh, thank you very much; and you, what have you to eat? "

" I've had some milk. They bought me six kopecks' worth of milk. And, father, why do gnats suck blood? "

Zaikin suddenly felt as though something heavy were rolling down on his liver and beginning to gnaw it. He felt so vexed, so aggrieved, and so bitter, that he was choking and tremulous; he wanted to jump up, to bang something on the floor, and to burst into loud abuse; but then he remembered that his doctor had absolutely forbidden him all excitement, so he got up, and making an effort to control himself, began whistling a tune from " Les Huguenots."

" Father, can you act in plays? " he heard Petya's voice.

" Oh, don't worry me with stupid questions! " said Zaikin, getting angry. " He sticks to one like a leaf in the bath! Here you are, six years old, and just as silly as you were three years ago. . . . Stupid, neglected child! Why are you spoiling those cards, for instance? How dare you spoil them? "

" These cards aren't yours," said Petya, turning round. " Natalya gave them me."

" You are telling fibs, you are telling fibs, you horrid boy! " said Zaikin, growing more and more irritated. " You are always telling fibs! You want a whipping, you horrid little pig! I will pull your ears! "

Petya leapt up, and craning his neck, stared fixedly at his father's red and wrathful face. His big eyes first began blinking, then were dimmed with moisture, and the boy's face began working.

" But why are you scolding? " squealed Petya. " Why do you attack me, you stupid? I am not interfering with anybody; I am not naughty; I do what I am told, and yet . . . you are cross! Why are you scolding me?"

The boy spoke with conviction, and wept so bitterly that Zaikin felt conscience-stricken.

"Yes, really, why am I falling foul of him?" he thought. "Come, come," he said, touching the boy on the shoulder. "I am sorry, Petya . . . forgive me. You are my good boy, my nice boy, I love you."

Petya wiped his eyes with his sleeve, sat down, with a sigh, in the same place and began cutting out the queen. Zaikin went off to his own room. He stretched himself on the sofa, and putting his hands behind his head, sank into thought. The boy's tears had softened his anger, and by degrees the oppression on his liver grew less. He felt nothing but exhaustion and hunger.

"Father," he heard on the other side of the door, "shall I show you my collection of insects?"

"Yes, show me."

Petya came into the study and handed his father a long green box. Before raising it to his ear Zaikin could hear a despairing buzz and the scratching of claws on the sides of the box. Opening the lid, he saw a number of butterflies, beetles, grasshoppers, and flies fastened to the bottom of the box with pins.

All except two or three butterflies were still alive
and moving.

"Why, the grasshopper is still alive!" said Petya
in surprise. "I caught him yesterday morning, and
he is still alive!"

"Who taught you to pin them in this way?"

"Olga Kirillovna."

"Olga Kirillovna ought to be pinned down like
that herself!" said Zaikin with repulsion. "Take
them away! It's shameful to torture animals."

"My God! How horribly he is being brought
up!" he thought, as Petya went out.

Pavel Matveyitch forgot his exhaustion and hunger, and thought of nothing but his boy's future.
Meanwhile, outside the light was gradually fading.
. . . He could hear the summer visitors trooping
back from the evening bathe. Some one was stopping near the open dining-room window and shouting: "Do you want any mushrooms?" And getting no answer, shuffled on with bare feet. . . . But
at last, when the dusk was so thick that the outlines
of the geraniums behind the muslin curtain were lost,
and whiffs of the freshness of evening were coming
in at the window, the door of the passage was thrown
open noisily, and there came a sound of rapid footsteps, talk, and laughter. . . .

"Mamma!" shrieked Petya.

Zaikin peeped out of his study and saw his wife, Nadyezhda Stepanova, healthy and rosy as ever; with her he saw Olga Kirillovna, a spare woman with fair hair and heavy freckles, and two unknown men: one a lanky young man with curly red hair and a big Adam's apple; the other, a short stubby man with a shaven face like an actor's and a bluish crooked chin.

" Natalya, set the samovar," cried Nadyezhda Stepanovna, with a loud rustle of her skirts. " I hear Pavel Matveyitch is come. Pavel, where are you? Good-evening, Pavel!" she said, running into the study breathlessly. " So you've come. I am so glad. . . . Two of our amateurs have come with me. . . . Come, I'll introduce you. . . . Here, the taller one is Koromyslov . . . he sings splendidly; and the other, the little one . . . is called Smerkalov: he is a real actor . . . he recites magnificently. Oh, how tired I am! We have just had a rehearsal. . . . It goes splendidly. We are acting ' The Lodger with the Trombone ' and ' Waiting for Him.' . . . The performance is the day after to-morrow. . . ."

" Why did you bring them? " asked Zaikin.

" I couldn't help it, Poppet; after tea we must rehearse our parts and sing something. . . . I am to sing a duet with Koromyslov. . . . Oh, yes, I was almost forgetting! Darling, send Natalya to get some sardines, vodka, cheese, and something else. They will most likely stay to supper. . . . Oh, how tired I am! "

" H'm! I've no money."

" You must, Poppet! It would be awkward! Don't make me blush."

Half an hour later Natalya was sent for vodka and savouries; Zaikin, after drinking tea and eating a whole French loaf, went to his bedroom and lay down on the bed, while Nadyezhda Stepanovna and her visitors, with much noise and laughter, set to work to rehearse their parts. For a long time Pavel Matveyitch heard Koromyslov's nasal reciting and Smerkalov's theatrical exclamations. . . . The rehearsal was followed by a long conversation, interrupted by the shrill laughter of Olga Kirillovna. Smerkalov, as a real actor, explained the parts with aplomb and heat. . . .

Then followed the duet, and after the duet there was the clatter of crockery. . . . Through his drowsiness Zaikin heard them persuading Smerkalov to read " The Woman who was a Sinner," and heard him, after affecting to refuse, begin to recite. He hissed, beat himself on the breast, wept, laughed in a husky bass. . . . Zaikin scowled and hid his head under the quilt.

" It's a long way for you to go, and it's dark," he heard Nadyezhda Stepanovna's voice an hour later.

"Why shouldn't you stay the night here? Koromy-slov can sleep here in the drawing-room on the sofa, and you, Smerkalov, in Petya's bed. . . . I can put Petya in my husband's study. . . . Do stay, really!"

At last when the clock was striking two, all was hushed, the bedroom door opened, and Nadyezhda Stepanovna appeared.

"Pavel, are you asleep?" she whispered.

"No; why?"

"Go into your study, darling, and lie on the sofa. I am going to put Olga Kirillovna here, in your bed. Do go, dear! I would put her to sleep in the study, but she is afraid to sleep alone. . . . Do get up!"

Zaikin got up, threw on his dressing-gown, and taking his pillow, crept wearily to the study. . . . Feeling his way to his sofa, he lighted a match, and saw Petya lying on the sofa. The boy was not asleep, and, looking at the match with wide-open eyes:

"Father, why is it gnats don't go to sleep at night?" he asked.

"Because . . . because . . . you and I are not wanted. . . . We have nowhere to sleep even."

"Father, and why is it Olga Kirillovna has freckles on her face?"

"Oh, shut up! I am tired of you."

After a moment's thought, Zaikin dressed and went out into the street for a breath of air. . . .

He looked at the grey morning sky, at the motionless clouds, heard the lazy call of the drowsy corncrake, and began dreaming of the next day, when he would go to town, and coming back from the court would tumble into bed. . . . Suddenly the figure of a man appeared round the corner.

" A watchman, no doubt," thought Zaikin.

But going nearer and looking more closely he recognized in the figure the summer visitor in the ginger trousers.

" You're not asleep? " he asked.

" No, I can't sleep," sighed Ginger Trousers. " I am enjoying Nature. . . . A welcome visitor, my wife's mother, arrived by the night train, you know. She brought with her our nieces . . . splendid girls! I was delighted to see them, although . . . it's very damp! And you, too, are enjoying Nature? "

" Yes," grunted Zaikin, " I am enjoying it, too. . . . Do you know whether there is any sort of tavern or restaurant in the neighbourhood? "

Ginger Trousers raised his eyes to heaven and meditated profoundly.

1887

TYPHUS

TYPHUS

A young lieutenant called Klimov was travelling from Petersburg to Moscow in a smoking carriage of the mail train. Opposite him was sitting an elderly man with a shaven face like a sea captain's, by all appearances a well-to-do Finn or Swede. He pulled at his pipe the whole journey and kept talking about the same subject:

"Ha, you are an officer! I have a brother an officer too, only he is a naval officer. . . . He is a naval officer, and he is stationed at Kronstadt. Why are you going to Moscow?"

"I am serving there."

"Ha! And are you a family man?"

"No, I live with my sister and aunt."

"My brother's an officer, only he is a naval officer; he has a wife and three children. Ha!"

The Finn seemed continually surprised at something, and gave a broad idiotic grin when he exclaimed "Ha!" and continually puffed at his stinking pipe. Klimov, who for some reason did not feel well, and found it burdensome to answer questions, hated him with all his heart. He dreamed of how

nice it would be to snatch the wheezing pipe out of
his hand and fling it under the seat, and drive the
Finn himself into another compartment.

" Detestable people these Finns and . . . Greeks,"
he thought.   " Absolutely superfluous, useless, detestable people.   They simply fill up space on the
earthly globe.   What are they for? "

And the thought of Finns and Greeks produced a
feeling akin to sickness all over his body.   For the
sake of comparison he tried to think of the French,
of the Italians, but his efforts to think of these
people evoked in his mind, for some reason, nothing
but images of organ-grinders, naked women, and the
foreign oleographs which hung over the chest of
drawers at home, at his aunt's.

Altogether the officer felt in an abnormal state.
He could not arrange his arms and legs comfortably
on the seat, though he had the whole seat to himself.   His mouth felt dry and sticky; there was a
heavy fog in his brain; his thoughts seemed to be
straying, not only within his head, but outside his
skull, among the seats and the people that were
shrouded in the darkness of night.   Through the
mist in his brain, as through a dream, he heard the
murmur of voices, the rumble of wheels, the slam-
ming of doors.   The sounds of the bells, the
whistles, the guards, the running to and fro of passengers on the platforms, seemed more frequent

than usual. The time flew by rapidly, impercept-
ibly, and so it seemed as though the train were stopping at stations every minute, and metallic voices
crying continually:

" Is the mail ready? "

" Yes ! " was repeatedly coming from outside.

It seemed as though the man in charge of the
heating came in too often to look at the thermometer,
that the noise of trains going in the opposite direction and the rumble of the wheels over the bridges
was incessant. The noise, the whistles, the Finn,
the tobacco smoke — all this mingling with the
menace and flickering of the misty images in his
brain, the shape and character of which a man in
health can never recall, weighed upon Klimov like
an unbearable nightmare. In horrible misery he
lifted his heavy head, looked at the lamp in the rays
of which shadows and misty blurs seemed to be dancing. He wanted to ask for water, but his parched
tongue would hardly move, and he scarcely had
strength to answer the Finn's questions. He tried
to lie down more comfortably and go to sleep, but
he could not succeed. The Finn several times fell
asleep, woke up again, lighted his pipe, addressed
him with his " Ha ! " and went to sleep again; and
still the lieutenant's legs could not get into a comfortable position, and still the menacing images stood
facing him.

At Spirovo he went out into the station for a drink of water.   He saw people sitting at the table and hurriedly eating.

" And how can they eat! " he thought, trying not to sniff the air, that smelt of roast meat, and not to look at the munching mouths — they both seemed to him sickeningly disgusting.

A good-looking lady was conversing loudly with a military man in a red cap, and showing magnificent white teeth as she smiled; and the smile, and the teeth, and the lady herself made on Klimov the same revolting impression as the ham and the rissoles.   He could not understand how it was the military man in the red cap was not ill at ease, sitting beside her and looking at her healthy, smiling face.

When after drinking some water he went back to his carriage, the Finn was sitting smoking; his pipe was wheezing and squelching like a golosh with holes in it in wet weather.

" Ha! " he said, surprised; " what station is this? "

" I don't know," answered Klimov, lying down and shutting his mouth that he might not breathe the acrid tobacco smoke.

" And when shall we reach Tver? "

" I don't know.   Excuse me, I . . . I can't answer.   I am ill.   I caught cold today."

The Finn knocked his pipe against the window-frame and began talking of his brother, the naval officer. Klimov no longer heard him; he was thinking miserably of his soft, comfortable bed, of a bottle of cold water, of his sister Katya, who was so good at making one comfortable, soothing, giving one water. He even smiled when the vision of his orderly Pavel, taking off his heavy stifling boots and putting water on the little table, flitted through his imagination. He fancied that if he could only get into his bed, have a drink of water, his nightmare would give place to sound healthy sleep.

" Is the mail ready? " a hollow voice reached him from the distance.

" Yes," answered a bass voice almost at the window.

It was already the second or third station from Spirovo.

The time was flying rapidly in leaps and bounds, and it seemed as though the bells, whistles, and stoppings would never end. In despair Klimov buried his face in the corner of the seat, clutched his head in his hands, and began again thinking of his sister Katya and his orderly Pavel, but his sister and his orderly were mixed up with the misty images in his brain, whirled round, and disappeared. His burning breath, reflected from the back of the seat, seemed to scald his face; his legs were uncomfortable; there was a draught from the window on his back; but, however wretched he was, he did not want to change his position. . . . A heavy nightmarish lethargy gradually gained possession of him and fettered his limbs.

When he brought himself to raise his head, it was already light in the carriage. The passengers were putting on their fur coats and moving about. The train was stopping. Porters in white aprons and with discs on their breasts were bustling among the passengers and snatching up their boxes. Klimov put on his great-coat, mechanically followed the other passengers out of the carriage, and it seemed to him that not he, but some one else was moving, and he felt that his fever, his thirst, and the menacing images which had not let him sleep all night, came out of the carriage with him. Mechanically he took his luggage and engaged a sledge-driver. The man asked him for a rouble and a quarter to drive to Povarsky Street, but he did not haggle, and without protest got submissively into the sledge. He still understood the difference of numbers, but money had ceased to have any value to him.

At home Klimov was met by his aunt and his sister Katya, a girl of eighteen. When Katya greeted him she had a pencil and exercise book in her hand, and he remembered that she was preparing for an examination as a teacher. Gasping with fever, he walked

aimlessly through all the rooms without answering
their questions or greetings, and when he reached his
bed he sank down on the pillow. The Finn, the red
cap, the lady with the white teeth, the smell of roast
meat, the flickering blurs, filled his consciousness, and
by now he did not know where he was and did not
hear the agitated voices.

When he recovered consciousness he found himself in bed, undressed, saw a bottle of water and
Pavel, but it was no cooler, nor softer, nor more
comfortable for that. His arms and legs, as before,
refused to lie comfortably; his tongue stuck to the
roof of his mouth, and he heard the wheezing of the
Finn's pipe. . . . A stalwart, black-bearded doctor
was busy doing something beside the bed, brushing
against Pavel with his broad back.

"It's all right, it's all right, young man,"
he muttered. "Excellent, excellent . . . goo-od,
goo-od . . . !"

The doctor called Klimov "young man," said
"goo-od" instead of "good" and "so-o" instead
of "so."

"So-o . . . so-o . . . so-o," he murmured.
"Goo-od, goo-od . . . ! Excellent, young man.
. . . You mustn't lose heart!"

The doctor's rapid, careless talk, his well-fed
countenance, and condescending "young man," irritated Klimov.

"Why do you call me 'young man'?" he moaned. "What familiarity! Damn it all!"

And he was frightened by his own voice. The voice was so dried up, so weak and peevish, that he would not have known it.

"Excellent, excellent!" muttered the doctor, not in the least offended. . . . "You mustn't get angry, so-o, so-o, so-o. . . ."

And the time flew by at home with the same startling swiftness as in the railway carriage. . . . The daylight was continually being replaced by the dusk of evening. The doctor seemed never to leave his bedside, and he heard at every moment his "so-o, so-o, so-o." A continual succession of people was incessantly crossing the bedroom. Among them were: Pavel, the Finn, Captain Yaroshevitch, Lance-Corporal Maximenko, the red cap, the lady with the white teeth, the doctor. They were all talking and waving their arms, smoking and eating. Once by daylight Klimov saw the chaplain of the regiment, Father Alexandr, who was standing before the bed, wearing a stole and with a prayer-book in his hand. He was muttering something with a grave face such as Klimov had never seen in him before. The lieutenant remembered that Father Alexandr used in a friendly way to call all the Catholic officers "Poles," and wanting to amuse him, he cried:

" Father, Yaroshevitch the Pole has climbed up
a pole!"

But Father Alexandr, a light-hearted man who
loved a joke, did not smile, but became graver than
ever, and made the sign of the cross over Klimov.
At night-time by turn two shadows came noiselessly
in and out; they were his aunt and sister. His sister's shadow knelt down and prayed; she bowed
down to the ikon, and her grey shadow on the wall
bowed down too, so that two shadows were praying.
The whole time there was a smell of roast meat and
the Finn's pipe, but once Klimov smelt the strong
smell of incense. He felt so sick he could not lie
still, and began shouting:

" The incense! Take away the incense!"

There was no answer. He could only hear the
subdued singing of the priest somewhere and some
one running upstairs.

When Klimov came to himself there was not a
soul in his bedroom. The morning sun was stream-
ing in at the window through the lower blind, and
a quivering sunbeam, bright and keen as the sword's
edge, was flashing on the glass bottle. He heard
the rattle of wheels — so there was no snow now in
the street. The lieutenant looked at the ray, at
the familiar furniture, at the door, and the first
thing he did was to laugh. His chest and stomach

heaved with delicious, happy, tickling laughter. His whole body from head to foot was overcome by a sensation of infinite happiness and joy in life, such as the first man must have felt when he was created and first saw the world. Klimov felt a passionate desire for movement, people, talk. His body lay a motionless block; only his hands stirred, but that he hardly noticed, and his whole attention was concentrated on trifles. He rejoiced in his breathing, in his laughter, rejoiced in the existence of the water-bottle, the ceiling, the sunshine, the tape on the curtains. God's world, even in the narrow space of his bedroom, seemed beautiful, varied, grand. When the doctor made his appearance, the lieutenant was thinking what a delicious thing medicine was, how charming and pleasant the doctor was, and how nice and interesting people were in general.

"So-o, so, so. . . . Excellent, excellent! . . . Now we are well again. . . . Goo-od, goo-od!" the doctor pattered.

The lieutenant listened and laughed joyously; he remembered the Finn, the lady with the white teeth, the train, and he longed to smoke, to eat.

"Doctor," he said, "tell them to give me a crust of rye bread and salt, and . . . and sardines."

The doctor refused; Pavel did not obey the order, and did not go for the bread. The lieutenant could not bear this and began crying like a naughty child.

"Baby!" laughed the doctor. "Mammy, bye-bye!"

Klimov laughed, too, and when the doctor went away he fell into a sound sleep. He woke up with the same joyfulness and sensation of happiness. His aunt was sitting near the bed.

"Well, aunt," he said joyfully. "What has been the matter?"

"Spotted typhus."

"Really. But now I am well, quite well! Where is Katya?"

"She is not at home. I suppose she has gone somewhere from her examination."

The old lady said this and looked at her stocking; her lips began quivering, she turned away, and suddenly broke into sobs. Forgetting the doctor's prohibition in her despair, she said:

"Ah, Katya, Katya! Our angel is gone! Is gone!"

She dropped her stocking and bent down to it, and as she did so her cap fell off her head. Looking at her grey head and understanding nothing, Klimov was frightened for Katya, and asked:

"Where is she, aunt?"

The old woman, who had forgotten Klimov and was thinking only of her sorrow, said:

"She caught typhus from you, and is dead. She was buried the day before yesterday."

This terrible, unexpected news was fully grasped by Klimov's consciousness; but terrible and startling as it was, it could not overcome the animal joy that filled the convalescent. He cried and laughed, and soon began scolding because they would not let him eat.

Only a week later when, leaning on Pavel, he went in his dressing-gown to the window, looked at the overcast spring sky and listened to the unpleasant clang of the old iron rails which were being carted by, his heart ached, he burst into tears, and leaned his forehead against the window-frame.

"How miserable I am!" he muttered. "My God, how miserable!"

And joy gave way to the boredom of everyday life and the feeling of his irrevocable loss.

1887

A MISFORTUNE

A MISFORTUNE

SOFYA PETROVNA, the wife of Lubyantsev the notary, a handsome young woman of five-and-twenty, was walking slowly along a track that had been cleared in the wood, with Ilyin, a lawyer who was spending the summer in the neighbourhood. It was five o'clock in the evening. Feathery-white masses of cloud stood overhead; patches of bright blue sky peeped out between them. The clouds stood motionless, as though they had caught in the tops of the tall old pine-trees. It was still and sultry.

Farther on, the track was crossed by a low railway embankment on which a sentinel with a gun was for some reason pacing up and down. Just beyond the embankment there was a large white church with six domes and a rusty roof.

" I did not expect to meet you here," said Sofya Petrovna, looking at the ground and prodding at the last year's leaves with the tip of her parasol, " and now I am glad we have met. I want to speak to you seriously and once for all. I beg you, Ivan Mihalovitch, if you really love and respect me, please make an end of this pursuit of me! You follow me about like a shadow, you are continually

looking at me not in a nice way, making love to me,
writing me strange letters, and . . . and I don't
know where it's all going to end!   Why, what can
come of it?"

Ilyin said nothing.   Sofya Petrovna walked on a
few steps and continued:

"And this complete transformation in you all
came about in the course of two or three weeks,
after five years' friendship.   I don't know you, Ivan
Mihalovitch!"

Sofya Petrovna stole a glance at her companion.
Screwing up his eyes, he was looking intently at
the fluffy clouds.   His face looked angry, ill-humoured, and preoccupied, like that of a man in pain
forced to listen to nonsense.

"I wonder you don't see it yourself," Madame
Lubyantsev went on, shrugging her shoulders.
"You ought to realize that it's not a very nice part
you are playing.   I am married; I love and respect
my husband. . . . I have a daughter. . . . Can
you think all that means nothing?   Besides, as an
old friend you know my attitude to family life and
my views as to the sanctity of marriage."

Ilyin cleared his throat angrily and heaved a sigh.

"Sanctity of marriage . . ." he muttered.   "Oh,
Lord!"

"Yes, yes. . . . I love my husband, I respect
him; and in any case I value the peace of my home.

I would rather let myself be killed than be a cause
of unhappiness to Andrey and his daughter. . . .
And I beg you, Ivan Mihalovitch, for God's sake,
leave me in peace! Let us be as good, true friends
as we used to be, and give up these sighs and groans,
which really don't suit you. It's settled and over!
Not a word more about it. Let us talk of something
else."

Sofya Petrovna again stole a glance at Ilyin's
face. Ilyin was looking up; he was pale, and was
angrily biting his quivering lips. She could not understand why he was angry and why he was indignant, but his pallor touched her.

"Don't be angry; let us be friends," she said
affectionately. "Agreed? Here's my hand."

Ilyin took her plump little hand in both of his,
squeezed it, and slowly raised it to his lips.

"I am not a schoolboy," he muttered. "I am
not in the least tempted by friendship with the woman
I love."

"Enough, enough! It's settled and done with.
We have reached the seat; let us sit down."

Sofya Petrovna's soul was filled with a sweet
sense of relief: the most difficult and delicate thing
had been said, the painful question was settled and
done with. Now she could breathe freely and look
Ilyin straight in the face. She looked at him, and
the egoistic feeling of the superiority of the woman

over the man who loves her, agreeably flattered her.
It pleased her to see this huge, strong man, with his
manly, angry face and his big black beard — clever,
cultivated, and, people said, talented — sit down
obediently beside her and bow his head dejectedly.
For two or three minutes they sat without speaking.

"Nothing is settled or done with," began Ilyin.
"You repeat copy-book maxims to me. 'I love
and respect my husband . . . the sanctity of marriage. . . .' I know all that without your help,
and I could tell you more, too.   I tell you truthfully
and honestly that I consider the way I am behaving
as criminal and immoral.   What more can one say
than that?   But what's the good of saying what
everybody knows?   Instead of feeding nightingales
with paltry words, you had much better tell me what
I am to do."

"I've told you already — go away."

"As you know perfectly well, I have gone away
five times, and every time I turned back on the way.
I can show you my through tickets — I've kept them
all.   I have not will enough to run away from you!
I am struggling.   I am struggling horribly; but what
the devil am I good for if I have no backbone, if
I am weak, cowardly!   I can't struggle with Nature!   Do you understand?   I cannot!   I run
away from here, and she holds on to me and pulls
me back.   Contemptible, loathsome weakness!"

Ilyin flushed crimson, got up, and walked up and down by the seat.

"I feel as cross as a dog," he muttered, clenching his fists. "I hate and despise myself! My God! like some depraved schoolboy, I am making love to another man's wife, writing idiotic letters, degrading myself . . . ugh!"

Ilyin clutched at his head, grunted, and sat down.

"And then your insincerity!" he went on bitterly. "If you do dislike my disgusting behaviour, why have you come here? What drew you here? In my letters I only ask you for a direct, definite answer — yes or no; but instead of a direct answer, you contrive every day these ' chance ' meetings with me and regale me with copy-book maxims!"

Madame Lubyantsev was frightened and flushed. She suddenly felt the awkwardness which a decent woman feels when she is accidentally discovered undressed.

"You seem to suspect I am playing with you," she muttered. "I have always given you a direct answer, and . . . only today I've begged you . . ."

"Ough! as though one begged in such cases! If you were to say straight out ' Get away,' I should have been gone long ago; but you've never said that. You've never once given me a direct answer. Strange indecision! Yes, indeed; either you are playing with me, or else . . ."

Ilyin leaned his head on his fists without finishing. Sofya Petrovna began going over in her own mind the way she had behaved from beginning to end. She remembered that not only in her actions, but even in her secret thoughts, she had always been opposed to Ilyin's love-making; but yet she felt there was a grain of truth in the lawyer's words. But not knowing exactly what the truth was, she could not find answers to make to Ilyin's complaint, however hard she thought. It was awkward to be silent, and, shrugging her shoulders, she said:

" So I am to blame, it appears."

" I don't blame you for your insincerity," sighed Ilyin. " I did not mean that when I spoke of it. . . . Your insincerity is natural and in the order of things. If people agreed together and suddenly became sincere, everything would go to the devil."

Sofya Petrovna was in no mood for philosophical reflections, but she was glad of a chance to change the conversation, and asked:

" But why? "

" Because only savage women and animals are sincere. Once civilization has introduced a demand for such comforts as, for instance, feminine virtue, sincerity is out of place. . . ."

Ilyin jabbed his stick angrily into the sand. Madame Lubyantsev listened to him and liked his conversation, though a great deal of it she did not un-

derstand. What gratified her most was that she, an
ordinary woman, was talked to by a talented man on
" intellectual " subjects; it afforded her great pleasure, too, to watch the working of his mobile, young
face, which was still pale and angry. She failed
to understand a great deal that he said, but what
was clear to her in his words was the attractive boldness with which the modern man without hesitation
or doubt decides great questions and draws conclu-
sive deductions.

She suddenly realized that she was admiring him,
and was alarmed.

" Forgive me, but I don't understand," she said
hurriedly. " What makes you talk of insincerity?
I repeat my request again: be my good, true friend;
let me alone! I beg you most earnestly! "

" Very good; I'll try again," sighed Ilyin. " Glad
to do my best. . . . Only I doubt whether anything
will come of my efforts. Either I shall put a bullet
through my brains or take to drink in an idiotic way.
I shall come to a bad end! There's a limit to everything — to struggles with Nature, too. Tell me,
how can one struggle against madness? If you
drink wine, how are you to struggle against intoxi-
cation? What am I to do if your image has grown
into my soul, and day and night stands persistently
before my eyes, like that pine there at this moment?
Come, tell me, what hard and difficult thing can I

do to get free from this abominable, miserable condition, in which all my thoughts, desires, and dreams
are no longer my own, but belong to some demon
who has taken possession of me? I love you, love
you so much that I am completely thrown out of
gear; I've given up my work and all who are dear
to me; I've forgotten my God! I've never been in
love like this in my life."

Sofya Petrovna, who had not expected such a
turn to their conversation, drew away from Ilyin
and looked into his face in dismay. Tears came
into his eyes, his lips were quivering, and there was
an imploring, hungry expression in his face.

" I love you! " he muttered, bringing his eyes near
her big, frightened eyes. " You are so beautiful!
I am in agony now, but I swear I would sit here all
my life, suffering and looking in your eyes. But
. . . be silent, I implore you! "

Sofya Petrovna, feeling utterly disconcerted, tried
to think as quickly as possible of something to say
to stop him. " I'll go away," she decided, but before she had time to make a movement to get up,
Ilyin was on his knees before her. . . . He was
clasping her knees, gazing into her face and speaking passionately, hotly, eloquently. In her terror
and confusion she did not hear his words; for some
reason now, at this dangerous moment, while her

knees were being agreeably squeezed and felt as though they were in a warm bath, she was trying, with a sort of angry spite, to interpret her own sensations. She was angry that instead of brimming over with protesting virtue, she was entirely overwhelmed with weakness, apathy, and emptiness, like a drunken man utterly reckless; only at the bottom of her soul a remote bit of herself was malignantly taunting her: "Why don't you go? Is this as it should be? Yes?"

Seeking for some explanation, she could not understand how it was she did not pull away the hand to which Ilyin was clinging like a leech, and why, like Ilyin, she hastily glanced to right and to left to see whether any one was looking. The clouds and the pines stood motionless, looking at them severely, like old ushers seeing mischief, but bribed not to tell the school authorities. The sentry stood like a post on the embankment and seemed to be looking at the seat.

"Let him look," thought Sofya Petrovna.

"But . . . but listen," she said at last, with despair in her voice. "What can come of this? What will be the end of this?"

"I don't know, I don't know," he whispered, waving off the disagreeable questions.

They heard the hoarse, discordant whistle of the

train.   This cold, irrelevant sound from the everyday world of prose made Sofya Petrovna rouse herself.

" I can't stay . . . it's time I was at home," she
said, getting up quickly.   " The train is coming in.
. . . Andrey is coming by it!   He will want his
dinner."

Sofya Petrovna turned towards the embankment
with a burning face.   The engine slowly crawled by,
then came the carriages.   It was not the local train,
as she had supposed, but a goods train.   The trucks
filed by against the background of the white church
in a long string like the days of a man's life, and it
seemed as though it would never end.

But at last the train passed, and the last carriage
with the guard and a light in it had disappeared
behind the trees.   Sofya Petrovna turned round
sharply, and without looking at Ilyin, walked rapidly back along the track.   She had regained her
self-possession.   Crimson with shame, humiliated
not by Ilyin — no, but by her own cowardice, by the
shamelessness with which she, a chaste and high-
principled woman, had allowed a man, not her husband, to hug her knees — she had only one thought
now: to get home as quickly as possible to her villa,
to her family.   The lawyer could hardly keep pace
with her.   Turning from the clearing into a narrow
path, she turned round and glanced at him so quickly

that she saw nothing but the sand on his knees, and waved to him to drop behind.

Reaching home, Sofya Petrovna stood in the middle of her room for five minutes without moving, and looked first at the window and then at her writing-table.

" You low creature ! " she said, upbraiding herself. " You low creature ! "

To spite herself, she recalled in precise detail, keeping nothing back — she recalled that though all this time she had been opposed to Ilyin's love-making, something had impelled her to seek an interview with him; and what was more, when he was at her feet she had enjoyed it enormously. She recalled it all without sparing herself, and now, breathless with shame, she would have liked to slap herself in the face.

" Poor Andrey ! " she said to herself, trying as she thought of her husband to put into her face as tender an expression as she could. " Varya, my poor little girl, doesn't know what a mother she has ! Forgive me, my dear ones ! I love you so much . . . so much ! "

And anxious to prove to herself that she was still a good wife and mother, and that corruption had not yet touched that " sanctity of marriage " of which she had spoken to Ilyin, Sofya Petrovna ran to the kitchen and abused the cook for not having yet laid the table for Andrey Ilyitch. She tried to picture her husband's hungry and exhausted appearance, commiserated him aloud, and laid the table for him with her own hands, which she had never done before. Then she found her daughter Varya, picked her up in her arms and hugged her warmly; the child seemed to her cold and heavy, but she was unwilling to acknowledge this to herself, and she began explaining to the child how good, kind, and honourable her papa was.

But when Andrey Ilyitch arrived soon afterwards she hardly greeted him. The rush of false feeling had already passed off without proving anything to her, only irritating and exasperating her by its falsity. She was sitting by the window, feeling miserable and cross. It is only by being in trouble that people can understand how far from easy it is to be the master of one's feelings and thoughts. Sofya Petrovna said afterwards that there was a tangle within her which it was as difficult to unravel as to count a flock of sparrows rapidly flying by. From the fact that she was not overjoyed to see her husband, that she did not like his manner at dinner, she concluded all of a sudden that she was beginning to hate her husband.

Andrey Ilyitch, languid with hunger and exhaustion, fell upon the sausage while waiting for the soup to be brought in, and ate it greedily, munching noisily and moving his temples.

" My goodness ! " thought Sofya Petrovna. " I love and respect him, but . . . why does he munch so repulsively ? "

The disorder in her thoughts was no less than the disorder in her feelings. Like all persons inexperienced in combating unpleasant ideas, Madame Lubyantsev did her utmost not to think of her trouble, and the harder she tried the more vividly Ilyin, the sand on his knees, the fluffy clouds, the train, stood out in her imagination.

" And why did I go there this afternoon like a fool ? " she thought, tormenting herself. " And am I really so weak that I cannot depend upon myself ? "

Fear magnifies danger. By the time Andrey Ilyitch was finishing the last course, she had firmly made up her mind to tell her husband everything and to flee from danger !

" I've something serious to say to you, Andrey," she began after dinner while her husband was taking off his coat and boots to lie down for a nap.

" Well ? "

" Let us leave this place ! "

" H'm ! . . . Where shall we go ? It's too soon to go back to town."

" No; for a tour or something of that sort. . . ."

" For a tour . . ." repeated the notary, stretch-ing.   " I dream of that myself, but where are we to get the money, and to whom am I to leave the office ? "

And thinking a little he added:

" Of course, you must be bored.   Go by your-self if you like."

Sofya Petrovna agreed, but at once reflected that Ilyin would be delighted with the opportunity, and would go with her in the same train, in the same com-partment. . . . She thought and looked at her hus-band, now satisfied but still languid.   For some rea-son her eyes rested on his feet — miniature, almost feminine feet, clad in striped socks; there was a thread standing out at the tip of each sock.

Behind the blind a bumble-bee was beating itself against the window-pane and buzzing.   Sofya Pe-trovna looked at the threads on the socks, listened to the bee, and pictured how she would set off. . . . *Vis-à-vis* Ilyin would sit, day and night, never taking his eyes off her, wrathful at his own weakness and pale with spiritual agony.   He would call himself an immoral schoolboy, would abuse her, tear his hair, but when darkness came on and the passengers were asleep or got out at a station, he would seize the opportunity to kneel before her and embrace her knees as he had at the seat in the wood. . . .

She caught herself indulging in this day-dream.

"Listen. I won't go alone," she said. "You must come with me."

"Nonsense, Sofotchka!" sighed Lubyantsev. "One must be sensible and not want the impossible."

"You will come when you know all about it," thought Sofya Petrovna.

Making up her mind to go at all costs, she felt that she was out of danger. Little by little her ideas grew clearer; her spirits rose and she allowed herself to think about it all, feeling that however much she thought, however much she dreamed, she would go away. While her husband was asleep, the evening gradually came on. She sat in the drawing-room and played the piano. The greater liveliness out of doors, the sound of music, but above all the thought that she was a sensible person, that she had surmounted her difficulties, completely restored her spirits. Other women, her appeased conscience told her, would probably have been carried off their feet in her position, and would have lost their balance, while she had almost died of shame, had been miserable, and was now running out of the danger which perhaps did not exist! She was so touched by her own virtue and determination that she even looked at herself two or three times in the looking-glass.

When it got dark, visitors arrived.   The men sat down in the dining-room to play cards; the ladies remained in the drawing-room and the verandah. The last to arrive was Ilyin.   He was gloomy, morose, and looked ill.   He sat down in the corner of the sofa and did not move the whole evening. Usually good-humoured and talkative, this time he remained silent, frowned, and rubbed his eyebrows. When he had to answer some question, he gave a forced smile with his upper lip only, and answered jerkily and irritably.   Four or five times he made some jest, but his jests sounded harsh and cutting. It seemed to Sofya Petrovna that he was on the verge of hysterics.   Only now, sitting at the piano, she recognized fully for the first time that this unhappy man was in deadly earnest, that his soul was sick, and that he could find no rest.   For her sake he was wasting the best days of his youth and his career, spending the last of his money on a summer villa, abandoning his mother and sisters, and, worst of all, wearing himself out in an agonizing struggle with himself.   From mere common humanity he ought to be treated seriously.

She recognized all this clearly till it made her heart ache, and if at that moment she had gone up to him and said to him, " No," there would have been a force in her voice hard to disobey.   But she did not go up to him and did not speak — in-

deed, never thought of doing so.   The pettiness and
egoism of youth had never been more patent in her
than that evening.   She realized that Ilyin was unhappy, and that he was sitting on the sofa as though
he were on hot coals; she felt sorry for him, but at
the same time the presence of a man who loved her
to distraction, filled her soul with triumph and a
sense of her own power.   She felt her youth, her
beauty, and her unassailable virtue, and, since she
had decided to go away, gave herself full licence for
that evening.   She flirted, laughed incessantly, sang
with peculiar feeling and gusto.   Everything delighted and amused her.   She was amused at the
memory of what had happened at the seat in the
wood, of the sentinel who had looked on.   She was
amused by her guests, by Ilyin's cutting jests, by the
pin in his cravat, which she had never noticed before.
There was a red snake with diamond eyes on the
pin; this snake struck her as so amusing that she
could have kissed it on the spot.

Sofya Petrovna sang nervously, with defiant
recklessness as though half intoxicated, and she
chose sad, mournful songs which dealt with wasted
hopes, the past, old age, as though in mockery of
another's grief.   " ' And old age comes nearer and
nearer ' . . ." she sang.   And what was old age to
her ?

" It seems as though there is something going

wrong with me," she thought from time to time
through her laughter and singing.

The party broke up at twelve o'clock. Ilyin was
the last to leave. Sofya Petrovna was still reckless
enough to accompany him to the bottom step of the
Verandah. She wanted to tell him that she was
going away with her husband, and to watch the effect
this news would produce on him.

The moon was hidden behind the clouds, but it
was light enough for Sofya Petrovna to see how
the wind played with the skirts of his overcoat and
with the awning of the verandah. She could see,
too, how white Ilyin was, and how he twisted his
upper lip in the effort to smile.

"Sonia, Sonitchka . . . my darling woman!"
he muttered, preventing her from speaking. "My
dear! my sweet!"

In a rush of tenderness, with tears in his voice,
he showered caressing words upon her, that grew
tenderer and tenderer, and even called her "thou,"
as though she were his wife or mistress. Quite
unexpectedly he put one arm round her waist and
with the other hand took hold of her elbow.

"My precious! my delight!" he whispered, kissing the nape of her neck; "be sincere; come to me
at once!"

She slipped out of his arms and raised her head
to give vent to her indignation and anger, but the

indignation did not come off, and all her vaunted
virtue and chastity was only sufficient to enable her
to utter the phrase used by all ordinary women on
such occasions:

" You must be mad."

" Come, let us go," Ilyin continued. " I felt just
now, as well as at the seat in the wood, that you are
as helpless as I am, Sonia. . . . You are in the same
plight! You love me and are fruitlessly trying to
appease your conscience. . . ."

Seeing that she was moving away, he caught her
by her lace cuff and said rapidly:

" If not today, then tomorrow you will have to
give in! Why, then, this waste of time? My precious, darling Sonia, the sentence is passed; why put
off the execution? Why deceive yourself? "

Sofya Petrovna tore herself from him and darted
in at the door. Returning to the drawing-room, she
mechanically shut the piano, looked for a long time
at the music-stand, and sat down. She could not
stand up nor think. All that was left of her excitement and recklessness was a fearful weakness,
apathy, and dreariness. Her conscience whispered
to her that she had behaved badly, foolishly, that
evening, like some madcap girl — that she had just
been embraced on the verandah, and still had an uneasy feeling in her waist and her elbow. There was
not a soul in the drawing-room; there was only one

candle burning. Madame Lubyantsev sat on the round stool before the piano, motionless, as though expecting something.   And as though taking advantage of the darkness and her extreme lassitude, an oppressive, overpowering desire began to assail her. Like a boa-constrictor it gripped her limbs and her soul, and grew stronger every second, and no longer menaced her as it had done, but stood clear before her in all its nakedness.

She sat for half an hour without stirring, not restraining herself from thinking of Ilyin, then she got up languidly and dragged herself to her bedroom. Andrey Ilyitch was already in bed. She sat down by the open window and gave herself up to desire. There was no " tangle " now in her head; all her thoughts and feelings were bent with one accord upon a single aim. She tried to struggle against it, but instantly gave it up. . . . She understood now how strong and relentless was the foe. Strength and fortitude were needed to combat him, and her birth, her education, and her life had given her nothing to fall back upon.

" Immoral wretch!   Low creature! " she nagged at herself for her weakness.   " So that's what you're like ! "

Her outraged sense of propriety was moved to such indignation by this weakness that she lavished upon herself every term of abuse she knew, and told herself many offensive and humiliating truths. So, for instance, she told herself that she never had been moral, that she had not come to grief before simply because she had had no opportunity, that her inward conflict during that day had all been a farce. . . .

"And even if I have struggled," she thought, "what sort of struggle was it? Even the woman who sells herself struggles before she brings herself to it, and yet she sells herself. A fine struggle! Like milk, I've turned in a day! In one day!"

She convicted herself of being tempted, not by feeling, not by Ilyin personally, but by sensations which awaited her . . . an idle lady, having her fling in the summer holidays, like so many!

"'Like an unfledged bird when the mother has been slain,'" sang a husky tenor outside the window.

"If I am to go, it's time," thought Sofya Petrovna. Her heart suddenly began beating violently.

"Andrey!" she almost shrieked. "Listen! we . . . we are going? Yes?"

"Yes, I've told you already: you go alone."

"But listen," she began. "If you don't go with me, you are in danger of losing me. I believe I am . . . in love already."

"With whom?" asked Andrey Ilyitch.

" It can't make any difference to you who it is! "
cried Sofya Petrovna.

Andrey Ilyitch sat up with his feet out of bed and
looked wonderingly at his wife's dark figure.

" It's a fancy! " he yawned.

He did not believe her, but yet he was frightened.
After thinking a little and asking his wife several
unimportant questions, he delivered himself of his
opinions on the family, on infidelity . . . spoke list-
lessly for about ten minutes and got into bed again.
His moralizing produced no effect. There are a
great many opinions in the world, and a good half
of them are held by people who have never been in
trouble!

In spite of the late hour, summer visitors were
still walking outside. Sofya Petrovna put on a light
cape, stood a little, thought a little. . . . She still
had resolution enough to say to her sleeping husband:

" Are you asleep? I am going for a walk. . . .
Will you come with me? "

That was her last hope. Receiving no answer,
she went out. . . . It was fresh and windy. She
was conscious neither of the wind nor the darkness,
but went on and on. . . . An overmastering force
drove her on, and it seemed as though, if she had
stopped, it would have pushed her in the back.

" Immoral creature! " she muttered mechanically. " Low wretch! "

She was breathless, hot with shame, did not feel her legs under her, but what drove her on was stronger than shame, reason, or fear.

1886

A TRIFLE FROM LIFE

A TRIFLE FROM LIFE

A WELL-FED, red-cheeked young man called Nikolay Ilyitch Belyaev, of thirty-two, who was an owner
of house property in Petersburg, and a devotee of the
race-course, went one evening to see Olga Ivanovna
Irnin, with whom he was living, or, to use his own
expression, was dragging out a long, wearisome romance. And, indeed, the first interesting and en-
thusiastic pages of this romance had long been
perused; now the pages dragged on, and still dragged
on, without presenting anything new or of interest.

Not finding Olga Ivanovna at home, my hero lay
down on the lounge chair and proceeded to wait for
her in the drawing-room.

"Good-evening, Nikolay Ilyitch!" he heard a
child's voice. "Mother will be here directly. She
has gone with Sonia to the dressmaker's."

Olga Ivanovna's son, Alyosha — a boy of eight
who looked graceful and very well cared for, who
was dressed like a picture, in a black velvet jacket
and long black stockings — was lying on the sofa
in the same room. He was lying on a satin cushion
and, evidently imitating an acrobat he had lately
seen at the circus, stuck up in the air first one leg

and then the other.   When his elegant legs were exhausted, he brought his arms into play or jumped up impulsively and went on all fours, trying to stand with his legs in the air.   All this he was doing with the utmost gravity, gasping and groaning painfully as though he regretted that God had given him such a restless body.

"Ah, good-evening, my boy," said Belyaev. "It's you!   I did not notice you.   Is your mother well?"

Alyosha, taking hold of the tip of his left toe with his right hand and falling into the most unnatural attitude, turned over, jumped up, and peeped at Belyaev from behind the big fluffy lampshade.

"What shall I say?" he said, shrugging his shoulders.   "In reality mother's never well.   You see, she is a woman, and women, Nikolay Ilyitch, have always something the matter with them."

Belyaev, having nothing better to do, began watching Alyosha's face.   He had never before during the whole of his intimacy with Olga Ivanovna paid any attention to the boy, and had completely ignored his existence; the boy had been before his eyes, but he had not cared to think why he was there and what part he was playing.

In the twilight of the evening, Alyosha's face, with his white forehead and black, unblinking eyes, unexpectedly reminded Belyaev of Olga Ivanovna

as she had been during the first pages of their romance. And he felt disposed to be friendly to the
boy.

"Come here, insect," he said; "let me have a
closer look at you."

The boy jumped off the sofa and skipped up to
Belyaev.

"Well," began Nikolay Ilyitch, putting a hand
on the boy's thin shoulder. "How are you getting
on?"

"How shall I say! We used to get on a great
deal better."

"Why?"

"It's very simple. Sonia and I used only to
learn music and reading, and now they give us
French poetry to learn. Have you been shaved
lately?"

"Yes."

"Yes, I see you have. Your beard is shorter.
Let me touch it. . . . Does that hurt?"

"No."

"Why is it that if you pull one hair it hurts,
but if you pull a lot at once it doesn't hurt a bit?
Ha, ha! And, you know, it's a pity you don't have
whiskers. Here ought to be shaved . . . but here
at the sides the hair ought to be left. . . ."

The boy nestled up to Belyaev and began playing
with his watch-chain.

" When I go to the high-school," he said, " mother is going to buy me a watch. I shall ask her to buy me a watch-chain like this. . . . Wh — at a loc — ket! Father's got a locket like that, only yours has little bars on it and his has letters. . . . There's mother's portrait in the middle of his. Father has a different sort of chain now, not made with rings, but like ribbon. . . ."

" How do you know? Do you see your father? "

" I? M'm . . . no. . . . I . . ."

Alyosha blushed, and in great confusion, feeling caught in a lie, began zealously scratching the locket with his nail. . . . Belyaev looked steadily into his face and asked:

" Do you see your father? "

" N-no! "

" Come, speak frankly, on your honour. . . . I see from your face you are telling a fib. Once you've let a thing slip out it's no good wriggling about it. Tell me, do you see him? Come, as a friend."

Alyosha hesitated.

" You won't tell mother? " he said.

" As though I should! "

" On your honour? "

" On my honour."

" Do you swear? "

" Ah, you provoking boy! What do you take me for? "

Alyosha looked round him, then with wide-open eyes, whispered to him:

" Only, for goodness' sake, don't tell mother. . . . Don't tell any one at all, for it is a secret. I hope to goodness mother won't find out, or we should all catch it — Sonia, and I, and Pelagea. . . . Well, listen. . . . Sonia and I see father every Tuesday and Friday. When Pelagea takes us for a walk before dinner we go to the Apfel Restaurant, and there is father waiting for us. . . . He is always sitting in a room apart, where you know there's a marble table and an ash-tray in the shape of a goose without a back. . . ."

" What do you do there? "

" Nothing! First we say how-do-you-do, then we all sit round the table, and father treats us with coffee and pies. You know Sonia eats the meat-pies, but I can't endure meat-pies! I like the pies made of cabbage and eggs. We eat such a lot that we have to try hard to eat as much as we can at dinner, for fear mother should notice."

" What do you talk about? "

" With father? About anything. He kisses us, he hugs us, tells us all sorts of amusing jokes. Do

you know, he says when we are grown up he is
going to take us to live with him. Sonia does not
want to go, but I agree. Of course, I should miss
mother; but, then, I should write her letters! It's
a queer idea, but we could come and visit her on
holidays — couldn't we? Father says, too, that he
will buy me a horse. He's an awfully kind man!
I can't understand why mother does not ask him
to come and live with us, and why she forbids us to
see him. You know he loves mother very much.
He is always asking us how she is and what she is
doing. When she was ill he clutched his head like
this, and . . . and kept running about. He always
tells us to be obedient and respectful to her. Listen.
Is it true that we are unfortunate?"

"H'm! . . . Why?"

"That's what father says. 'You are unhappy
children,' he says. It's strange to hear him, really.
'You are unhappy,' he says, 'I am unhappy, and
mother's unhappy. You must pray to God,' he says;
'for yourselves and for her.'"

Alyosha let his eyes rest on a stuffed bird and
sank into thought.

"So . . ." growled Belyaev. "So that's how
you are going on. You arrange meetings at restaurants. And mother does not know?"

"No-o. . . . How should she know? Pelagea
would not tell her for anything, you know. The day

before yesterday he gave us some pears. As sweet as jam! I ate two."

"H'm! . . . Well, and I say . . . Listen. Did father say anything about me?"

"About you? What shall I say?"

Alyosha looked searchingly into Belyaev's face and shrugged his shoulders.

"He didn't say anything particular."

"For instance, what did he say?"

"You won't be offended?"

"What next? Why, does he abuse me?"

"He doesn't abuse you, but you know he is angry with you. He says mother's unhappy owing to you . . . and that you have ruined mother. You know he is so queer! I explain to him that you are kind, that you never scold mother; but he only shakes his head."

"So he says I have ruined her?"

"Yes; you mustn't be offended, Nikolay Ilyitch."

Belyaev got up, stood still a moment, and walked up and down the drawing-room.

"That's strange and . . . ridiculous!" he muttered, shrugging his shoulders and smiling sarcastically. "He's entirely to blame, and I have ruined her, eh? An innocent lamb, I must say. So he told you I ruined your mother?"

"Yes, but . . . you said you would not be offended, you know."

" I am not offended, and . . . and it's not your business. Why, it's . . . why, it's positively ridiculous! I have been thrust into it like a chicken in the broth, and now it seems I'm to blame! "

A ring was heard. The boy sprang up from his place and ran out. A minute later a lady came into the room with a little girl; this was Olga Ivanovna, Alyosha's mother. Alyosha followed them in, skipping and jumping, humming aloud and waving his hands. Belyaev nodded, and went on walking up and down.

" Of course, whose fault is it if not mine? " he muttered with a snort. " He is right! He is an injured husband."

" What are you talking about? " asked Olga Ivanovna.

" What about? . . . Why, just listen to the tales your lawful spouse is spreading now! It appears that I am a scoundrel and a villain, that I have ruined you and the children. All of you are unhappy, and I am the only happy one! Wonderfully, wonderfully happy! "

" I don't understand, Nikolay. What's the matter? "

" Why, listen to this young gentleman! " said Belyaev, pointing to Alyosha.

Alyosha flushed crimson, then turned pale, and his whole face began working with terror.

"Nikolay Ilyitch," he said in a loud whisper. "Sh-sh!"

Olga Ivanovna looked in surprise at Alyosha, then at Belyaev, then at Alyosha again.

"Just ask him," Belyaev went on. "Your Pelagea, like a regular fool, takes them about to restaurants and arranges meetings with their papa. But that's not the point: the point is that their dear papa is a victim, while I'm a wretch who has broken up both your lives. . . ."

"Nikolay Ilyitch," moaned Alyosha. "Why, you promised on your word of honour!"

"Oh, get away!" said Belyaev, waving him off. "This is more important than any word of honour. It's the hypocrisy revolts me, the lying! . . ."

"I don't understand it," said Olga Ivanovna, and tears glistened in her eyes. "Tell me, Alyosha," she turned to her son. "Do you see your father?"

Alyosha did not hear her; he was looking with horror at Belyaev.

"It's impossible," said his mother; "I will go and question Pelagea."

Olga Ivanovna went out.

"I say, you promised on your word of honour!" said Alyosha, trembling all over.

Belyaev dismissed him with a wave of his hand, and went on walking up and down. He was absorbed in his grievance and was oblivious of the boy's presence, as he always had been.   He, a grown-up, serious person, had no thought to spare for boys. And Alyosha sat down in the corner and told Sonia with horror how he had been deceived.   He was trembling, stammering, and crying.   It was the first time in his life that he had been brought into such coarse contact with lying; till then he had not known that there are in the world, besides sweet pears, pies, and expensive watches, a great many things for which the language of children has no expression.

1886